<small>ACCLAIM FOR</small> *Richard Bausch's*

THE LAST GOOD TIME

"Superb. . . . There are no gimmicks here, just drama, human beings caught in the act of being human, characters who care and make choices and face consequences. . . . If you want beauty, if you want substance without glitter, if you yearn for a well-told story worth telling, this is your novel."   —Tim O'Brien

"A novelist with superb psychological and narrative instincts . . . as well as an appetite for unexpected revelations."   —*Boston Globe*

"*The Last Good Time* is the most compassionate view of the modern world that I have ever read. . . . Bausch finds grace and joy in the midst of the inevitable and the terrible."   —Mary Lee Settle

"Bausch reads like Raymond Carver or Andre Dubus. . . . [He is] a sublime orchestrator of his material."   —*Los Angeles Times*

"Bausch's strengths are prodigious."   —*San Francisco Chronicle*

"Bausch's writing is so solidly detailed that the reader cannot escape his characters' pangs of anguish."   —*Philadelphia Inquirer*

Richard Bausch

THE LAST GOOD TIME

Richard Bausch is the author of five other novels and two volumes of short stories, including the novels *Violence, Rebel Powers,* and the collection *The Fireman's Wife and Other Stories,* his most recent works. His stories have appeared in *The Atlantic Monthly, Esquire, Harper's, The New Yorker, The Southern Review, Prize Stories: The O. Henry Awards, New Stories from the South, The Granta Book of the American Short Story,* and *The Best American Short Stories.*

THE LAST GOOD TIME

▲

Richard Bausch

VINTAGE CONTEMPORARIES

Vintage Books

A Division of Random House, Inc.

New York

CELEBRATING
10
Years of

VINTAGE CONTEMPORARIES

FIRST VINTAGE CONTEMPORARIES EDITION, AUGUST 1994

Library of Congress Cataloging-in-Publication Data
Bausch, Richard, 1945-
The last good time / by Richard Bausch. – 1st Vintage Contemporaries ed.
p.   cm.
ISBN 0-679-75556-X
1. Title
[PS3552.A846L3   1994]
813´.54–dc20   94–17943
CIP

Author photograph © Jerry Bauer

Manufactured in the United States of America
10 9 8 7 6 5 4 3 2

For Karen again,
with new love and sweet old affection.

I would like to thank the National Endowment for the Arts for providing needed time and support during the writing of this novel.

THE LAST GOOD TIME

1

▲

On the outskirts of a great northern city there lived an old man who kept a small apartment, alone, because that was the way his life had gone. The apartment was one of two rooms on the second floor of an old brownstone house, and he liked it clean and neat. . He was retired, he lived on a monthly pension check from the city's symphony orchestra—along with the regular Social Security payments—and he considered that his standard of living was adequate. He was not an extravagant man; he kept to himself, mostly. The nurses who lived across the hall from him called him Cakes, which made him uneasy. It was his name, in fact, but he knew they were having fun with the jaunty sound of it as opposed to his dour, wordless presence in the building. He saw them on the stairs now and again, and sometimes during the day he heard them laughing and talking and playing their rock 'n' roll. They had odd schedules, always shifting, and they were apt to be awake and making their noise at any hour of the day or night. He never complained, though. He was afraid of what they might think and say about him. If the music was too loud, he simply let himself out of the apartment and went for a walk. There was a café at the end of the block, and across the square at that intersection was the public library. He could sit in there and read during the early evening hours, or he could take a book to the café and lounge in one of the booths, drinking orange juice or coffee.

Sometimes, especially if it was very late, he just walked. He would walk down to the playground and stand in its peculiar nighttime quiet. It was a big playground, a park, really, with a fountain and pond at the center, and stone or wrought-iron benches here and there, amid yellow gravel paths and beds of flowers, with the baseball diamond and basketball courts off to one side. It was a very peaceful and solitary-feeling place at night.

During the day there were people, of course: the businesses around the square emptied out for lunch hours, and from the apartment houses in the surrounding neighborhoods scores of women brought their children to play, while they congregated under the trees to talk. In summer, on cool days, it was a vibrant place, and the old man liked to eat his lunch there, sitting under one of the willows beyond the outfield, with the food spread on a small blanket at his side—deli sandwiches, a little fruit, cold tea in a thermos, and, now and again, a single shot of whiskey, sipped slowly from a paper cup, to top it all off.

If, when the nurses were being noisy, he couldn't leave the apartment—because the weather was bad or because he was too tired or it was too late and he was too groggy from half sleep to move—he could still be patient in the almost certainty that the young man in the apartment just above his own would eventually do the complaining for him: the young man was a student, and needed the quiet to study in.

"Goddamnit," he would cry from the top of the stairs, "shut it off down there, I'm going to call the police!"

The music would be turned down, but it was never enough, and soon the hall would be reverberating with shouts, curses, threats. door slammings, thumps and the shrill answering voices of the nurses. And then all would be quiet.

The old man lay listening to these things, and when it was all over, he could read, or doze, or watch a little television without the constant undertow of the nurses' music, their talk—the wild, high laughter of their parties.

Sometimes, when it was peaceful, he could convince himself that no one else lived in the house, that he was alone there, with the occasional disturbances and eruptions of the city echoing out in the night—sirens, horns, voices—and the quiet would be like another kind of noise, an element of his aloneness as if he were the place where nothing happened, nothing made any noise at all.

But this story begins with an October afternoon—a cool, fragrant, summer-soft day full of the shouts of children in the park, where the shadows on the grass seem splashed with the rich, autumnal coloration of the trees. The old man, Edward Cakes, walks down the street, having come from the library with another bunch of mystery novels, and as he approaches the old brownstone where he keeps his apartment, he sees the young man, the student, emerge from the front door with a pile of clothes and possessions stacked and bundled in his arms. There is a gleam of sweat on his very white, very smooth young face. He shoves everything, falls with it, into the back of a rust-pitted old Chevy station wagon that he had pulled up onto the sidewalk.

"Out of the way, Pops," he says to Edward Cakes.

The old man makes room for him, then goes on up to his room and drops the mystery novels on his bed, hears the student come lumbering past his door, carrying something heavy, no doubt. He decides to go down and find out what is happening, though he thinks he knows.

"Moving out?" he says to the young man, who meets him on the stairs.

"Outa the way, man."

Edward Cakes steps aside to let him pass.

One of the nurses comes down, then, and she and Cakes stand on the little porch, hearing the rumble and noise of the young man clearing himself out.

"I bet the cops are after him," the nurse says. Then she smiles; there is a gap between her front teeth. "Guess it's just going to be you and us for a while, Cakes."

They watch the young man come down the stairs, fighting with a rack of clothing. "Clear the goddamn doorway."

"Cops after you, dildo?"

"Right. I'm a drug ring."

"You?"

"Get the fuck outa the way."

They watch him pitch forward down the stairs, where he falls into the side of the car, braces himself, backs and staggers to the tailgate, and hurls himself, with the clothes, into the back. When he comes back up the steps, he is out of breath, but it is clear that he wants to say something to Cakes. "Can you—" he begins. "Can you—" He bends and puts his hands on his knees. "Can— you help me move a bookcase? It's my only piece of furniture." He is wheezing.

"You better do something about that asthma," the nurse says to him.

"It's the dust—moving. Will you—sir?"

Cakes follows him up to the room, which is smaller even than his own, the ceiling half an angle of roof on the one side, opposite the door; the bookcase is against the wall to the left, and it is heavy, cumbersome, coated with dust. They walk it out to the top of the stairs, and then the young man gets below it, guides it down. When they get it into the street, they must lift it to put it into the station wagon, and of course it doesn't fit, so the young man gets into the car and tries to rearrange everything, pushing it all toward the front seat. But the bookcase still won't go. It is just too big.

"I'm afraid it's just not going in there," Cakes says.

The nurse, sitting on the top step of the porch with her hands on her knees, laughs at them, chewing gum, blowing an occasional bubble and then closing her mouth over it.

"Fuck it," the young man says, and pulls the bookcase out on the street, toward the alley next to the house.

"I'll take it," says the nurse.

"You want it," the young man says, bending to lift it. In one motion, one powerful, continuous action, he raises it in his gleaming, straining arms above his head, and throws it down on the sidewalk; it lands with a sickening crack, like bones breaking, and one side of it splinters. "You can have it," he says.

For a moment no one says anything.

Then the young man closes the back of the station wagon, claps his hands together as if to knock the dust from them, swaggers to the driver's side of the car and gets in. He starts the car and it stalls. He tries again, and again it stalls. So he gets out and walks around to the front of it and kicks the grill, once, twice; he gets up on the hood and kicks the windshield and jumps up and down as if to stamp the whole car into the ground. When he tries to start it again, it catches, coughs, throws a cloud of black smoke out its exhaust pipe, but rumbles on, shaking, and slowly he pulls it off the sidewalk, down into the street, where, once more, it stalls. Now he gets out of it, comes back to the bookcase, picks it up and carries it, shoulder high, toward the car; he is going to smash it against the car, but then he falters, drops it, tries again to lift it. "Goddamn motherfucking shit-hole cock!" he screams. He manages to tip the bookcase back, to shove it so that it falls against the curb, where he kicks it, whirls and goes back to the car. This time it starts, and he gets it moving—pulls away in a swirl of street grit and squealing tires, on down to the end of the block and around the corner, screeching, out of sight.

"For somebody who likes quiet he can sure make a hell of a lot of noise," the nurse says.

The owner of the building was a very tall, stately-looking, dark-haired woman named Blackemore (pronounced Blake-a-more), and whenever anyone vacated one of the apartments, she made it an occasion to inspect the place. She rode out from downtown in a taxi, and made the driver wait for her while she walked through the building, inspecting first the vacated apartment and then all of the others; she looked for signs of abuse or carelessness, for repairs that needed attending to; she knew all the city building and wiring codes, and she checked everything for compliance to the letter of the law. To her tenants she was polite, vaguely supercilious, and efficient in the sense that she rarely wasted a word or a breath. She walked into Edward Cakes's room, nodded at him, then went about her work. When she was finished, she stood at his window and looked out.

"You keep a tidy apartment," she said.

"Thank you."

"Did you know the fellow who left us yesterday in such a hurry?"

"No."

"You wouldn't know where he intended to go, for instance."

"I'm sorry, no."

She turned from the window. "Very clean apartment."

"I like it," Cakes said.

"That young man left owing me more than a month's rent."

"I'm sorry, I didn't know him."

She seemed to study him a moment. "You keep to yourself, don't you."

He nodded.

"Are you happy here?"

He thought the question was odd. Again he nodded.

"No complaints?"

And now he understood. "The nurses," he said, "across the hall."

"Yes?"

"They keep me up all night."

She stared at him.

"They make too much noise."

After a moment she said, "I'll speak to them about it."

"The young man—the one who ran out—he used to get after them."

"I understand. I'll speak to them about it." She moved to the center of the room, stood gazing at the picture on the wall above his bureau. "Someone famous?"

"No."

"Looks like it should be someone famous. To think women used to dress like that. What did they call them?"

"Flappers," he said.

"That's it. Of course."

"I knew her," Cakes said.

"A girlfriend."

He nodded.

"Why don't you have other pictures on your walls?"

He could think of nothing to say.

"It's very clean, but barren in here," she said. Then she looked at the picture again. "A pretty girl like that. Do you mind if I straighten the picture? It seems crooked." She did not wait for his permission to do so. Then she nodded at him and went her way. He stood at the window and watched her get into the waiting taxi and ride off down the street, and when the cab was out of sight he turned and gazed for a long time at the picture on the wall. It had been straight. He set it right again, stepped back, stared at it. The girl in the photograph wore a dress he remembered to have been bright blue, with a low waist, and pleats at the hem; here was her lithe body in profile, with the one slender leg kicking back from the knee, the one arm up, as if she had just completed a pirouette—and her smiling lips and dark eyes. A perfect nineteen-year-old beauty, just a girl, a baby.

2

▲

This is what he could see from the window: across the street and ranked down a long hill to the left, blocks of row houses with little dirt yards and racks of clotheslines in back. To his right, at the end of the block, the square and the park, with, in winter anyway, the pond and fountain visible through the naked branches of the trees. Beyond the park, to the north, was an abandoned asphalt lot with a single island of rusted-out gas pumps, and from this lot one could see the widening perspective of the city, which seemed to have grown off in the opposite direction, away from these old buildings and the square. In fact, the square—and the park it contained—had once been an important part of the city, flanked by the old courthouse, the Municipal Hall, and the library. Now only the library was what it had once been; the Municipal Hall had been converted into a bank, and the courthouse had been torn down to make room for a computer school. The library was a fine old Romanesque building with a ponderous, gray dignity, but its holdings were fairly sparse, and every year fewer and fewer people used it.

Edward Cakes could spend entire afternoons there, sitting on the worn marble steps in front, or reading at one of the tables in its tall, columned rooms, without seeing another patron come through its doors. The one clerk, a woman with glasses thick as ice cubes, never spoke to him other than in her official capacity, never offered even the smallest crumb of recognition as if her myopia had made it impossible for her to remember a face from one day to the next. "Young lady," he had said to her once, "you don't like your work, do you." And the woman stared at him over the frames of the glasses.

"Do you wish to check books out or return them," she said.

One block past the square, facing an old Catholic church and a used-car lot, was a little restaurant called the People's Café, where, almost invariably, he had his dinner. It was a humble place, with checked tablecloths and wood-framed, plain pictures on the walls, but the food was always very good, and the choices were plentiful and interesting. One could go a long time without having the same thing twice there. On this afternoon he treated himself to pork chops and mashed potatoes with pork gravy, and then walked back to his room, wondering who the new tenant would be and if Mrs. Blackemore had found anyone yet. It was a fine, brisk fall day. When he got back to the room, he found the house empty—or at least quiet—and so he sat down in his chair by the window to read a chapter from one of the books he had checked out the evening before. He must have dozed off, for then it was dusk, and there was a knocking, someone calling a name. It was loud and seemed sudden, and he got up, went to his door, almost on tiptoe, and realized that someone was coming down the stairs from the room above. This someone now knocked on *his* door and brought a startled syllable up out of his throat.

"Hello?" A woman's voice.

He opened the door. She stood in the shadows of the landing, and he couldn't make out her features. "Yes?"

"Is—" The voice was distraught. "Excuse me—I'm—I'm looking for Terry. Do you—do you know where I might find Terry?"

"Terry," the old man said.

"Yes, Terry. Terry Dillard. Terry Dillard. I'm a friend of

Terry Dillard's and I'm looking for him. Do you know where he is."

"I'm afraid I don't know the name."

"Dillard," she said, loud, and came at him, or it seemed that way: the shadows fell away from her face and she stretched up on her toes to look beyond him at the room. "Dillard, are you in there?"

"I'm alone here," said Cakes.

"Well then—you must know him, mister. He lives right upstairs."

"That person—that person moved out. Yesterday evening. He was—he seemed very much in a hurry, too. He left without paying his rent."

Her face, as he spoke, registered something like recognition, as if this were only what she had expected. She pushed the hair back from her face, the features set in a kind of rueful acceptance. She was young, no more than twenty-five. Her eyes were deep-set, dark, almond-shaped, set above full lips the color of a faint bruise. It dawned on him that she was cold, her thin arms wrapped tightly about her chest, her shoulders quaking. She wore only a light denim jacket and jeans.

"You're shivering," he said, "come in here."

She put her hands to her face. "Goddamn. The bastard, I knew it."

"Come in here."

"You don't know where he went?"

He shook his head.

"The cold-blooded bastard." She began to cry. "He told me he'd meet me at the goddamn train station. He said he'd be waiting for me. He said when I got off he'd be there, waiting."

There seemed nothing else to say.

"Thanks," she said, turning from him.

"He was a student at the college," Cakes said. But she was already running down the stairs. He closed the door, went to the window and tried to find her in the dusky light of the street, but then she was on the stairs again. When he opened the door, she came past him, her hands shoved down into the pockets of the jacket. "Goddamn him," she said, pacing. "Goddamn him to hell." She halted, put her hands up to her hair, which was blond and very limp, as if she had just been doused with water. "I knew it. Goddamn him."

"Maybe you can find out where he went," Cakes said.

"It wouldn't make any difference. I should've known." She went to the window now, and he turned the overhead light on.

The room—bed and bedstand, bureau, table and chairs, stove and refrigerator, the one window, where this strange girl stood now, crying into her hands—seemed so much smaller somehow, so much meaner, with her in it. He moved to cover the rumpled sheets of the bed, feeling, oddly, that his pants were too short; he put his hands in his pockets and pushed down so the bottom cuffs met the tops of his shoes.

"Is there a way I can get into his room?" she asked.

"He took everything of his. There's just some old furniture that came with the room, I'm sure."

"The fucker." She sobbed.

He crossed the room to stand at her shoulder, and he thought he should touch her, yet couldn't, finally. He put his hand up, then withdrew it.

"I don't have anywhere to go," she said.

"You—you can stay here. Girls live across the hall."

She looked at him. "I'm going to have the son of a bitch's baby."

"You can stay across the hall," he said. "With the nurses. Until you can find something—they're nurses, across the hall—"

"No," she said, "fuck it."

Before he could do or say anything else, she had crossed to the door and was gone, leaving it ajar, running on the stairs and still crying. This time he saw her in the street below, and he watched her until she disappeared in the shadows at the end of the street.

3

▲

That night the nurses had some sort of party. They were up all hours, and their music pounded in the walls of the house. Edward Cakes lay sleepless, listening to it. The bass notes, repeating themselves like the tattoo of some primitive drummer, thrummed along his spine. It was not only too loud, it was completely without interest as music, as sound. He knew something about music—for almost forty years he had played violin as a member of the city's symphony orchestra; and if, all those years, he had never been quite good enough to be more than what people in the business called a tutti player, the orchestra was nevertheless a very fine orchestra, requiring that one be quite good to remain with it, and he had remained with it, had been a professional. He knew what music was when it was very good, and when it was very bad, he could be made physically sick by the sound of it.

As now.

He got up, finally, and composed a note to the nurses.

Please,
    The top room is empty, but I am still here, and I cannot sleep.

Sincerely,

    Edward Cakes

He went out into the hall, started to bend over and put the note under their door, but then thought better of it and retreated to his room. He would leave it for them in the morning, when they were not in such hilarious moods.

And so again he was lying quite still, listening to the awful music and the laughter, and when he finally went to sleep, he dreamed of women in some sort of aboriginal incarnation, dancing to the wild throbbing of drums. He woke in the watery light of predawn, in blessed quiet, got out of the bed and padded in his bare feet out into the hall and put the note under their door. Then he went back in his room, showered and dressed, hurrying a little because he did not want to meet them on the landing. He was faintly ashamed now as if he had done something sneaky or underhanded; all he wanted was a little consideration.

He breakfasted at the café, and then walked the five blocks past the square to visit an old friend who lived in a high-rise building called the Homestead. The Homestead was a place from which almost no one ever moved, once settled there. Arthur, aged eighty-nine, was settled there. Cakes had known him a long time; it was Arthur who had lived in the room above him before Terry Dillard occupied it. Arthur found one day that he could no longer get up and down stairs of any kind. He had a daughter who lived out in the suburbs, and she had arranged to have him placed, as it were, in the Homestead. She rarely came to see him there, but she was not a woman who could travel into the city with ease: she herself was past sixty years of age, and traffic frightened her.

"I must be dying," Arthur said to Cakes now, "my daughter sends me a plant." He sat in a padded chair, with a sweater folded over his knees like a shawl. He was very thin, brown and leathery, and he had no hair at all, but his bones were big—you could see he had once been a powerful man, and there was something about him, some element of outrage, that animated him, lighted his eyes and quickened the movements of his hands. "Look at this," he said. It was a potted plant with odd, facetless, round leaves. "Some kind of damned cactus, Edward." The plant was on the small table between his chair and the one Cakes now sat in. Both chairs faced the television set on the other side of the room. The screen was blank.

"From my daughter, a cactus."

"How is your daughter?"

"You want to know how Linda is. She's healthy enough and

she's got money enough to pay my rent here. That's how she is. And she sends me this plant. A cactus. That's how she is."

"Does it say what it is?" Cakes reached over and moved one of the leaves of the plant to see if there was a label on the rim of the pot, or a tag stuck into the very black, mulchy dirt around the waxy stem.

"It's a cactus," Arthur said. "I told you that."

"Yes, but what kind of cactus."

"Hell," Arthur grumbled, "a cactus is a cactus."

They were quiet for a few moments.

"A girl came to my room yesterday," Cakes said. "A young girl."

"Wonderful, Edward. Tell me."

"She wasn't extremely attractive, I must say."

"She was ugly?"

"No, not ugly."

"Once had a lovely woman name of Maxine. She was uglier than hell, Edward, but a lovely woman all the same. I almost married her. But now—this girl. She's good-looking."

"Kind of—sloppy," Cakes said.

"Agh. They dress so sloppy these days. It's the style." Arthur cleared his throat, staring off at the blank television screen. "Well, anyway—did you make love with her?"

"Don't be ridiculous."

"Hell," Arthur said. "Tell me about the flapper. It's been a while since we've talked about her."

"I was telling you about this girl who came to my room."

"Come on," said Arthur, nodding at him. "I'm in love with the flapper."

It was something Cakes had mentioned once, a memory, and Arthur had pressed him for the details—which were romantic. Quite so, in fact, though Arthur almost always wound up suggesting things about it, making it part of what was now an old argument between them: Arthur was crude, his version of romance too baldly sexual for his friend's sense of propriety and respect. The story about the flapper was not really a story; it was without any real narrative line. Cakes merely told of having spent a winter weekend in a cabin in Vermont with the flapper, the girl in the picture on his wall. That girl had become Edward's wife; her name was Ellen. In 1928 she was gorgeous and adventurous and she took Edward Cakes, nineteen years old and a virgin, to the cabin—it was owned by her parents, who were, then, in Europe on a holiday—and he made a fire in the fireplace while she changed into a chiffon nightgown with puffy fur collar and sleeve cuffs, and they had two days there alone, in the snow of the year 1928; they drank champagne and toasted poor Al Smith, and in the night she danced for him, naked in the firelight. She made love to him, the goddess of his wildest dreams, lying back on the thick-piled white rug with her long legs open, those dancer's legs, and outside it snowed and the wind blew as if the world were empty. Cakes told the story with a kind of fanatical excitement, because it was perhaps the best memory of his life. "I took her picture—the one on my wall—that year."

"Ah," Arthur said. "The look of a young woman—the way a woman moves."

"One came to my room yesterday."

Arthur sighed. "I married young. I might've told you this. My Angela was a pretty person, but you know she never wanted me to look at her. It was because she was so big, of course. But I loved her. I would have liked a little oral sex, though."

Cakes looked at him. "I'm not going to talk about this."

"What's wrong with talking about a little oral sex?"

"Please," Cakes said.

"You didn't get any oral sex that night?"

"I don't know why I let you talk me into telling you about it."

"I'm just asking you."

"It's a ridiculous, filthy question."

"Then you didn't."

"I didn't say that," Cakes said.

"You said you did everything. That's the way you tell the story—you say you went up to this cabin in the mountains and you built a fire and the two of you spent the whole weekend there and you did everything—right in front of the fire."

"All right," Cakes said.

Arthur looked at him out of one eye, the other squinting, pulling the corner of his mouth up. "Well?"

"Look, there's magazines that have what you want. I'll buy you one of those magazines the next time I come over."

"I couldn't use it now, anyway," Arthur said. "I got these nurses coming in and out of here all day long."

"You know what your trouble is," said Cakes, "you don't have any sense of romance. You have absolutely no sense of romance at all."

"I think a thing like that is romantic," Arthur said.

"Well, there you are."

Arthur sighed, unfolded his hands and ran them along his thin thighs. "I'm probably not going to leave this place, Cakes. Couldn't you just humor me a little bit and let it go at that? I mean, where's the harm. It's just talk."

"I don't like that kind of talk," said Cakes. "I never have."

"Yeah—well, you don't like convalescent homes either, do you. Here you are."

"Let's change the subject," Cakes said.

"Anything for a friend," said Arthur.

4

▲

The nurses were in their early thirties. One was blond, very thin, with a shrill, unpleasant voice and a manic, cackling laugh. Her name was Denise, and Cakes knew this because she was always addressing herself: "Denise, you need a date tonight," she would shout, coming up the stairs. "Denise, you are home at last."

The other was Spanish-looking, with opaque black eyes and a round, flat-nosed face. She chewed gum constantly, it seemed, and sang in a rich alto voice to the radio; she was very good—seemed to understand harmony. She could pick eighth notes out of the air. She was sitting on the top step of the porch as he came walking home after dinner at People's Café. She was filing her nails. The afternoon sun had been warm, and now it was cooling, an enormous red disk beyond the far houses at the end of the street. "Hey," she said, "getting cold."

He said, "Good evening."

"Got your note," she said. "We didn't know we were causing you any trouble, Baby Cakes. You never complained before—we thought you might be hard of hearing."

"Mrs. Blackemore didn't mention to you that I was disturbed by the noise?"

"Sure didn't."

"Well," he said.

She blew a bubble and popped it, looking directly at him. "Listen, you got levels we never thought about before, Baby Cakes."

"I'm afraid I don't know what you mean," he said. "I'm tired, I need a good night's sleep."

"Well, I hope you get it tonight, I'll tell you."

He climbed the steps.

"There's somebody waiting for you," she said. "Somebody young, Baby Cakes."

"I don't remember your name," Cakes said.

"Paula."

"Paula, please don't call me Baby Cakes."

"Whatever you say." She smiled at him.

Upstairs, just outside his door, sitting down with her knees up and her back against the wall, was the young girl.

"I'm back," she said.

He opened his door, entered the room, and she came in behind him. She was wearing the same clothes, the same jacket. When she put her hands up to her long hair and set it back over her ears, he saw that the hands were bony and thick-knuckled, like a man's; she shoved them into the pockets of the jacket.

"I thought I'd take you up on your offer," she said, "till I get a place to settle."

He said, "Pardon me?"

"You know." Something in her gaze seemed to poke at him, and he looked away. "The room. A place to stay."

He looked at her again.

"Come on," she said, "don't leave me hanging here—I spent the last day and a half on the street."

"You—you want to stay here?"

She said, "Yeah. Here."

"I meant for the night," he said.

"I have to stay somewhere, all right? I mean, is it all right with you?"

"Yes," Cakes said, "No—you don't understand."

"I'll do anything you want," said the girl.

"No. When you were here before—I meant you could stay across the hall, with the nurses. Just for the night."

"Look, I don't care," she said, and seemed about to cry again.

He went to the door and closed it. She had sat down at the table and folded her arms; she looked like someone waiting to be talked to, scolded perhaps, given instructions about ways of conduct.

"I only have this bed."

"I'll sleep on the floor."

"I don't understand," he said. "Why here? Why would you want to stay here?"

"I don't know anybody else. You seemed nice. What do you want?" She spread her fingers out on the polished surface of the table. "Maybe you got lucky, who knows."

"What about your family?"

She was looking at her hands. "I don't have a family."

"You're an orphan?"

"Not exactly."

"Mother, father—tell me." He was getting impatient; he stood over her and felt the strangeness of having her there, and then he remembered that she was pregnant. Quite suddenly, with a feeling like memory, he knew he wanted her to stay.

"I came up from Virginia," she said. "Mother, father. Brothers and sisters. All older than me. My nearest brother is thirty. I came along late in life, see."

He merely nodded. He was afraid to say the wrong thing.

"Mother promptly had a nervous breakdown."

"Lord," Edward Cakes said. He sat down across from her, adjusted his chair. "Go on."

"That's all. I'm the baby and I fucked everything up. I hate them all and I'm sure they hate me right back."

"What brought you—I mean, I know what brought you—"

"You want to know about Terry-and-the-Pirates Dillard, right?"

He nodded.

"Terry is from Virginia, too. We went to the same high school and graduated together and all that, and this year we got me pregnant. He came back from college and I sort of went for him—" she put her fist up to her mouth, and then sniffled. "He said, you know, that he wanted me to get on the goddamn train, and come up here, and we'd try it. He was going to meet me at the station. Well, I just should've known better." She was crying now, spitting the words out. "But I went for it. Hook, line and sinker. You should've seen me at the station, walking around looking for him. I just kept walking around that station, looking at all the faces, and not one of them is him. The son of a bitch. I left all my things there and just started out and came here and he's—gone."

"Maybe he just got scared," Cakes said.

"Of course he got scared. He got cold feet. Of course—anybody could guess that."

"Then maybe he'll come back."

"Maybe." She sniffled again. "Ha."

"Maybe he—maybe he went to Virginia to find you."

She shook her head. "You know he fucking dropped out of school? Right in the middle of the semester. That's how much he wanted to see me." She was staring at nothing now, the rough, mannish hands in the jacket pockets. "He's probably a thousand miles away by now."

"I'm sorry," Cakes said.

She only glanced at him, and she did not speak.

"Do you—do you need money to go home?"

"There's no such place."

"I'm sorry to hear that," Cakes said.

She was wiping her nose with the flat of her hand. "I slept in the park last night."

"Lord," Cakes said, "that's not safe."

She looked at him. "I'll sleep in that chair by the window. I'll be gone most days—I have to get settled in somewhere, you know, and find a place. A job. And this can be where I come to hide. I have a little money, but I don't want to spend it too fast, so I can pay you some other way, maybe."

"You don't have to pay me," he said.

"I'd clean up or something."

"You don't have to."

"No, I will."

"You can use the bed, too," he said, feeling warm and generous and glad. "I'll sleep in the chair."

"Oh no."

"It's all right. I nap in it all the time."

"It looks like a comfortable chair."

"If you'd rather have the chair—" he began.

"No, that's fine. The bed's fine—it looks like a comfortable bed."

"Very good," he said.

She stood, ran her hands through her hair, then seemed suddenly confused, even embarrassed. She sat down again.

"Very good," he said again.

"My name's Mary."

He told her his, and they shook hands across the table. "And you're from Virginia."

"Virginia born and bred."

"My friend Arthur is from Virginia. A place called Point Royal."

"I know it. I have an aunt lives there."

"Well, I'll tell him."

She sighed. They both looked at the room. It was as if, now that she would be staying in it, something about it—the measurements, the lines of it, the walls and the angles of ceiling and cornice and corner—had changed. "Cakes," she said. "That's an unusual name, isn't it."

He agreed.

"I bet you got teased a lot when you were a kid."

"I still do," he said.

Again they were looking at the room. Her gaze settled on the picture above the bureau. "Who's that?"

"A woman I knew when I was young."

She got up and walked over to the bureau and stood with her hands in the back pockets of her jeans, studying the picture. "Very pretty."

"Thank you."

"She had nice eyes."

"Yes."

"A pretty face."

"I thought so."

"I always loved those kinds of clothes."

He said nothing.

"A regular flapper, huh. Was it your wife?"

"Later she was, yes."

"Lucky for you."

"Yes," he said.

She turned. "Well—guess we better make this bed. You know —fresh sheets?"

"Of course."

They worked together. She had removed her jacket, revealing a soft pink blouse, far too thin for the chilly weather; she wore no bra, and the light, at certain angles, showed the shadow of her breasts through the cloth.

"What're you looking at," she said suddenly.

He stammered, "I'm sorry."

"They're sore," she said.

"Where are the—rest of your things?"

"Still at the train station—in the—you know, the baggage place. Wherever they keep that stuff. I mean I just left it there and went looking for Terry and came all the way here. And I haven't been back to the station." She fluffed the pillow and laid it down at the head of the bed, then tucked the open end of the slip under it. "There," she said. "Now, do you mind if I crawl in?"

"No."

"Great," she said.

He watched her pull the spread down and arrange herself under it, using it to cover her as she removed her jeans. Then she lay back on the pillow, not looking at him, somehow not even aware of him as if she had thought he had left the room. This shook his nerves loose, and now he was conscious, in a strange way, of the whole thing, this turn of events, like a sudden fall, and so he had to excuse himself and go into the bathroom. There, he tried to make no noise, and he remembered how his wife would run the water in the tub whenever she used the bathroom; he had always thought it a ridiculous thing, yet now he did so himself. He would take a shower, or a bath. He would take a slow bath, soak himself.

5

His wife and son had died within a year of each other, the son of a wound through the heart during the police action in Korea; the wife of a heart attack seven months later. She had been in frail health since the first years of the marriage, and the doctors said it was heart failure that killed her, but Edward Cakes knew it was grief. His own grief almost killed him. He lay sleepless many nights, thinking of the ways he might die, thinking of the rest of his life as a thing he lacked strength to do, and his heart would move in his chest as if to get out from under the weight of his sorrow. This all took place in a house, on a clean, quiet street in the suburbs of the city. There were wide patches of shade on well-kept lawns, and little explosions of color where flower gardens bloomed. It was the forty-fourth spring of his life. There were neighbors and friends who loved him, worried over him, tried to console him, keep him busy, interest him in other women. He told them he wanted to be left alone; he hoped they understood. His wife's sister came all the way from California to help him settle things—sell the house, decide what he should do next. She was a garrulous, religious woman with no sense of horror at all. She talked about her sister in a silly, half-teasing way, as if her spirit were standing in the room, and he hated her for it, hated her for trivializing the death of his wife, though he knew that this was her only way of dealing with it, that she was barely holding on to this large article of faith: that the dead woman was with God, broken heart and all.

"Edward," she said, "she's probably laughing at us right now."

"Yes," he said, "of course."

The sister's name was Jane. She was married to a doctor—a gynecologist from Austria, whose German accent reminded Cakes of the death camps: the man opened his mouth to ask for the sports page in the morning and Edward Cakes saw piles of bones, the horrifying sepia photographs of ovens and bodies. For the doctor this journey east was an occasion, apparently, of much needed rest. He spent most of each day in bed in the guest room of the house, reading the newspapers and going over some financial reports that he had brought with him. He had never met Cakes, had never seen his dead sister-in-law, and so he could hardly be expected to mourn very deeply. Yet it bothered Cakes the way he asked for the sports page every morning, the way he sat daubing his lips with the napkin after each bite of a meal, the cold blue of his eyes. There was something too precise about him as if he were one of those amazing German clocks that ran perfectly for seventy-five years without losing a second. Jane bustled around the house, trying to keep too busy to think, and her husband lay behind the closed door of the guest room, turning the pages of a financial report and, no doubt, dreaming of money.

One night, near the end of their stay, Jane and the Austrian had an argument over something—it was the sort of smoldering, bitter, muted unpleasantness that results when there is no privacy, and emotions are tamped down to preserve the sense of decorum and harmony. The Austrian was sullen and uncommunicative most of the day. After dinner he excused himself in a small, controlled voice and went to bed, and poor Jane began to get drunk. Cakes had brought out a box of family photographs. After a while he and Jane sat together on the sofa in the living room, going through all the old pictures of Edward's wife: Ellen sitting on the low rail of a porch, in the shade of an awning, her hands lightly on her lap—some bright summer day of her girlhood; Ellen with Jane in a group of young women at the beach; Ellen alone, posing in white tulle, pensive, a dancer.

"This one," Jane kept saying, handing him the photographs. "Oh, and this one." She was drinking brandy from a snifter, and from time to time she offered him some of it. Each time he refused, and she would pour herself some more.

"You can't believe how beautiful she was here." She held a picture of Ellen smiling from a window of the house in Hudson Bay, where the two girls had grown up. "There was something special about her from the start," Jane said. "You can see it here. The will, the—the impulsiveness."

"Yes," Cakes said.

"And here she is in that flapper outfit."

"Yes," he said.

Jane sighed. "Nineteen twenty-eight." She sat back and sipped the brandy. "I wish we could've seen more of each other over the years. Time gets away from you."

"I know," he said.

"Did she—did Ellen talk about me?"

"Of course she did."

"Tell me."

"Oh, come on, Jane. This is hard enough for me—"

"Of course it is. Of course it is."

They were quiet for a moment.

"I'm going to tell you something I never told anyone before," Jane said. "I loved Ellen so much. She was absolutely the most wonderful person in this world."

Cakes could not look at her, yet he could not quite look away either. She poured more brandy for herself, and he watched this.

"I loved her to distraction."

"It's late," he said.

"Only if you're German."

He thought she had spoken too loud. "For the love of God, Jane."

"It's true. Germans go to bed like small towns. Nine o'clock sharp. Unless, of course, there's a village to plunder."

He stared at Ellen's face in the photograph that, so many years later, would hang on his wall.

"Don't you like the word 'Teutonic'?" Jane asked.

"I don't want to talk about this."

"Of course you don't."

A moment later she said, "I didn't really know her after she was married to you."

"Well—" he began.

"We were all the way out there in California."

"Yes."

She poured more of the brandy for herself. "When we were kids, you know, we were very close."

He said nothing.

"Did she tell you how close we were?"

"Of course."

"I'm drunk," Jane said, and took a long drink of the brandy.

"I think I'll go to bed," said Cakes.

"Don't go yet. Did I tell you how much I loved Ellen?"

"You did."

"She was my favorite person—she had the courage the rest of us didn't have."

"Why don't you go on to bed now," he said.

"Loved her—I'll tell you. We were not ordinary sisters."

He waited.

"She was the dancer, though. She was the one who had all the talent. You know, like you with the violin. I mean I always knew she'd wind up with somebody like you—a musician or an artist or something. An author. She had all the talent and the looks. I bet you were never disappointed in her."

"No." It was all he could say.

"Eh. See?" Jane put the glass down hard, and let her hands fall in her lap. "Everything she wanted she could have. From the time she was a baby. Everybody loved her."

He sat nodding, looking at the pile of photographs in his lap.

"Something—something special about her."

"Yes."

"I mean when she was young, of course." She picked the glass up again, took a loud swallow from it.

"Of course," Edward said.

"As to how she was later—well, I wish I knew. I wish I'd been able to see her a little."

He said nothing.

"Well," Jane sighed, "she's in a better place, anyway. She's probably laughing at us right now."

This irritated him, and he sought to change the subject. "I'm moving into the city."

"She's probably sitting right there in that chair laughing at us."

"Why would she be laughing."

Jane waved the hand that held the snifter of brandy, and the liquid almost splashed over the rim of it. "You don't find this funny? The older sister, who never had the looks or the personality and who married Hitler just so she could be reminded of her shortcomings every day of her life—you don't find this funny? The older sister, still a little envious of the younger?"

There wasn't anything to say to this, and he was a little surprised to find himself nodding as if in agreement.

"So she's sitting there laughing."

"No," he said. He could not allow this ridiculous vision of his wife. "She's not sitting anywhere, all right? She's dead, Jane."

At this, Jane began to cry. She made no sound at all, sitting with the glass of brandy tilted precariously in her lap, the tears streaming down her cheeks. "I hated her," she said low. "Jesus

Christ. I was glad every time something bad happened to her—
every time she hurt herself."

"You ought to go to bed," he said to her. Then he gently
lifted the glass from the relaxed fingers of her hand, and almost at
once she stiffened, as if to gather herself for a shout or scream.

She looked at him, blinked, then blinked again. "Where's my
drink." Her voice was quiet but petulant, almost whining. "I want
my brandy."

"It's right here," he said.

And then the doctor was standing above them, blond and
impassive and superior. He did not drink. One could almost tell
merely by looking at him. He wore his robe tied neatly, and his
hair was combed straight back, like the physical manifestation of
the order and symmetry of his soul. "Jane," he said.

"What." She did not look at him.

"Come to bed now, Jane." His voice was soft, but firm.

"You go fuck yourself, Adolf."

"Jane, zis vill get you nowhere. Zis anger all ze time."

"It gets me somewhere, Fritz."

"You stop zis, Jane."

"You got it, Hans."

"She iss drunk," the Austrian said to Cakes. Then he reached
down and took her wrist. "She iss upset. Zis has been a shock to
her."

"Hands off, Heinie."

The ɯoctor let go of her and put his hands in the pockets of
his robe.

"Go to bed, Hermann."

"Ze name iss Thomas."

"No shit."

"Jane, you know zis iss not befitting you."

She sat sipping the brandy, and Cakes got up to leave them
there. "Don't go, Edward," she said.

He made no answer, nor did he show that he had heard her.
He went to the bedroom and closed himself in, sat on the bed that
for more than twenty years had been his and Ellen's, and began to
cry quietly, hearing the low muttering on the other side of the

door. It was dark. There was nothing but these voices troubling the quiet. He listened to them, and abruptly he was filled with a black horror, that he was alone, that these people arguing so un-happily in the other room were going to be leaving him soon, and then there would be no one. For a searing minute it was as if he could feel the lonely curve of the planet, spinning away from the sun. He lay back on the bed, closed his eyes and heard Jane crying in the guest room. In the morning she would remember every-thing, and perhaps she would stop talking about heaven and about Ellen as though Ellen were sneaking through the rooms of the house, a friendly spirit, smiling blissfully beyond strife. . . .

But the next morning, the morning she and the Austrian left for California, she was her old self. The only sign that there had been anything between them was her continuing attention to the photographs; she wanted some of them, wanted to have them to remember her sister by. Her eyes grew moist as she expressed this wish, and her husband touched her shoulder; it was a caress. He put his arm around her and led her to the sofa, where she sat picking through the photographs, marveling at what they pre-sented to her memory. Cakes was still feeling the fright of the night before over the prospect of being alone, and he asked them to stay another week.

"We couldn't," said the Austrian.

Edward said, "I understand," and felt the lining of his stom-ach begin to burn.

In an odd way his fear about being alone had something to do with his insistence, that morning so long ago, that Jane take the photographs with her. There was some wordless corner of his mind which understood that the photographs would serve to keep him in touch with Jane, and the connection, any connection, was quite suddenly more important than anything else, including his discomfort with the doctor, who, just before he and Jane stepped out the door, took Edward's hand and said, "You haf to go on wid life now."

"Yes," Edward said, wondering how one was to set about going on with life, what actions one was to take to start.

As far as Cakes knew, Jane and the Austrian were still living somewhere out on the West Coast. For a few years they had kept a desultory correspondence; but it had lapsed sometime before Cakes rented his room in Mrs. Blackemore's old brownstone house.

Once, long ago, with Ellen, he had traveled to Washington, D.C.—and in a museum there he had seen a coral-encrusted sword and scabbard in a glass case. The plaque explaining the exhibit said: *This Spanish Sword and Scabbard remain just as they were when removed from the sea off the coast of Florida in 1936.* Sometime after he had settled into the room, he thought about this: he was buried somehow, oxidizing, gathering coral. He had formed friendships with women and then been frightened away by them, by something of their need for him, some element of their loneliness; he had gradually cut himself off from old friends, old comforts. He took a bus each day to Symphony Hall, where he sat among players far younger than he, most of whom would move on to become principals, if not soloists, and they rarely spoke to him; he had become this lone person, stopped here, in bitter solitude. He played his violin and grew tired of the sound. It was an effort to play it with any enthusiasm at all. He realized, one afternoon while practicing for a concert in which a famous soloist would do the Beethoven Violin Concerto, that this sound of the violin was often the only sound that issued from him in the course of a day.

He went home that night, and when he saw Arthur going up the stairs ahead of him, he said, "Good evening, sir."

Arthur turned around, holding onto the banister. "Excuse me?"

"I said good evening."

"Oh, good evening."

"My name is Edward Cakes." He offered his hand.

"Arthur Hagood," said Arthur, smiling, "pleased to meet you. We've been passing on these stairs for more than two years, and now all of a sudden you want to talk."

"I'll buy you a whiskey," Cakes said.

"Are you desperate? I don't like to be with desperate people."

"I am not desperate. I just felt like speaking to you. We've been passing each other on the stairs for two years, and I thought it was high time."

Arthur nodded at him. "Then you can come up in my room and we'll have a little whiskey."

That first night Cakes did most of the talking. He talked about how the years seemed to blur and run together, and how he was almost sixty and couldn't remember what he had done with all that time, since the death of his family. He had worked, he had traveled, acquired a few possessions; he was alone now, and he had been alone for a very long time.

"You're lucky," Arthur said. "You don't have anybody to take care of you."

"I don't understand."

"I'll tell you sometime."

They were quiet.

"Some people call me Max," said Arthur. "I never liked it much. Close friends, if they want to sometimes—they can call me Max. Okay?"

Cakes nodded.

"Not all the time though."

"Were you ever close to getting married again?" Cakes asked him.

"Once. A lovely woman, too. She had a daughter, too. And the daughter wanted to take care of her. I'll tell you sometime."

"You have a daughter."

"She worries about me," Arthur said.

A moment later he said, "What about you. You ever get close again?"

"A couple times."

"What happened?"

Cakes shrugged. "I couldn't do it."

"Why not?"

He shrugged again.

"Yeah," Arthur said, "who ever knows."

6

▲

"There's a girl sleeping in my room," he said.

Arthur was lying down, propped on pillows, the bed cranked up so that he could eat the fruit and green salad that lay on the tray before him. The television was on, the sound turned low, and it flickered at the foot of the bed.

"Did you hear me?"

"I heard you," Arthur said. "Eat some of this, will you? I'm not hungry."

"I don't want any."

"So you have a girl sleeping in your room."

"Sleeping in my bed."

"With *you?*"

"I sleep in the chair."

"She's desperate."

"Do you want me to tell you about it or not?"

"I'd rather see for myself."

"Maybe I'll bring her here to visit you."

"Could you talk her into something for me—"

Cakes interrupted him. "None of your filthy talk, Max."

"I was going to ask if she had a friend—or a sister, maybe."

"She has a big family."

"Children?"

"No. She's just a baby."

"How young is she?"

"Twenties."

"And so why is this baby staying with you?"

"She's expecting."

"She's staying with you because she's going to have a child?"

Cakes began to explain.

"Ah," Arthur said suddenly. "Tell me about the flapper."

"I was telling you about Mary—"

"I *know* you were. It's uninteresting—it's got no beauty. It's happening to you right now. Don't bore me with what's happening to you right now."

"Do you want me to stop coming over here?"

"I want you to stop boring me with this girl."

"Well, then *you* talk. You talk and I'll listen to you."

"I'm going to close my eyes," Arthur said, "and look at her face, and you tell me about it. Come on. It was snowing outside, you had a fire in the fireplace—"

"Eat your supper," Cakes said. "I'm going."

"Don't go."

"Well, let me talk about what I want to talk about."

"You know what they say?" Arthur asked him.

He waited.

"They say that when two men talk about their sexual experiences, it's a sign of deep friendship."

"Who says that."

"*They.* Whoever *they* are—the authorities. It's like *anonymous* in the books, you know. This poem was written by anonymous. *They* say a man is closest friends with another man when they talk about sexual experience together."

"I'm not talking about sexual experience," Cakes said, "I'm talking about romance, for God's sweet sake."

"You're having a romance with this girl."

"No, no, no, no, no. I was talking about Ellen."

"Don't call her Ellen. She's your wife when you call her that. For me, she has to be the flapper."

"She was my wife, you know."

"Forget it," Arthur said, "Let's just drop the whole thing."

"You see a pretty woman and even at your age all you can think of is having her, like a—like a dinner or something. No wonder your wife wanted to keep the lights out when you were together that way—"

Arthur's eyes narrowed. "You can leave Angel out of this."

They were quiet for a moment.

"You know what I think of your romance," Arthur said. "Shit. That's what I think of it. Your romance is totally without body. Now me, I sit in this place and think of beautiful women. What's wrong, I'd like to know, with that? The knights in shining armor, Edward, they bathed once or twice every five years. The damsel in distress wore a veil so she could cover her nose."

"You have a right to your opinion," Cakes said.

"I do. And to my dreams, too. Even if they're about somebody's wife."

Again they were quiet.

"I'm sitting here waiting to die, and I can think what I damn well please."

"You're not going to die," Cakes said.

"Of course I am. Good God, what a stupid thing to say."

"You know what I mean," Cakes said. "Not now. You're not going to die now."

"I didn't say I was going to die now," said Arthur. "Now please leave. Leave me alone."

"I'll bring the girl to visit with you."

"Don't bother."

"It's no bother," Cakes said. "You can look at her and think what you please."

"You always thought you were better than I am, didn't you?"

"I never thought any such thing."

"Sure you did. Because I was older and my health wasn't good."

"Come on."

"You always thought I was vulgar."

"That's not so," Cakes said. "Come on, I'm leaving now. Let's be friends again."

But Arthur lay staring at the flickering television screen and would not answer him. When you offended Arthur, you created a sulking child; in an hour he would be himself again, and he would probably wish he had not sent his friend away so rudely. Cakes got on the elevator and rode the six floors to the lobby, where a crowd of people were returning from some outing or other. Somewhere in the suburbs was Arthur's one daughter and her family.

When Cakes first knew Arthur, there had been occasional trips out to have dinner with them. Since Arthur had been placed in this home, the only person who came to see him at all was Cakes, and there were times when it seemed that Cakes must bear the resentment and anger that those who were so conspicuously absent had caused. There was an understanding between the two friends, wordless and in some way almost timid: they had never spoken before about how close they were; no talk had passed between them about what good friends they were or what they meant to each other—there were no signs, no words of affection. They seldom bothered even to greet each other: when Cakes visited him they simply began talking as though picking up from a previously interrupted conversation. During the time that Arthur had resided at Mrs. Blackemore's house, they would often pass each other going in or coming out of the building—they were friends by this time, they might have made plans to spend the evening together—yet they would barely speak. It was as if there was something they had to be surreptitious about. They would exchange a look of recognition, and that was all; anyone watching them would have said they did not know each other. Cakes would go on up to his room, and a few minutes, or a few hours—or a few days—later, Arthur would knock on his door and, when the door was opened, begin to speak:

"If you had a television, you wouldn't be so jumpy all the time."

"I'm not jumpy."

"You don't sleep well at all."

"I never did."

"You never had a television."

"Of course I did."

"Well, why don't you get one?"

As he was leaving the home, Edward Cakes remembered Arthur talking about being closest friends—the business about sexual experience. What had Arthur wanted to tell him? He thought about the other man's eyes and saw again the way Arthur had stared at the television. He was standing outside the building. There was a bright sun, and a blustery wind that shook the stop sign on the corner and bent his coat collar up against the side of his neck. He looked back at the building, which rose straight up, fourteen floors, in gray stone somberness, and the nerve of anyone to call it a home. Now it seemed alive, breathing, a thing that could swallow. Arthur would never leave this place.

Cakes turned and went back in, walked down to the elevators and pushed the glowing button and waited, feeling oddly the need to hurry, as if something might prevent him from getting to his friend's room in time.

Arthur was still staring at the television screen, where a fire engine sped around a corner.

"Maybe it'll be a short winter," Cakes said.

The other man said nothing.

"I'd like to see some warm weather."

Arthur sighed, looked at him. "What did you forget?"

"Nothing."

"Don't tell me. I've been unconscious—you were here three days ago."

"No. I was just here. I came back."

"Why?"

"I don't know. I just felt like it."

"You don't have anything better to do."

Cakes was silent.

"Get lost. I don't need your pity."

"I don't know what you're talking about," Cakes said. "Why don't you turn this television off. You lay here and waste electricity."

"I like to look at the colors."

"You like to look at the girls."

"That too—why did you come back?"

"Because I wanted to—"

"Yes, but why did you want to."

"What is this anyway?" Cakes said.

"You feel sorry for me. Right? I won't allow it, Cakes. I'd rather be alone here."

"I'm not feeling sorry for you. I love you."

"Good God, he's turned queer."

Cakes tried to laugh. "You know, Max."

"Just remember, you spoke to me first. You came to me. Just remember that. You didn't have anyone. Not a soul."

"I won't forget it," Cakes said. "You'll remind me."

"I hope I don't have to," said Arthur. "I just hope I don't have to." And again he began to stare, petulantly and with his mouth drawn down, at the television.

7
▲

The girl had been gone all day, and she was not yet there when he returned from his visit with Arthur. He sat by the window with a glass of orange juice and watched the street below. An old woman hurried against the wind, holding onto her hat. In the park, up the other way, some boys were playing a game of tackle football; they had put their coats down to serve as markers—out of bounds and goal line. Edward Cakes watched them for a time, sipping the orange juice. He was beginning to wonder if the girl would return. It was growing dark; the wind had grown colder, no doubt. He watched the football game break up, and then he started thinking about dinner. He would cook it himself tonight. He would set two places at the table. This seemed so strange, trying to decide what to cook for dinner. He set the table, whistling softly. One plate he tossed behind his back and over his shoulder, to catch it with his other hand; he bowed, smiling, put the plate down with a gliding motion, stood straight and rubbed the palms of his hands together. It would be so much fun to cook for someone else. But when he heard a noise on the stairs, he was abruptly aware of the possibility that he would seem foolish in this assumption that she would want to eat with him. So he hurriedly put everything away again. Just as he got the last piece into the drawer by the sink, he heard the nurses out in the hall, talking loud. The girl had not

even come, then, and here he was, out of breath, ridiculous, leaning on the sink. He went to the door, looked out. Denise and
Paula were laden down with bags of groceries.

"What's with you, Baby Cakes," Paula asked him.

"Looking for his girlfriend," said Denise.

"Here," Paula said, thrusting her hip at him. "Reach in my
purse and get the key out and open the door for us, will you?"

"Hurry up," said Denise, "I'm dropping these."

The purse dangled on Paula's hip. Cakes reached into it, and
Paula gave a little sexual groan through the popping of her chewing gum. Denise laughed, like a shriek, because Cakes, lifting the
keys out of the deep pockets of the purse, had hooked a piece of
silklike cloth, and brought it out with the keys.

"My God," Paula said, "open the door, will you?"

He couldn't get the cloth untangled, couldn't find the right
key. He turned in a small circle there in the hall, with the nurses
moving and laughing and breathing at his sides, bags falling, cans
bouncing, the voices echoing unpleasantly along the walls; finally
he got the key, Paula shouting at him that it was the one, and he
put it into the lock and got the door open. The two women stumbled and faltered into the apartment, and he bent down to pick up
the fallen cans. It was beer. "Better not open these," he said, to no
one in particular. Then he tried to get the key out of the lock,
holding one of the beers under his arm. The key would not come
out; he pulled, jiggled it, pulled again. There was a lot of confusion and noise; Denise was beginning to empty the bags and Paula
was looking through them.

"Where's the beer. Did you forget the damn beer?"

"It's here." Cakes held up the two beers. "Two of them,
anyway."

"It's cold. I gotta have it *ice* cold."

Cakes handed her the two beers and then realized that there
was no reason for him to be standing in the doorway now; they
seemed already to have forgotten him. Paula had opened one of
the beers, which foamed and spouted, sending her to the sink,
laughing. "Goddamn."

"Hey, Cakes," Denise said, "you want a beer?"

"No thank you," he said.

"Come on and get loud," said Paula. "Can't you get the key out of the door?"

"It seems to be stuck."

"They had my undies hooked to them. Ain't that the damnedest thing?"

"Who puts her underpants in her purse, for God's sake," Denise said.

"The elastic came off today, Cakes. I shoved it all in my purse. Come on and have a beer. Let's be friends."

"I have to make something for dinner," he said.

"For you and the little honey, huh."

"She your granddaughter or something?" Denise asked.

He said, "She's a—friend."

"Woo-woo."

"Does she like to party?" asked Paula.

"I couldn't say."

"Poor Cakes. You're really flustered, ain't you. Do we keep you awake a lot? Poor idda bidda ting?"

"Well," he said, "if you'll excuse me." He turned to leave.

"What's cooking anyway? What're you making for dinner?" Denise asked.

"I haven't started yet."

"Is there enough for us, too?" asked Paula. "You want to eat dinner over here with us?"

He was uncertain, looking at one and then the other.

"Really," Paula went on, "why not. We got all this damn food. We went shopping hungry, you know? Don't ever go to the goddamn grocery store when you're hungry. Look—look here," she said, opening the top of one of the bags, "you want to see what I got? Look at this." She put both hands down into the bag and brought up a small frozen turkey. "See this? Hard as a rock." She set it down with a thud. "I couldn't pass it up, see, because I was so hungry when I went into the store."

"Famished," Denise said. "That's my new word for the day, by the way. 'Famished.' "

"Every day Denise learns a new word and uses it in a sentence."

"I learned a word a day last year, and that makes three hundred sixty-five words."

"But look here, Cakes," said Paula, "we got all kinds of stuff that we could fix quick. So what do you say?"

"You're very kind." Cakes looked over his shoulder into the hall. "But I—"

"Ah, come on. Where's the harm. What'll you make tonight, anyway? We got a feast right here on this table. Let's have a feast."

"You like seafood?" Denise asked. "We got seafood galore."

"Denise loves seafood, right Denise?"

"We both do," Denise said.

"Your girlfriend can join us, Cakes."

"She's not my girlfriend," said Cakes.

There was a pause.

"That's all right with us," Paula said. "You know, whatever. Right, Denise?"

"We'll have seafood," Denise said.

It was a strange evening. Edward Cakes sat on their sofa, his hands on his thighs, while they bustled and argued over the preparations for dinner; they had a plastic room divider between the living area, and the kitchen area, and so from where he sat he could see only their watery outlines in the plastic. Their apartment was larger than his; they had two small bedrooms, into one of which Paula went two or three times, smiling at him as she passed. Each time she came out she had something different over her hair—first it was a net, then it was a scarf. On the other side of the plastic divider, the two women whispered, laughed, giggled, bickered over seasonings, whether to use butter or margarine, what to do for dessert. Occasionally one of them would peak around the partition and smile at him, ask if he would have a beer, something, anything to drink or snack on or smoke. He didn't want anything; he would wait. He listened for the girl, and once he stood at the window of this strange living room and looked out at the street. Finally Paula came into him and began to talk about what it was like growing up in West Texas. She showed him her stereo, put music on—some dreadful disco thing, with a lot of falsetto and the same pounding chords, over and over, and while it blared, she told him the stereo was a gift from her mother, who was one fancy old lady, and the talk of West Texas because, for her seventh marriage, she had hooked up with a black man named Raymondo, whom everyone knew as Rabies and who had once run a whorehouse, like a regular madam or something. Paula said all this, and then she walked into the kitchen to get herself another beer.

The actual meal began very quietly; they waited for a few moments as if unsure about starting without the girl. It was awkward. Cakes poured his beer too quickly into the frozen mug they had given him, and the foam flowed over the lip and down the sides.

"Man, we got all the foam in the world tonight," Paula said.

He got up to find a washcloth, and she told him to sit down, not to mind it. He did so. There was a pool of spilled beer next to his plate, and twice he put his elbow down in it. They ate quietly for a while. The whole thing felt like a mistake. The flounder Paula had broiled was dry, and the baked potatoes were not quite done. Paula apologized for these things, and the other two protested, and again there was nothing to say.

Finally Paula said, "How long have you lived here, Cakes?"

He didn't know at first: he had to think about it. He said, "A long time." Then he said, "Almost fifteen years."

"That is a long time."

Again they were quiet.

"So where's your—where's your friend?" Paula asked.

"I don't know," he said. "I thought she'd be back by now."

"Is she really just a friend?"

"Yes," he said.

"You don't want to tell us anything, do you, Cakes."

"I wish you wouldn't call me that."

"What should we call you?" Denise asked.

"He wants to be called Edward."

"Oh, but Cakes is so cute."

"Maybe he doesn't want to be cute," Paula said.

"Do you have a family?" Denise asked him.

He said, "No."

"You don't have *anybody?*" Denise's wide, frankly incredulous gaze fixed him.

"Denise is *terrified* of being alone," said Paula. "She'd marry *you* if she thought she'd be alone."

"Paula."

"Well, you would."

There was an exchange, then, of gestures between the two women, and this was followed by another long silence.

"Where'd your friend go, anyway?" Paula asked.

"I'm afraid I don't quite know," Cakes said. "She left early this morning. I suppose she's out looking for work. And, you know, she'd left all her things at the train station."

"It's a little late to be looking for work."

"To tell you the truth," Cakes said, "I'm a little worried."

"Maybe she met a friend," Denise said.

The silence this time was long enough to become awkward; it was, finally, rather oppressive, like a form of humidity. There came a moment when it was clear that the meal, the evening, was over. Cakes thanked them for everything, excused himself for bowing out so early, and made his way, with relief, back to his room. It was past eight o'clock now, and he really was worried. He sat in his chair by the window and looked out at the lights in the street—the warm red window of one of the row houses down the hill, and the faint scattering of lamps through the leafy shadows of the trees in the square. A sudden gust of wind shook the branches, and leaves flew out of them like night birds. When he heard her on the stairs, he was amazed that he could have missed seeing her from the window. He went to the door and almost stumbled over himself getting out on the landing. She was carrying something—a striped kitten. She held it in the crook of her arm, petting it; her fingers trembled over the puffed curve of the back. Her eyes caught him, and she stopped, and gradually her lips curled into a broad smile. She held the kitten toward him in her open palms. "Isn't it sweet?" she said.

8

"Where have you been?" he asked.

She had poured milk into a saucer and set it on the floor; the kitten stood there lapping up the milk, tottering a little, while she sat with her legs crossed, watching it, her head turned curiously to the side as if she had never seen anything like this before—a kitten drinking milk.

"Where were you all day," he said.

"The college."

"I was beginning to worry."

"Don't worry."

"I was going to make something for dinner, maybe."

"I ate," she said.

Presently he said, "Where did you find the cat?"

"Oh." She reached down to touch the kitten's little spike of a tail. "He was hiding behind a trash can by the curb."

"Where was this?"

"Downtown."

Cakes pulled a chair around from the table and seated himself. "You were looking for work?"

"I was at the college. It turns out old Terry-and-the-Pirates Dillard is still hanging around the college."

Cakes rubbed his eyes and said nothing.

"They probably don't allow pets here, do they," she said. She was not looking at him. Her slender, rough fingers toyed with the kitten's tail. "Do they allow pets here?"

"No," Cakes said, "they don't."

"Poor thing. You were hungry," she said to the kitten. The saucer was licked dry. She held it up and smiled. "Can we have some more milk?"

Cakes poured it, and then spilled it as he set it down into her hands. She gave a little shout and then laughed, put the saucer on the floor and lifted the kitten, letting it lick the spilled milk from her fingers. "I guess you'll want us to leave now," she said.

He thought for a moment that she was still addressing the kitten. "No," he said.

"Poor thing," she said to the kitten.

"Listen," he said, "what good does it do to see—to find your young man if he ran away from you?"

"What makes you think I'm looking for him?"

"You said you were at the college all day."

"Maybe I'm thinking of taking a class or two."

"Are you?"

"Not now, no."

"I don't understand."

"Maybe I'm looking for work at the college, too."

"Are you?"

"I'm thinking about it, sure."

"Were you at the college all day?"

"Yes."

A moment later she said, "There's a lot to see and do at a college in the middle of the big city, right?"

"What about your things?" he asked.

"What about them?"

"I thought you might've gone to get them."

She frowned. "Guess I should have."

"Of course, that's not the safest neighborhood for a woman by herself."

"Yeah—right." She seemed to study him. "How old are you?"

"I'm seventy-five."

She pointed at the picture on the wall. "And that was your wife?"

"Yes."

"I'd like to see other pictures of her. Do you have other pictures of her?"

"Three or four," he said. "Not many."

"Did you love her?"

He nodded.

"My father plays around, I think. Did you play around?"

"No."

"Not even a little?"

"Not even a little."

"Were you tempted?"

"Of course I was tempted."

"I think my father plays around. I think he feels bad about it, too, but my mother's such a basket case, really. I mean I don't think I blame him."

"What makes you think he plays around?" Cakes asked.

She shrugged. "Just a feeling." Then she looked at him and smiled tolerantly, as if he had told her something about himself that she already knew. "Like now. You say you never played around, and you look guilty as hell."

"Well, if your feeling is all you have to go on, perhaps you shouldn't trust it very much."

"Tell me about your wife," she said.

"Why would you want to know about my wife?"

"Why not?"

He sighed. "It was all so long ago."

"Tell me about her." She sat back, hugging her knees.

"What do you want to know?"

"Everything."

"Well, of course I won't tell you everything."

"Tell me how you met her."

"I met her on a dance floor," he said.

"Did you ask her to dance?"

"No."

"But you fell in love right away."

"In fact, it wasn't right away—I was interested in her, yes. Why are you so anxious to know all this, anyway?"

"What was she like?" the girl asked.

"She was—she was very bright. Very—*smart*. And she loved very much to dance. When I met her, I was in college, studying music—"

"You play music?"

"I did, yes."

"What did you play?"

He told her.

"We call it a fiddle where I come from," she said. "Did you play in, like, a band?"

"I played in an orchestra, yes."

"No, I mean a band, you know—jazz and stuff. For dances and stuff."

"A little," he said.

"Do you like jazz?"

"I love jazz."

"Me, too," she said.

"I never played it very much, of course. But I liked to listen."

She smiled. "So go on—you were studying music."

"I was studying music, and for extra money I was playing bass in a—well, a kind of jazz band, really. This was when jazz was—younger. We just played jumpy kinds of things, so people could dance and bounce a little."

"The Jazz Age," said the girl.

"You know about that."

"Are you kidding? I love that whole thing. I read F. Scott Fitzgerald when I was sixteen."

"All those years ago," he said, and smiled.

"Well—it was, you know. *The Great Gatsby.* After I saw the movie."

"Yes."

"But I wished a hundred times before that I could've lived back then and taken a bath in gin, and go to speakeasies and all that. You lived then, didn't you—you know all about that."

He nodded.

"Did you take a bath in gin and play in speakeasies?"

"I suppose I saw a speakeasy or two. But I don't recall bathing in any gin. There were a couple of speakeasies I played in, I guess."

"Oh, wow. No kidding."

"The speakeasies paid pretty well, as I recall."

"Perfect—that's perfect. Tell me about it."

There was a pause, then. She was sitting there waiting, hugging her knees; the kitten had curled up next to the saucer and gone to sleep.

"You were playing in a speakeasy."

"I'm sorry," he said.

"How you met your wife."

"Oh—that wasn't a speakeasy. That was a frat house at a college. And—and anyway, I was in the middle of a number and she came dancing out on the floor with her blouse pulled up, you know, showing her belly, and did a belly dance. She'd taken bets from her friends that she wouldn't have the nerve to do it."

"And she won the bets."

"She won the bets. And when I saw her—that first second I saw her—"

"It was love at first sight."

"I guess it was as close to it as anyone ever comes," he said.

"And did she love you back?"

"No," he said. "Didn't even like me, as a matter of fact."

"This is like a movie or something."

"She wasn't interested in marriage, or in any one man, at that time in her life. She was young—younger than you are—and she was very good, you see, as a dancer. She wanted to do it professionally."

"And did she?"

"For a time, yes. A very short time."

"What happened?"

They were both looking at the photograph now, and their voices had softened, as if in reverence. Somewhere out in the night an ambulance sent up its odd, terrifying wail.

"She married me," Cakes said. "For one thing."

The girl lay on her side, arranged herself. "She gave it up."

"No." He began to try to pick through the memories, gazing at the photograph. "No, that isn't how it was at all, I'm afraid."

"Don't you want to tell me?"

"First," he said, "you have to know that she was very, very good. I mean she could have made a career out of it, because apart from her talent she was—she was quite beautiful."

"So tell me," the girl said.

He rose from the chair, his bones creaked, and the awareness of his age came to him like a rude remark; straightening, ignoring the stiffness in his legs, he walked over to the bureau and stood there, elbows resting on the bitten surface, staring at the picture, the face that was almost recognizable. "There's not that much to tell, really. I sort of took to following her around. She had a lot of friends, a world of her own. She—took me up to the mountains with her once, just for fun, she said. It was a cabin that belonged to her parents—they'd both gone to Europe on some sort of holiday." He laughed softly. "Her father wanted to leave the country because the Democrats were running a Catholic for president. It was a joke she made. Her parents—anyway, they'd locked this cabin up. Ellen—her name was Ellen. Ellen was supposed to be studying in New York. We had to break into the cabin. We were a couple of kids, you know." He reached up, touched the frame of the picture. "It was a very wonderful time for me. We were in love." He turned, moved back to the table, sat down. The girl lay on her side, with her head on her arm, sleepily blinking at him.

"And then?"

"Well," he said, "then she sort of dropped me—went off to do her dancing."

The girl sighed, lay over on her back. "She must've been something."

"I couldn't talk her into coming with me, or even—I couldn't even get her to see me. She just—closed me off. And then one day about a year or so later she came to me. She walked up to my door and knocked on it, and when I opened it, she said something that simply bowled me over."

"She said she loved you."

He shook his head. "She sort of smiled at me, you know, like it was an old joke between us, and said, 'Cakes, if you still want to get married, I think I'll just take you up on it.' "

"She called you Cakes?"

He said, "Yes."

"How neat."

"You see," he said, "she had this trouble with her heart. She couldn't keep dancing. She'd been to this doctor—"

"What was wrong with her heart?"

"When she was a child, she'd had scarlet fever—she'd almost died of it. And it damaged her heart. She'd started having these palpitations with the dancing, and so the doctors told her she'd better stop. She wasn't supposed to have any children, you know. But we had the boy the next year. She wanted it—she wanted to have one child, at least. Oh, she doted on that baby, too. It made me jealous the way she doted on him."

"Where is he now?" the girl asked.

"He died in Korea."

"I'm sorry."

"It was a long time ago," Cakes said.

"You really loved each other."

He reached down and touched the kitten's ear. "I'm very tired," he said.

"I've never loved anybody like that."

"You're young."

"Did she—did Ellen—did she die young?"

Cakes sat back and rubbed his eyes, then looked at her. "You wouldn't say so."

"When did she die?"

"A long time ago."

"Have you been alone all that time?"

He said, "Well—mostly."

"God."

A moment later he said, "Well," and made as if to rise.

"Isn't it funny?" she said. "We're talking like this, and you're —you were fifty years old when I was born."

Now he did rise. He went to the refrigerator, got out the milk again and poured himself a glass. There had been the shuffling sound of his feet on the bare floor. The girl lay back and folded her arms over her chest.

"Why don't you get up on the bed?" he asked.

"I'm comfortable."

The kitten had rolled over on its side, stretched both paws, shuddered and settled.

"How long were you together?" the girl asked.

"A long time," he said. "Not long enough."

She was staring at the ceiling. He thought her face, in the light, was rather pretty. "I think I would've got along great with that lady. Even if I can't dance a lick."

"Perhaps you would have," Cakes said.

She sighed. "I thought Terry Dillard was pretty cool."

"He seemed so serious to me," Cakes said.

"Well, anyway, I'm finally out of the great Bellini household."

"That's your last name?"

"Mary Virginia Bellini. Sounds like a cosmetic company, doesn't it." She smiled that broad smile. "Lip Love, by Mary Virginia Bellini."

"I think, just—Virginia Bellini. Mary Virginia sounds like a nun."

She laughed. He thought it was a warm, rich laugh. "You're right," she said. "Oh, God, that's great."

Presently, he said, "So you wanted out of your family."

"I *was* out."

"How old are you?"

"I'm old enough, Cakes."

There was a moment when neither of them spoke; he cleared his throat. "I'd appreciate it if you wouldn't call me that."

"I'm twenty-four," she said. "I'll be twenty-five on November 2. I didn't mean to hurt your feelings."

"No harm done."

"How long have you lived here?" she asked.

"You're the second person to ask me that today."

She sat up and leaned on her hands. "It seems so lonesome here."

"I watch television," he said. "I spend a lot of time at the window."

"Don't you have any friends?"

"I have friends."

"Any girlfriends?" she smiled.

"I have known a few women," he said.

"You want to know about *my* friends?" She looked around the room, and her eyes wandered down to the sleeping kitten. "Here's a friend."

"Why don't you go to sleep now," he suggested.

She looked at him. "Why?"

"I don't know—I thought you might be tired."

"You go ahead." She yawned.

"I have this milk I poured for myself."

She gave a little shrug, ran one hand lightly over the kitten's bony flank. "Too bad, for kittens and puppies."

He drank the milk.

"Too bad, too bad, too bad."

"I'm going to go to sleep now," he said, rising.

"I wish you wouldn't."

He paused.

"Can we talk some more?"

"I'm very tired," he said.

"I don't like to be alone." She spoke through a pout, like a little girl.

"There's nothing to be afraid of."

"It's not being afraid. I just don't like being alone. I'm one of those people, you know, that don't like their own company all that much."

"I'm sorry to hear that," he said, and sat down again.

"Oh, listen," she said, "I'm not asking for any pity."

He said, "I understand."

"It's just that I wanted to keep talking."

"Tell me about your family."

"There's nothing to tell. You can go for weeks in that house without saying a single goddamn word to anybody, or getting one said to you. You know what my mother and father do all day?

They go about their business. They eat breakfast together when he's—when Daddy's home—and they have lunch, they putter around in the yard, in the garden—my father feeds his fish. He's got this huge set of aquariums in a room, like a—like a marina, you know? Anyway—they do all these things pretty much together, and they don't say anything. I mean they don't speak. It's like there's nobody there. They just completely ignore each other. If they say anything at all, it's like strangers. My mother—I told you she had a nervous breakdown after I was born. Well, that was just the first one. I got her started, see, and she just never quite got over it. Every time she didn't feel quite right about things, she'd start getting odd, and it was like she just slid down a hole or something. She'd start staying in bed longer in the mornings, and then one day she wouldn't get up at all. She'd lay there, curled up like a baby. And so, you know, this would go on. Then, sometimes, if she was beginning to feel like she might start down, she'd go on a shopping spree, or join six million different clubs, or talk everybody to death no matter who was there or who was listening or what was going on. When it got like this, my father would find a way to get himself a trip out of town, of course."

"What—what does your father do," Cakes said.

"He's a professor. He travels a lot."

"And what does he teach?"

"Geology."

Cakes stifled a yawn and rubbed his eyes again.

"I've got two brothers who don't work, and they stay home. One watches TV all the time. He's a walking television commercial and he's thirty-two years old. My father hates him."

"I really have to get some sleep," said Cakes. He put the empty milk glass in the sink and made his way to the chair by the window. At some point during the previous night he had got an extra blanket from the closet and lay it over his legs. He arranged it now while the girl cooed and warbled at the kitten.

"You won't leave me alone, will you, just because you get a little sleepy. . . ."

His back ached, the tendons behind his knees were sore from having slept with the knees locked, legs straight out, the night before. It had been, in fact, an extremely uncomfortable night; it was why he was so very tired now. As he settled into the chair, something caught in his back, just below the shoulder blade. He shifted his weight, carefully, but there was no position—and he knew there would be none—that eased the discomfort. He lay his head back, sighing, giving in.

"Cute thing," the girl was saying. "Aren't you the cutest little thing." She laughed. The kitten mewed, was apparently wide awake now. It mewed again, and she laughed again.

"Please," Cakes said, "I'm sorry."

"It's so early," said the girl, "It's not even ten o'clock."

"Why don't you take the kitten for a walk?"

"Outside?"

"There's a couch downstairs—in the hall."

"You want me to sleep down there?"

"No," he said.

"We'll be quiet—really."

"You could read if you want."

"I don't see anything but these—mysteries."

He stretched his legs out, felt the throb in the tendons. Then he stood. "I'm sorry, but I think I'll have to use the bed tonight. Is it all right if we alternate nights?"

She had the kitten in her lap and was stroking it, not looking at him.

"Do you mind?" he said.

"No."

"Thank you."

He couldn't sleep. In the bed, breathing the faint afterodor of her body, feeling the sore places in his back and along the back of his legs, he lay hearing her try to be quiet. The kitten would not sleep now, and mewed continuously, so that her efforts to make it stop became funny for her; she began to laugh, and her efforts to stifle the laughter only made things worse. "It's all right," he said at last, "I'm not asleep."

"Kind sir," she said.

Then he was asleep. It was dark, he had been gone in it, and he was coming out of it, hearing someone in the room, something moving nearby, and she was getting into the bed with him.

"Please," she said.

She was shaking. She burrowed into the warmth at his side, put her head into the hollow of his shoulder.

He said, "Mary—"

Outside, the sirens and horns and trains made their noise, the airport roared, and he was aware only of how quiet it was.

"I'm just like anybody else," she murmured, crying. "I just want somebody to hold me."

He held her, patting her shoulder gently, breathing the odor of her hair, and in a little while she was asleep.

9

Sometime before dawn it started to rain. He lay awake, listening to it come sighing out of the dark, and as it increased, he thought, for some reason, of death. The thought blew through him like a chill, then was gone. The girl lay breathing in sleep, her mouth open, one hand lying in the hollow of her pale neck. Edward Cakes remained quite still, and the rain came down hard, ran on the window and changed the quality of light in the room—the dawn arriving, a faint, moving grayness. He heard cars go by in the street, and there was the muffled, fading rumble of a jet plane in the distance. The girl stirred, opened her eyes and looked at him. She was a white shape there next to him in the bed. "It's early," she said.

He told her in a whisper, as though to soothe a child, to go back to sleep.

"Oh," she said, "Raining."

"It'll stop soon," he said.

But it did not stop; it poured, out of a flat gray sky, without increase or let up, all day, and the girl stayed with him. In the morning they foraged in Mrs. Blackemore's storage room downstairs to find an old packing crate, which they made into a litter box for the kitten, using old newspaper. She tore one side of the box away, so that it was like a small room with one wall missing, and the kitten crawled in and went to sleep in a corner of it.

"Poor thing," she said, standing over the box, "he thinks it's a bed."

"He'll figure out what it's for," Cakes said.

"Poor thing."

They ate lunch together—clam chowder Cakes made from a can—and then the girl sat in his chair with the kitten curled up in her lap and watched television. She was restless, she told him finally, and there wasn't anything to do about it except sit like a lump in front of the television set. She only wished there was something good on—even the movies were dull, and there were far too many commercials.

In the afternoon she went across the hall and knocked on Paula and Denise's door, but the two nurses had apparently been gone all day. Cakes watched her come back into the room, head bowed, looking for all the world like a disappointed child.

"Don't you have any cards or anything?" she said.

"I'm sorry."

"I hate rain," she said. "Why couldn't it just rain at night?"

This did not seem to require an answer.

She sat down at the table across from him and folded her arms over her breasts. "Ever play trivia?"

"How do you play," he said.

"I say the initials of someone famous, and you try to guess who it is."

"I see."

"Anyway, that's one way to play it."

"All right," he said.

"You want me to start?" she asked.

He nodded.

She sat forward, bit her lower lip, looking over his shoulder

at nothing, obviously struggling to come up with a name. "Okay.
I have it." She sat back and smiled. "P.F."

"P.F.," he said.

She nodded.

"P.F.," he said again. His mind was blank. "P.F."

"P.F.," she said.

"Is it a man or a woman?"

She shook her head. "I'm not supposed to say."

"P.F.," he said. "I can't think of anyone."

"He's *famous,*" she said.

He grinned at her. "It's a he, huh."

"All right. Yes. And he's *famous.*"

"Let me see," Cakes said. He could think of nothing, no
names at all, and this was beginning to embarrass him. Finally he
shrugged, holding his hands up in a gesture of surrender. "I'm
sorry, I can't think of a single person."

"Percy Faith," she said, "what about Percy Faith?"

"Is *that* who it is?" He was surprised.

"No. It's a person—a famous person who's name makes the
initials P.F. You're supposed to guess people with those initials
until you get the right one. Can't you think of *anyone?*"

"Now wait a minute," he said, "let me try now. Let me just
think here a minute."

"I'll give you another hint. He's in music."

"And it's not Percy Faith."

"No," she said. "It's not Percy Faith."

"Music." He frowned, touched his chin.

"Jesus," she said suddenly, "you can't even think of *one?*"

"I'm sorry."

"Not one name?"

"I really am drawing a blank."

"I guess I shouldn't have picked him," she said, looking
down at her hands. "It's Peter Frampton."

"Who?"

"Never mind—you don't know the name. Peter Frampton.
He's a rock 'n' roll star."

"Oh."

"I should've picked somebody else."

"I like the Beatles," he said.

"Everybody likes them." She stood, went to the window and looked out. "We could go to the train station and pick up my stuff."

"I suppose we should."

"It's just one bag."

"Do you want to?"

"I'm grubby," she said, and pulled at the cloth of her blouse. "I should never have let it go this long."

"Do you want to go, then?"

She bent down to pick up the kitten. She patted its back and kissed the top of its head. "Maybe if it stops raining."

"I have a robe you could wear."

She sat in the chair again and held the kitten in the crook of her arm. "I'm so sleepy," she said to it, and then she lay her head back.

"Would you like the television on?" he asked.

"If you want it on."

In only a moment she was asleep.

He read for a while, dozed for a while in the bed and finally got up to put something together for dinner. There was hamburger meat, and he made patties, peeled and cut potatoes, working quietly, so as not to disturb her; but then she awakened anyway, yawned, stretched, moved to the window and gazed out, holding the kitten up to her cheek.

"Poor thing," she said, "I don't think he feels good."

"Let's give him some milk," Cakes said.

But the kitten seemed uninterested in anything; it lay panting, eyes half closed, in the newspaper-lined box.

"Poor thing," said the girl. As she spoke, she shuffled over to the bed and lay down. "I'm so grubby."

"Will you have something to eat?" he asked.

"Sure."

But she fell asleep again, and he had to wake her when the dinner was ready. His soft nudging of her shoulder brought a small cry up out of her throat, and for a moment she sat with one hand over her heart, breathing.

"I didn't mean to startle you," he said. "Forgive me."

"God—I couldn't remember where I was."

"I've got dinner—there's hamburgers—"

"What a scary thing. I didn't even know I'd gone to sleep."

He waited, feeling quite awkward and doltish while she washed her face and then—carefully as if uncertain what was expected of her—settled herself at the table, napkin open on her lap beneath her folded hands. It was as though she were waiting for instructions to begin eating. The two of them sat there looking at each other.

"Well?" she said.

"Oh," said Cakes, "of course." And he began to dish out his own portions, passing the plates across to her as he finished; it dawned on him that this was probably wrong, that he should let her have each plate first. When he tried to give her the cottage cheese first, she said, "Don't you want any?"

"Of course," he said, and doled his own out, then handed her the container.

"Thank you," she said.

They were quiet.

She had begun to pile things onto her hamburger, and he sat watching her: onions, pickles, lettuce, tomatoes, cheese, mustard and ketchup. She used liberal amounts of each item, building the hamburger, tier on tier.

"Good," she said, chewing.

He thanked her.

"At home," she said, "nobody could talk at the table."

"That's the rule in a lot of houses," said Cakes.

"What about in your house?"

He shook his head. "No."

"Were you handsome?"

"Pardon me?"

"Did you get a lot of girls."

"Oh," he said, "millions."

"No—really."

He shrugged. "I don't know."

"I'll bet you had plenty, didn't you."

He smiled, shook his head.

"My father says it's the quiet guys who really get a lot of women—the ones who don't talk about it all the time."

"Well, in my case, I'm afraid the theory is disproved."

They ate in silence for a time, and then she said, "How many women have you had sex with?"

He put his fork down and pretended to be counting off on his fingers. Then he said, "I'm afraid there's too many to count."

"I'm serious," she said.

Again he shrugged. "There have been a few."

"When was the last time?"

"Oh, please," he said.

"Really—when?"

"Don't ask rude questions." He couldn't look at her now; he turned his fork in a buttery pile of potatoes.

"Would you like to have sex with me?"

"I would rather not discuss it like a problem in mathematics," he said.

"I'm embarrassing you."

He said nothing. He could feel the blood in his face and neck.

"I think you're very nice."

"Thank you," he said.

"I'll bet you're a tender lover, too."

Again he was silent.

"Want to go for a walk in the rain?"

"Where would we go."

"Oh, just—you know, for a little walk."

"I'm afraid I'm not as robust as I used to be."

"You're afraid you'll get sick."

"Well—yes."

"It's just a little rain. We could be romantic—we'll come back and take a warm bath." She smiled at him and then fixed him with her eyes, seemed to look into him somehow, and he felt all the faults and the faded powers of his body, all the eloquent aches and failures and erosions. It was as if he were rooted to the chair by his very age. She stood and extended her hand. "Come on," she said.

Outside, the rain was falling exactly as it had all day, and they walked together over to the park. At one point he took her hand, but saw immediately that this had surprised her, so he let go. He was bewildered. He did not know what to do or say or think. The rain went down his shirt collar, and it was cold; it began to drench through his clothes.

"Isn't this great?" she said. But she was shaking.

They went to the center of the park, to the fountain, where she cupped her hands in the water and laved it over her face. Her hair was wet and heavy now, lying on her neck and shoulders like a soaked blond rag.

"Let's go back," he said.

"Isn't it like being—baptized?"

"I've got to get back."

"Wait," she said. "Isn't it? Isn't it like being baptized?"

"Yes," Cakes told her.

"Sometimes I wish I was clean as Jesus," she said.

He turned, started back. He was soaked through to the skin. She came up beside him, hooked her arm in his.

"Kind sir," she said.

"Madame," said Cakes.

She laughed. "You're funny."

"I'm cold."

"I wish things were different," she said.

"I wish it wasn't raining." He had spoken before her words had quite sunk in. Now he looked at her, striding along at his side, her rainy face in profile. "What did you say?"

"Not a thing, kind sir."

"You said you wished things were different."

"Did I?" She was looking at the sidewalk.

"Why did you say that."

She stopped. The rain was pouring from her nose and chin, and it made her eyes blink. "I don't know. I was just talking—you said you wished it wasn't raining."

"Yes."

She hooked her arm in his again. "Shall we go, monsieur?"

They walked along toward Mrs. Blackemore's tall shadow of a house.

In the room she undressed, talking gaily to the kitten about rain, then she went into the bathroom and hung her wet clothes on the shower curtain rod. Her body was thin, like a boy's body, and Cakes busied himself with his own wet clothes, embarrassed by her nakedness. She ran water in the tub, steaming the window and the mirror, and climbed in, talking about how there was nothing like a scalding hot bath to relax a person. Cakes had put a robe on, and remained beyond the open door, and now she called to him.

"Come on, it's just right."

He carried his wet clothes in and put them with hers on the shower curtain rod, aware of her eyes on him, of his robe, his nakedness under the robe.

"Getting in?" she said.

"Of course." He wanted to seem relaxed, sure of himself. But his hands faltered over the robe, and she laughed softly.

"Come on, Cakes." She was looking at him without expression, as if she already knew everything, every wrinkle and bump and contour of his body. He dropped the robe, stepped into the water, which was too hot, and burned his feet, his ankles.

"Warm you right up," she said.

Slowly, painfully, he let himself down, he was finally sitting, his knees up, his hands behind him under the water, and she reached over, parted his knees, took his prick, very gently, into her hand.

"Oh," he said.

"Such a funny smoothness," she said.

The clothes above them dripped; it was very quiet.

"Lay back," she said.

He managed to do so, and she maneuvered herself so that she could take him into her mouth.

"Oh," he said again.

She moved slowly, licked, kissed, sucked. He laid his head back and closed his eyes.

"Come on," she said finally. "Let's dry off and go to bed."

It was dark at the window; the rain kept coming, the same unvarying fall, and Edward Cakes lay in his bed with this strange, this shining girl, whose breath smelled of soap, who was not beautiful, or, really, very attractive, and who now led him, like a boy trying sex for the first time, into her young body. He kissed her shoulder, buried his face in the damp, musty tangle of her hair.

"Good," she said. "Oh. Good, good."

Later she went into the bathroom and ran water, and he lay with his hands behind his head, not thinking. There was just the rain at the window and the sound of her in the bathroom. When she came out, she went around the room, calling the kitten, found it under the bed, bundled it in the blanket on the chair, then shut the lights off, got into the bed and lay with her back against him. "I guess I did say maybe you'd got lucky."

"Pardon me?" he said.

She laughed. "Pardon me. You're so polite—pardon me."

"I didn't understand you," he said.

"Let's go to sleep."

"I think you're beautiful."

"Right," she said.

"Will you stay with me?"

"Jeez."

"Will you?"

She rolled over on her back, and he turned toward her, kissed her cheek. "You're sweet," she said.

He kissed her again, and then oddly, almost boyishly, he was telling her about himself—his career with the symphony, his travels, his friendship with Arthur. He did not talk about Ellen or his lost son; he did not talk about grief at all, or about loneliness. He got the violin down out of the closet and showed it to her, explained a little about how one made music on it, even played a few bars of the Mendelssohn concerto for her. It wasn't at all like riding a bike, he told her: if you don't play all the time the skills begin to leave you, and of course his fingers had grown so old and stiff, he was so rusty. During all this, she lay curled in the blankets, sleepily blinking at him.

"You must've been real good," she said.

"I'm afraid I was never more than average—but average for a very good symphony is pretty good, really."

"That's what I said. You must've been real good."

He nodded, almost shyly.

"It's a pretty instrument," she said.

"Yes."

"I always liked it."

"You know," he said suddenly, "I could teach you to play it."

She smiled. "What a funny old man. You look so funny there, naked and holding a fiddle."

He put the violin back in the case, back on the top shelf of the closet, then got back into the bed.

"I didn't hurt your feelings did I?"

"Oh," he said, "no."

"You forgot the lights."

"I'm sorry."

"I'll do it," she said, rising. "I think I better try to give the kitten some milk again." Then she stood quite still, as if some sound had startled her into listening. "Hey—it's stopped. It's not raining anymore." She went to the window and looked out. "I was beginning to think it would never let up. The sky is clearing already—I can see the moon, Cakes."

"Please," he said, "call me Edward."

"Edward," she said. "That's so formal. Edward."

"I prefer it to Cakes."

"What about Eddie?"

"No."

She turned from the window, pranced before him, one arm up as if she held a veil before her eyes. "What if I said I wanted you to call me the Queen of Sheba."

"I'd call you the Queen of Sheba."

"Ah, but see—I'm not picky. I'm not picky at all. So why are you picky?"

"I guess I was born that way," he said.

"All right, then—Edward it is." She put his robe on, poured milk into a saucer for the kitten, then let the robe drop, shut the lights off and got into bed again. "Good night, Edward."

"Good night, Queen of Sheba."

"Kind sir," she said, and burrowed into the blankets at his side.

10
▲

In the morning he went to the library and checked out all the F. Scott Fitzgerald they had. It was a sunny, cold day, without wind, and the puddles of rain in the streets and along the curbs were like bright sheets of glass. There was a crisp fall smell in the air, and the trees of the park looked burnished in their autumnal colors against the sky. He had left the girl lying curled in the bed, with the kitten behind her knees, and that was the way he found her when he returned. He put the books down on the table and began to make breakfast—he would make bacon and eggs. From across the hall he heard the sound of Paula's stereo. He thought it was a perfect morning, and the frying bacon made his mouth water, made him think of other mornings, when Ellen had been alive and there was something happening in a given day, something to be excited about.

Before the first strips of bacon were done the girl had awakened, sat up yawning, stretching her arms out. "I'm not hungry."

"I got you some books," he said, "on the table. You won't have breakfast?"

"Okay, maybe a little." She got up and padded in her bare feet across the floor, picked up one of the books and opened it, yawning again. He kept his eyes on the frying bacon, though she was a shape in his peripheral vision. He felt somehow that to look at her now would be to take away her dignity. "Great," she said.

"You mentioned that you liked him."

"I said I read him. I read him already."

Cakes said nothing.

"I guess it'll be fun to read someday." She went into the bathroom and closed the door.

He called to her. "What shall we do today?"

"We?"

He said, "Of course."

"Well, I've got to get my things, you know. At the train station."

"I meant after we did that."

She was silent.

"We have to take a cab," he said. "I don't have a car. I stopped driving when I moved in here."

The water ran.

He drained the bacon, made coffee. "Almost done?"

She was splashing and humming in the bathtub. He waited, hearing Paula's radio faintly, and the small complaining of the kitten somewhere in the rumple of blankets on the bed. After a few minutes he knocked on the bathroom door. "It's almost time."

"Could I borrow your robe?" she said. "These clothes are still a little damp."

He got the robe from the closet, opened the bathroom door and held it in. "How do you like your eggs?"

"Turned over and stepped on," she said.

He broke two eggs into the pan, watched them both whiten, and when they were done he sat at the table and waited, everything set and ready, the bacon cooling on a plate at the center, the eggs steaming, the toast buttered and sliced and stacked. It was pleasant to sit there, waiting, while she made her water-roiling sounds, gargling and rinsing her mouth out. And then, in a strange way, it made him sad. He got up and poured more milk in the saucer for the kitten.

"Hey," she called, "do you feel married?"

"Excuse me?" he said.

"I feel married."

He said, "Your breakfast is getting cold."

"I'm coming."

She came out in his robe, and as she moved to the table and took her place, he remembered that she was pregnant. The fact went through him like an electric charge.

"I need to borrow some bucks from you," she said. "Do you have any cash?"

"A little."

"What's the matter."

"Nothing," he said.

She pulled her chair closer to the table. "Hey, really—doesn't this feel like being married? I mean we've even got a cat."

He smiled. "Eat your breakfast."

"Yes, Daddy."

"Would you call your husband Daddy?"

"I don't know. If he was a sugar daddy I guess I would." She began to eat. There was something almost prim about the way she held her fork, the way she used it to pick up the smallest morsels of egg, the daintiest bites, and so delicately touched her lips with the napkin after each one. "What would you call your wife?"

"Honey," he said.

"Honey."

"I suppose so, yes."

"I hate that."

He said nothing.

"How could you call anybody *that?*"

He shrugged. "It's a common endearment."

"I hate it."

"What do you want me to call you," he said.

"Not honey. That's for sure."

"Well, all right. What about all the other forms of endearment."

"Like what?"

"Oh—*darling, sweetheart, dear.*"

She had begun to shake her head with the first word. "All crap. They're all just—crap. I hate them all."

"Why?"

"I just do. People call each other that while they tear each other to pieces. Darling—*stab*. Sweetheart—*slice*. Deary—*rip*. No thank you, that's all I can say. Just, no thank you."

"What about people who love each other," he said.

"What about them?"

He was at a loss. Again he simply shrugged.

"I don't know anybody like that."

They ate in silence for a while.

"Do you know anybody like that?"

"I've known plenty of people like that—you're awfully young to be talking that way."

"I'm older than you know, Cakes."

"How old are you, exactly?"

"I don't mean that."

"I know it," he said. "I'm just asking. How old are you?"

"Twenty-four. I told you that."

"I would've said you were younger."

"You would've been way wrong."

Again they ate in silence. The cat walked around and complained, lay on its ribbed side and pulsed, mewing, licking its paws.

"I don't want to spend all my money before I get settled," she said. "So if you could lend me a few bucks, I'd be grateful."

He had ten dollars, and he gave it to her.

"I need a little more than this."

"I'll write you a check."

"I'm sorry to have to ask you, but you know how it is. Once I get settled, I'll pay you right back."

"You're staying here," he said. "Right?"

"Looks that way."

"We'll go down to the train station right after we eat," he said.

There were no taxis in the street, and so he had to call one; and then they had to wait for it. They sat on the steps, and Paula and Denise came down on their way to work. Paula introduced herself, shook hands with the girl, and introduced Denise. The girl seemed wary of them as if she thought they might begin to ridicule her at any moment. The conversation was general, and then it was simply awkward, and when the cab arrived, Cakes was relieved. "Well," Paula said. "Nice meeting you. Anytime."

"Anytime," said Denise, "anytime."

The driver of the cab was a big, dark-haired man with some sort of growth on the side of his neck. He wanted to talk; there was too much violence in the city: you couldn't trust anyone anymore. It was particularly dangerous for cabbies, what with robberies and murders and the like, knifings and beatings and strangulations. "When I was a kid," he said, looking back at his passengers, "you didn't have these things." He had grown up in the city; he knew it like the back of his hand, and it was a shame the way the politicians had let it go to hell. He kept looking at Edward as if to gauge the reaction of the older man, and Edward wondered if he weren't the type of person who just tries to say what he hopes his listeners want to hear. The assumption would be that, since Edward was an old man, he would be harboring grievances and angers and nostalgias about the way things used to be. And perhaps this was true: perhaps Edward felt exactly as this cab driver felt, and perhaps he might have even discovered some affection for him, since the cab driver reminded him slightly of Arthur—the way Arthur must have looked as a younger man. But the fact was that there was a lot of traffic, and the cabbie, with all his gregariousness, was not watching the road. There were trucks backing out of alleys or parked along curbs; cars were double-parked or sped across lanes; people crossed the street— and the cab sailed through it all on bad shocks, barely missing mayhem, the cabbie straining his neck to establish eye contact with his new friends, as it were. Edward Cakes felt as though he must watch the road *for* the cabbie, and finally, in spite of the warm talk and the smiles and the heartiness, he told him so.

"Oh, I can see it just fine, sir," the cabbie said.

"Whoops," the girl said as they bounced over a bad place in the road. "That got my stomach."

"You like that," said the cabbie, "like the old tummy ticklers, right?" He sped up.

"Please, slow down," Cakes said.

"I'm going the limit, sir."

"I used to love tummy ticklers when I was a kid," the girl said.

"Just like the amusement park." The cabbie looked back at her.

"Please," said Cakes, "will you watch the road."

Now the cabbie looked back at him. "You don't live in the city, do you, sir."

"Just please slow this car down."

"This is normal. Suppose you just let me do the driving— okay?"

"Well, *drive,*" Cakes said.

They were all quiet, then, as the cabbie swerved and zig-zagged around the back end of an unloading beer truck. Edward had closed his eyes.

"Nothing to it," the cabbie said.

"This is fun," said the girl.

"Get this one, coming up here."

They went sailing out into the air and then dropped with a jolt that bounced them and made the girl grab Edward's arm.

"How about that one?"

"You stop this car," Edward said. "You stop it right now."

"The train station's right up here."

"I said stop it."

"Don't," said the girl.

But Cakes sat forward in the seat. "Did you hear me? I said for you to stop this car right now, goddamnit!"

"Whoa," said the girl as they went over another sudden dip in the road. This time Edward struck his head on the roof of the car; it was not a severe blow, but it fed his anger.

"Stop this cab right now," he said, "or I'll report you to your superiors."

"You hurt yourself?" the girl asked him.

The cab slowed, then halted along the curb. "Three fifty-one," said the driver.

"I'm not paying you," Cakes said, "not for that—that *ride.*"

"Come on, old buddy."

He got out, and so did the cabbie. They were on one side of the car, and the girl, getting out too, now, was on the other. The cabbie stood over Cakes and put one finger on his chest.

"Don't make me take it from you, gramps."

"You won't lay a hand on me," Cakes said. The girl was watching them.

"I'll count to three," said the cabbie.

"Pay him," the girl said, "and let's go."

"I'm filing a complaint," Cakes said.

The cabbie poked him twice, hard, in the chest. "You do what you want, *shithead.* But now, you pay."

"Pay him, will you?" the girl said.

"I'm going to have him removed for reckless driving," said Cakes. Then he was off, falling down somewhere, spitting something. There was something in his mouth he couldn't spit out, and now his ears were ringing, and a weight pressed against the side of his face—a grainy pressure along the curve of the bone. He remembered the way the cabbie's lips had twisted, and as he opened his eyes, he saw the face floating above him at an odd angle. It changed, was gone, and the girl's face was there. She was saying something to him that he couldn't hear because of the ringing. He opened his eyes again, it seemed, or he had blinked, been gone. Her hands were on his shoulder; he had rolled over on his back, or she had moved him.

"I'm sorry," he said, "did he hurt you?"

"Jesus," she was saying, "don't die now."

"Where is he?"

"Lay there," she said, "I'll go get help."

He was getting up. "I don't need any help. I can get up—"

"Let me help you—"

"No," he said. He had come to a sitting position. His mouth was bleeding; it felt as though part of his lip had been torn. He touched the place. The inside of his mouth was swollen already, tasted of pennies; again he spit something out, or tried to. A strand of blood dropped from his mouth to the pavement between his outstretched legs.

"Hit an old man like that . . ." the girl was saying. "Here." She had produced a handkerchief from somewhere, and as she daubed his mouth with it, he realized it was his own, had been folded neatly in the pocket of his coat. "I never saw so much blood."

"Let me stand up," he said.

She put her arm under his, trying to help, and when he was on his feet, he had to lean on her for support.

"I'm sorry," he said.

"The bully," she said, "the fucking ape."

"Where are we going?" he asked.

"I don't know—I don't know what to do. I'm afraid he'll come back. He didn't get his money . . ."

They turned in a small circle there on the sidewalk. The cabbie had left them within a few blocks of the train station; it was in sight, across a wide expanse of gravel and broken asphalt ribbed with long clumps of crabgrass and strips of sand, as if the whole area had been claimed from a shoreline. Beyond the asphalt was an abandoned railroad car and a few feet of rusty track. The station rose behind this, new and white, with windows gleaming in the sun.

"Come on," the girl said.

They made their way with difficulty across the asphalt, and then through a curving alley, like a culvert, on either side of which children had drawn names and obscene words in chalk. Here, out of any wind, it was warm, and they stopped to rest a moment. Above them little swirls of dust blew, and there was the sound of the trains in the station.

"His name," Cakes said, "I can't remember his name. What was the name."

She was quiet. She sat with her hands in the pockets of her jacket and looked at the walls of the station.

"Do you remember the name?"

"I don't think we can get in there this way," she said, standing.

"Damnit," he said, "what was the cab number?"

"Will you forget it?" she said.

"I'll get him fired from his job."

She paced before him. "We didn't pay the man, okay? Are you all right? Can you stand up? I want to get out of here before he comes back."

"I hope he does come back."

She took his wrist, and he stood. He was dizzy for a moment, and then he was confused. They seemed to be going back the way they had come.

"What're you doing?" he said, trying to stop.

She pulled him forward. "Come on. You can't get in there that way. It just ends in a ditch and a wall. We have to go around to it, down the block."

"Wait," he said, and when she would not wait, he wrenched himself free.

"Will you stop it?" she said.

"Go," Cakes said. "Just—you go."

"What're you going to do?"

"I don't know." He couldn't look at her, knew his face was bloody and swollen, that he was an abject, beaten figure, shivering with cold, a fool, talking tough. "I'll go home."

"Oh, that's great—you'll go home. In a cab, maybe?"

"Yes," he said.

They were facing each other across a patch of grass and gravel at the edge of the road. The wind was strong now and blew her hair into her face.

"What's the matter with you," she said. "What did *I* do."

"You remember that cabbie's name, don't you," he said.

"What if I do."

"Just—just go on," he said, turning. He was moving away from her, walking into the wind.

"Wait," she said. She came up to him, and the two of them walked on for a few feet. Above them was an overpass, and when they entered the shade of it the wind sliced at them, was colder, stronger. "Where are you going?"

He stopped again. There was blood on the front of his coat, and he tried to wipe it off, turning away from her.

"Will you let me help you," she said.

He did not resist now. She had taken his arm above the elbow and gently began to guide him toward the end of the block. Neither of them spoke. The street led around in a curve and gave off onto a walking bridge over the railroad tracks. There they stopped and rested again; she stood gazing out at the tracks, the vista of railroad yards and warehouses and smokestacks in the distance. He sat on a small stone bench with his back to all this.

"Look," she said, "I wish you'd tell me what *I* did wrong."

"You don't understand," he said.

"Try me."

He said, "I'm humiliated." He looked at her and shrugged. "Humiliated."

"Why?"

"You think I'm too old for humiliation?"

She was silent.

"I'm a man," he said, "for the love of God." He stood and pulled the collar of his spattered coat tight. "Let's go. Let's get your things—and take another taxi home."

"If I had looked at his name," she said, "really, I'd help you get him fired. I would."

"It doesn't matter," he said vaguely. "I just want to get home now. Please. I've had enough excitement for one day."

She grasped him above the elbow again, and they moved carefully along the span of the walking bridge. Edward Cakes wondered what sort of shadow they made for anyone who happened to be walking below them.

11

▲

There were three cuts inside his mouth, his bottom lip was
bruised, and two bottom teeth (he still had all his teeth) were
loose. The girl was worried about a concussion, and when they
came back to the room, she got him to lie down, then went across
the hall to ask for help from Paula and Denise. Only Paula was
home. She came into the room wearing a thick, padded nightgown, like a quilt or comforter, and looked him over. He wanted
no help, and he might've resisted if he had not been almost sick
with dizziness and nausea from the taste of his own blood. Paula
looked in his mouth and whistled. "What happened to you," she
said.

The girl had been telling her.

He sat listening to them talk about concussions, blows to the
head and face, cuts and bleeding. He was lying on his bed, and
there was cold sun at the window and the room spun. Paula put
something on his lips, some ointment or other that stung him, and
then she asked him to watch her finger, moved it erratically in the
air before his face.

"Okay," she said finally.

"Please," he mumbled through the swelling, "leave me
alone."

"You know what, Cakes? The empty room's been rented."

He said, "Fine."

"Now ask me who the new tenant is."

He shook his head.

"It's another woman." Paula touched his chest. "I tell you,
Cakes, you're a lucky man, ain't you? Man, you're just surrounded by women."

"Did you know the—the person who rented the room before?" the girl asked.

"Hell yes. Are you kidding? We had a lot of conversations. Didn't we, Cakes."

He nodded.

"What about?" asked the girl.

"About my damn stereo for one thing," Paula said. She was chewing the ever present gum, and now she brought out a bubble, popped it and smiled. "He didn't like my stereo at all."

"I'm pregnant with his baby."

There was the slightest pause.

"Jesus Christ," Paula said.

Cakes sat around and put his feet on the floor. He wanted Paula to leave.

"Goddamn," Paula said, looking at the room for apparently the first time. "This is the first time I've seen your room, Cakes."

"Please," he said, "thank you for your help."

"Who's this?" Paula stood before the photograph.

"That's his wife," the girl said.

"Aw, ain't that nice." Paula took the picture off the wall, held it at arm's length as if to memorize something about it. "A damn nice-looking girl, too."

"Please, put it back," Cakes said. He couldn't get his lips to function; the words came garbled and blurred.

"If I was born back then, I bet I'd dress like that, too, if I had the money." Paula tried, unsuccessfully, to put the picture back. "Damn," she said, and tried again.

"Here," said the girl, and made an attempt to take it from her.

"Wait, I got it."

Cakes shouted. "Don't drop it!"

"We're not gonna drop it," Paula said. The girl had let go. "What's your name, honey?"

The girl told her.

"Long before the fashions came, right, honey?"

"Let me have the picture," Cakes said.

Paula went on talking, trying again to hang the picture on its nail. "I swear I never thought old Dillard would look at a girl twice, unless it was to say something shitty to her. You sure he's not a fag, honey?"

"He's not a fag."

"There," said Paula, and stepped back.

"It's crooked," the girl said.

"I'll be damned if it ain't."

Cakes moved to his chair and sagged down into it; everything creaked. He felt all his bones, all the muscles and the connecting tissues of his back and hips. He hadn't even got in a blow, not even a missed one, a swing. He had simply wound up sitting on the ground, bleeding into the asphalt. Outside, the wind blew leaves out of the trees and slanted the clouds like tatters of smoke.

"Cakes, are you okay?"

He mumbled, "Yes." His back was to them.

"I guess this is a hint that we should get out of here," Paula said.

"I'm sort of staying here," said the girl.

"I guess you are, honey—I guess 'sort of' must be the word, all right. You don't even have a radio, do you, Cakes. Hey, Cakes. Is this it? Is this what you do for fun—just sit there and stare out the window all damn day? Does that TV work?"

"Thank you for your help." He turned part way, giving her the side of his face.

"Any time, Cakes."

Looking out the window again, he felt the strangeness of being who he was—this man in a chair by a window, hearing two young women talk about clinics, doctors. He thought of the night before, and then he thought about the cabin in Vermont. The way he had kissed the girl in the room behind him, the way she had made him lie back, and done those things to him with her mouth —it was all a confusion for a moment, and he seemed to be far away in time and place; but then he was sitting straight up. It was real; the two women were talking at his back. Last night, at the girl's touch, he had realized how unlike anything one remembered about it the feel of love was, the messy and tactile merging of bodies. The sounds, odors, textures. He had not appreciated it enough; he hadn't appreciated anything enough.

Behind him, now, the girl gave a little cry.

He turned. "What is it?"

"The kitten."

They were silent a moment. Then she got down on her hands and knees to look under the bed, the bureau, the chair. He had stood; he thought the kitten must be gone. There was the heavy quiet into which the girl's voice simply dropped. "Here kitty, kitty, kitty, kitty." And, like good news, she brought the kitten out from beneath the chair.

"Poor thing," she said, "doesn't know where it is."

12
▲

What was true?

The truth was that the two days in the cabin in Vermont had been tempered with pain. He did not remember the pain, any more than, he knew now, he could really remember the pleasure; it was lost, then. He had lost it forever. He remembered someone strange, a nineteen-year-old boy, nervous, scared and clumsy, making a fire, shoving lighted newspapers under a grate full of sticks and logs; a draft caught the flames and sent them licking along the back of the boy's hand. He remembered it. The flesh there had blistered almost at once, and Ellen had laughed at him, at his shaking anticipation of her, as if she had had many lovers and were not, as he was, a virgin. Their lovemaking was awkward; it tantalized rather than satisfied them. It presaged things. The truth was that in all the years of their marriage he had felt that she withheld something from him. He had spent his energy trying to reach her where she secretly was, and wound up feeling starved, somehow, never quite sated or even, really, loved. He believed that, secretly, she was only making do with him, that he was a part of her failure, the heart condition that had forced her to give up her dreams. There were long frustrations, chronic angers, silences that lasted too long.

"What do you want from me," she would say.

And he could not find the words to express it.

"This is the only way I know how to love someone," she would say. "You tell me what you want and I'll change. I love you."

It wasn't enough. It was never what he needed, and so he had waited—it really became a thing he thought about in that way: something he was anticipating, like a wedding day, a day when she would truly love him. He thought about it all the time, and when he was angry with her for any reason, this other thing, this other anger—that he was still waiting, still having always to miss something in his relation to her—rose to the surface, like a larger fish feeding on smaller ones.

Part of it, he supposed, was the way she was about the boy. It was obsessive. The child was almost eight years old before he could tie his own shoes, and his features had begun to take on the slack, spoiled appearance of uncurbed appetite. His mother waited on him, satisfied his whims, listened to him with something bordering on thralldom, recorded every milestone of his growing up. Her conversation at times became a sort of litany beginning with the boy's name. "Ian this and Ian that, I know," she would say. "But you wouldn't believe what he did today." And she would go on to list everything. Except that it was not a list, it was a narrative with transitions. It was a running account of every waking minute in the life of Ian Edward Cakes. Most of this was, no doubt, the result of what the child had cost her, what risks had been involved in having him: Ellen had in fact bargained her life on the birth of this son. But the attention she lavished on him began to ruin him, and Edward Cakes would come home to look with repugnance upon the bored, self-satisfied, half-contemptuous face of his son, who at the age of thirteen was already completely without friends and rather insufferably angular. He collected comic books, read science fiction and kept his room full of all sorts of odd gadgetry: gyroscopes and wheels and elaborate gears and pulleys. None of these things were troublesome in themselves, of course, but he turned everything into a kind of morbid show: he liked to make things having to do with torture and execution, for instance, and was fascinated by gibbets, oubliettes, racks, guillotines, gallows, crosses. Forms of slaughter interested him immensely. He stayed in his room whole summer days, growing fat, drawing his machines of death, or building new extensions to the mechanical thicket on his desk, or simply buried in his tales of faraway planets and robots.

Once, at dinner, he looked at Cakes and said, "You know what I got in here?" indicating the inside of his left forearm.

"Tell me," Cakes said.

"Wires. Steel. Tubes. Batteries."

"For the love of God," Cakes said.

"There's no such thing," said the boy.

"He's precocious," Ellen said later.

"He's spoiled sick," said Cakes.

Yet he could not bring himself to do anything to reverse the damage: Ian was Ellen's more than his. He went to work, played the music, and when the orchestra traveled, he traveled; Ellen raised the child. Ian grew into a strange, supercilious youth, who was finally unable to feel much of anything for others. He got into trouble in school, and it was the kind of trouble that made for other trouble, that one got into alone, without the mitigating shape of loyalty or honor or any of the codes boys followed when they got into trouble together; there was something finally quite mean about him. And when his mother was hurt by what he'd done, he seemed to rejoice in it, as though he had really been aiming at her all along.

"I can't understand it," she said, "I can't believe it."

Ian had been caught cheating on a science test; in some ways he knew more about science than his teachers, yet he had cheated on the test, had done so blatantly, as if challenging the teacher to call him out for it. The teacher was a homely, fretful, bone-thin man named McCrackin, who was only a month away from retirement, had been teaching almost forty years and had never seen anyone quite like Ian Edward Cakes. He requested a conference with both parents.

By this time Ellen's heart had begun to weaken; her color was not good, and she grew tired too easily. There was an unmistakable air of defeat about her. She sat in a chair opposite Mr. McCrackin's desk and held her purse on her lap with both hands. Cakes, sitting next to her, thought of spinsters, women in the cramp of religion. The two of them waited for Mr. McCrackin. She cleared her throat, touched a handkerchief to her lips, clutched it in one hand. She *looked* cramped, held in.

He said, "Relax, Ellen."

And she began to cry, sniffing and clearing her throat. "I don't understand," she said. "I don't get it."

"Stop it," he said.

"Why does he hate me? I never did anything but love him."

"Be quiet. Nobody hates you."

Mr. McCrackin entered the room carrying a folder full of papers and looking hurried and scatterbrained and anxious; he wore a red tie, the end of which he had tucked down the front of his pants. He moved around the desk and busied himself for a moment arranging the folder among the papers and other folders there. Mr. McCrackin looked aghast about something, his face puffed and violet-colored, the mouth open as if in a grimace of pain. His glasses slid down to the end of his long nose and with one finger he pushed them back.

"Forgive me," he said, "for making you people wait."

"I've taken steps," Ellen said in a pitiful attempt to sound stern. "Ian will never cheat again."

"Yes, well." Mr. McCrackin sat down, adjusted his tie and folded his hands before him. "I'm sure you've done everything you could."

"We don't understand why a conference is necessary," Ellen said, barely able to keep her voice.

"Well, I would like to discuss the boy with both of you." McCrackin looked at Cakes.

"Certainly," Cakes said.

The other seemed to gather himself, to sit straighter. "He's a bad person, Mr. Cakes."

Through Ellen's horrified gasp, Edward Cakes said, "You mean he's hard to reach."

"No. I mean he's a bad person."

"Yes, but how do you mean it? You can't just say that—"

"I mean it just that way, sir. There's no other way I mean it. Your son is a bad, a terrible person."

"You can't tell me that," Ellen said, brushing the wings of her nostrils with the handkerchief.

"Wait a minute," Cakes said through her crying. "You can't just—just put him in a—say that about him and then just leave it at that. Ian is a bad person in what way?"

"In every way, sir." Mr. McCrackin began to count off on his fingers. "One, he's self-centered and unable to regard others with any sort of esteem or consideration; two, he has utterly no regard or esteem for authority of any kind or accomplishment of any kind; three, he's—well, stupidly cruel and disdainful; four, he's suspicious, and completely unable to believe anyone could sincerely be sincere and tell the truth simply because it's the truth; and, five, he's a bad person. I'm sorry, I can't put it any other way. He's a bad person. He has no friends, wants no friends, he has no loyalty, no pity, no real interest except his own sneering boredom with everything. And to top it all off—"

"That's all," Cakes said, standing.

"No, let me finish. I'm retiring, Mr. Cakes, and so I can say this to you. I know it's hard to listen to, and I know that nobody else has ever said these things to you, but I can say them so I'm saying them—somebody should've said it a long time ago, because now I don't know what can be done about Ian. I've tried everything, myself, as a teacher, short of getting someone to shoot him, or shooting him myself. But you see I'm just a—a *thing* to him."

Ellen simply sat there crying.

"Goddamnit," Cakes said.

"What I wanted to suggest to you both is that you get some professional help for the boy."

"Psychology," Cakes said as if they were discussing fields of study. He turned to his wife. "Please stop crying, Ellen."

She sobbed, sniffed, blew her nose. She was speechless, seemed, in fact, panic-stricken.

"He needs a psychologist, yes," said Mr. McCrackin. And then he straightened again, adjusted himself in the chair. "He needs somebody to gain some kind of control over him. Do you understand what I mean by that?"

"I understand that you're way out of bounds," Cakes said.

"I'm sorry, I don't have time to be polite. And I'm right about your boy, Mr. Cakes. And I think you know I'm right."

"It's not that simple," Cakes said, "It's wrong of you to put it that way."

"Maybe so, sir. But everything I've said to you is true. I'm leaving this job, I'm not teaching anymore ever again, and I have no reason to lie to you or to put it softly. I know you love the boy, and for that alone I think you have qualities of forgiveness that are nothing short of admirable."

"I will not forgive this," Cakes said.

He helped his wife leave the building. Ian was in class somewhere on the second floor; in the parking lot Ellen turned and looked at the building and cried, too loud. Her Ian there, among strangers. Cakes got her into the car and drove her home, bathed her, as you would a child, and put her to bed. Then he sat in his living room and counted up the number of years he had been married, how many years he had been playing violin, how long it had been since he had entered college.

He was almost forty years old.

Over the next four or five years he tried to get to know the boy, to teach him, change him. There were nights of terrible conflict in the house, Ian and Ellen forming a sort of alliance against him, though Ellen was often unable to do much of anything except stand between them and cry.

It all finally gave way to a silence, a strangeness between them all, as if they had never known anything tender and singular about each other. There seemed no coming back from it. Ian finished high school, entered a local college and lived at home. He was studying philosophy, and then he was studying botany, and on many nights he worked at the kitchen table, making notes and memorizing things from the textbooks. He was polite, as they were all polite; and when he ate dinner with them, or went with them to a movie, or to the store, they looked like a family. When the orchestra traveled, each winter, Edward Cakes was glad to go, and when it returned he was unhappy. Sometimes he thought he might explode with the tension. His wife and son were by now so repellent to each other that even the forms of ordinary practical communication were strained and difficult: they seemed to be groping for another language, somehow, merely to get through the business of the day: what would be eaten, laundered, dusted, renewed, put away, fixed, left alone.

Before he went into the army, Ian decided that he wanted to change his name. "I don't like Cakes," he said, "it's a silly name."

"It's your name," Edward Cakes said.

"Everybody teased me about it—all my life."

"A little teasing never hurt anybody."

"It wasn't a *little* teasing, and it hurt."

"All right," Cakes said, "what will you change it to?"

"From now on, I'm Ian Lance."

"That's ridiculous."

"No, it's not. Cakes is ridiculous."

"Cakes is your name."

"Not anymore."

"What's the matter with you?" Cakes said. "Why are you this way? What's been done to you to make you like this."

"You're asking where you went wrong?"

"I'm asking you where *you* went wrong, boy. Who do you think's been hurting you, anyway?"

"Don't yell," Ian said. "Don't get *her* into this."

"She gave you everything she had."

"Not so loud."

Edward Cakes lowered his voice. "You don't have any respect for her, no love. She's nothing to you, and she did everything for you."

"How much respect do you have?" Ian asked him. "How much have you ever had for her?"

"Why don't you tell me what your gripe is, Ian."

Ian blinked lazily. "Think about it, *Dad*. How much respect did you have for her? I grew up watching you, remember."

"All right," Cakes said, "you just say it. You tell me what you think is wrong."

Ian did not answer right away. He seemed to be trying to decide something. Then he sighed, half shrugged. "I don't like my name."

He joined the army under the name of Ian Howard Lance, and so the telegram informing them of his death, just seven months later, was mistakenly addressed to Mr. and Mrs. Edward Cakes Lance.

At some point during those weeks following his son's death, Cakes looked at his wife and felt something snap inside. She was standing near a window in the living room of the house, and the sun made a shade of her. The outline of her body in the light dress she wore showed how thin she had become; he saw this, he seemed to remember her—it was oddly as if she were already gone. There was a version of her in his mind, all the things he knew about her, everything she had done and said and been, and none of it quite added up to this woman across the room from him, a shadow in the bright rectangle of a window, listlessly wielding a dust cloth. He seemed to know, then, that when she died, it would be the last, the most terrible grief—that he had never really known her or loved her enough. And so he stood, walked over to her, touched her shoulder. There were words for it, words to tell her, something he should finally say, but when she looked at him, half smiling and with that great weariness in her eyes, he could not speak; he was, for that instant, the instant when the words, whatever they were, quivered on the end of his tongue, physically unable to utter a sound.

Finally he managed to say, "Come here." Then: "Sit down." Then: "You're working yourself to death."

"In a minute," she said, and turned from him.

It was then that he remembered the cool beauty who had

spirited him north to the cabin in Vermont in the winter of 1928, who had sung "Let's Misbehave," dancing for him in the firelight, wearing only the hat she was to wear, later, while posing for the photograph he would keep, all the years—it was then, that moment in the living room, sometime after Ian's death, that he had found the memory and known it for the memory of the loveliest time of his life.

Now, in the room on the second floor of Mrs. Blackemore's brownstone, blood in his mouth, and jaw throbbing, his body one long ache, the girl murmuring softly in sleep, he remembered everything and realized it was because of the music. He was hearing music. The new tenant played records, loud, on an old, scratchy phonograph. It was swing music, someone was singing "Elmer's Tune," and he sat listening to it. It was night. The street outside was quiet, empty; far off, a red light blinked, and a pair of headlights inched along the curb and went out. "Elmer's Tune" finished, and a new record began.

"Oh," the girl moaned from the bed, "what is that?"

Cakes leaned forward a little, listening. "It's something of Paul Whiteman's," he said.

"Who's that?"

"A bandleader, long ago."

"Are you coming to bed?"

He looked at her. "Yes."

It took him a long time to get out of the chair. She had rolled over, was asleep again, and so he sat back down, lay his head back, listening to the music. And then he was hearing something else. He sat forward again, looked at the ceiling.

There could be no mistaking it; it was the soft, rhythmic, shuffling sound of someone dancing alone.

13
▲

"Let me get this straight," Arthur said. "You got in a fight over her?"

"In front of her," said Cakes. "Not over her, in *front* of her."

"Are you sleeping with her yet?"

This was no one's business. "Don't be a fool."

"Then why fight over her?"

"It wasn't over her, Max. For the love of God."

They were sitting in the dayroom, facing a floor-to-ceiling window through which the red spires of the old wing of the building were visible. The sky beyond was the color of dirty water, and the air itself seemed gritty: black dust blew in the wind; it would snow.

"You look like a gangster with your face all banged up."

"I feel like an old man."

"Poor Edward."

"She got up this morning and went out without eating anything. I couldn't get her to tell me anything. She gets upset if I question her."

"Look at you," Arthur said.

Cakes touched, with his tongue, the sore places on the inside of his mouth. "I was knocked out."

"Fights," Arthur said. "I shake to think. I was never a fighter. Not even as a boy. In my block there were twenty, thirty boys, all tough, and me—I was the clown. Let me tell you, I didn't mind being the laughingstock. I made them laugh. I could tell a story."

"That wouldn't have done me much good yesterday," Edward said.

"You should keep your temper."

"I didn't even see it coming."

"You never see the one that gets you."

"I never even felt it."

"No."

"Have you ever been knocked out?" Cakes asked.

"I've passed out. It's the same thing."

"You mean from drinking?"

"I don't mean from the sight of blood."

They were quiet.

"So tell me about this girl."

"She left this morning without eating anything. I don't know where she went."

"And you got someone playing music and dancing all night."

"Yes."

"A woman."

"I haven't seen her."

Arthur chuckled softly. "He's surrounded by ladies now. What luck in his old age. I think you're making the whole thing up."

"I'm not—look at my face."

"So." Arthur laughed. "You walked into a door."

"I'm glad to see you're up and around," said Cakes, meaning to change the subject.

"Yeah," Arthur said, "maybe I'll get lucky, too." He grimaced and moved in his chair. "So, you're making love to the young girl."

"If you're going to talk that way, then I'll just leave."

Arthur looked at the ceiling as if to address someone there. "He talks like this, and I'm the one who's sitting here with nurses and doctors and a bad ticker."

"Why do you have to reduce everything to the body," Cakes said. "You reduce everything to your—your glands, for the love of God."

"I'm full of sap, Edward. I'm an old tree full of sap."

They were quiet again.

Behind them, on the far side of the room, two old women watched television, and the sound of it had made a sort of counterpoint to their talk: voices, an audience laughing, an occasional flourish of music.

"So," Arthur said, "what do you want from this, then?"

Cakes looked at him.

"Do you want to fall in love, maybe?"

"You're not making any sense."

"The *girl.* The *girl.*"

Cakes was silent.

"Look. Tell me you might be in love with the girl. You think you might be falling for her in a big way. No bullshit, no horsing around or anything—just say it. Say it. For me, like it's true. You think you might be in love with the girl. Then I'll say, 'Really?' and you say, 'Really.' Then I'll say, 'I'm happy for you,' and you say, 'But I'm miserable,' and I'll say, 'Why?' and you say, 'Because I don't think she loves me.' Which will be no surprise to anyone. And then you ask me for advice, see. And I'll give it, and it'll be very good advice, and maybe we'll toast for good luck. We'll get some of that chalky shit they serve here in the name of milk, and we'll have a toast, friends sharing good feeling and warmth and the birth of love with all its pangs and worries and upsets and sweetnesses. We'll get a little drunk, maybe, and laugh about it. And you'll show me a picture. Your new girlfriend. It'll be a nice-looking girl, not too attractive. Like you said, right? It'll be her. The young woman. What could be nicer? You say you'll bring her here to meet your old friend, the nice Jewish boy: Arthur. Each time you come you'll promise. And each time I'll say, 'Wonderful—I can't wait.' Only something will of course keep her from making the trip."

"If you know it's a fantasy, why do you want to keep it up?"

Arthur frowned at him. "You're serious."

"Look," Cakes said, "why can't you just talk about—well, about the things I tell you. I'm not a storyteller, Max. I'm not comfortable making things up."

"Now I'm depressed. You're surrounded with ladies and you're living like a celibate. It's true, isn't it—for God's sake, you're not trying to cover up."

Cakes sat quiet, gazing out at the first few flakes of snow.

"You know what I'm thinking?" Arthur said presently. "I'm wondering what you say to a terminal patient on New Year's Eve."

"You're not terminal," Cakes said.

"Of course I am."

"Like we all are."

"I could've made a better world, Edward. No rain except at night, very late. No disease. No death. A world big as the universe and all the food you could want. No aging, of course—no aging at all. And all the sex you could want. And everybody, if he wants to, could own a Vermeer." Arthur sat with his hands folded lightly over his belly and mused, staring out the window.

"Maybe, one time when I come here," Cakes said, "I could get them to let me take you out for a walk or something."

"It's snowing," said Arthur.

"It's early for it," Cakes said. "Supposed to get up to three inches."

"Winter," said Arthur. "He wants to talk about the weather."

"You mentioned that it was snowing."

"I'm sorry—you're right, I did."

"What do you want to talk about?"

"Who knows?"

Edward was silent.

"You say this new tenant dances all by herself at night?"

"She did last night. For hours."

"Maybe she had company."

"No, it was just her."

"Old records, too."

"Paul Whiteman."

"Maybe you should go upstairs and ask her to dance."

"Maybe I will," Edward said.

"That's the spirit."

"There's certainly no use trying to sleep."

"You got an eternity to sleep," said Arthur.

"It was Rudy Vallee at two o'clock this morning."

"My, my."

"Between that and the rock 'n' roll, I may lose my mind."

"Make friends with her," Arthur said. "Make friends with all women, Edward. That's what it's all about, and everything else is just chaff. Just chaff."

14

▲

When the time comes, Arthur will not let his friend go. He insists that Cakes stay for lunch, thinks of Cakes walking out of the building and down the street, away; thinks of how it would be to get up and go, to take a train somewhere, or a jet. He thinks of all the things he will never do again, and he is not morbid, but only a little nostalgic. It is too soon for things to be ending, as he knows they most certainly are, and he wants to tell someone about it, wants to say simply that even a long life, a rich life, as his has been, is tragic at the end, because it has had to lose so much. In the matter of this afternoon he knows his poor daughter is coming all the way into town to see him, and he doesn't feel like facing her and her family alone. This is because, no matter how hard he tries and she tries, something always makes them argue; they are always rubbing each other the wrong way, and there are plenty of reasons for it and so far nothing to be done about it; he cannot control himself with her, cannot keep a civil tongue in his head. She is an old woman now, past sixty. He doesn't really know her; he remembers her. She was a smart, sociable, but ordinary little girl who grew into a smart, sociable, but ordinary woman, and that is all right with him; it is just that he hates the way he is with her now, as he hates the breezy condescension she mostly shows him. So he talks his friend into staying with him, to wait for the daughter. They have lunch together in the cafeteria, and Arthur's daughter does not come, or is late. It is easy to see that Cakes is restless, and so Arthur tells him to go ahead and leave if he wants to.

"It's just that I'm worried about the cat," Edward Cakes tells him. "It isn't eating right, and it's all by itself."

"Too bad," says Arthur.

The implication is that Cakes is worried about a cat, and here is Arthur, not eating too well, all by himself. At night Arthur can't sleep. It gets harder the older you get, someone told him. He can't remember who, now. And then he can remember. It is a woman, his last love, his last good time, he tells Edward Cakes. And then he says how, my God, it was years ago. He has eaten a little, he is warm, he begins to doze. Cakes is sitting at his elbow, and someone has put the television on across the room. There is a television in every room of this building except the bathrooms and the laundry room and the crafts room. Arthur thinks the crafts are a bunch of shit, and he told that to someone, too. It was a nurse, he remembers, who caught him masturbating and was appalled—the nerve, the unmitigated nerve of her to be appalled. But he does like the nurses, he tells Cakes. He is sleepy, too. He thinks Cakes said something about going, and he says, "Wait." And then the two of them are simply sitting there at the table waiting, lunch finished with, for Arthur's daughter to arrive. Cakes watches television, and Arthur watches Cakes. A good man, a good friend, a little stuffy. A little afraid. Well, who can blame anyone for being a little afraid? What's maddening is someone who thinks he's not afraid. Arthur is afraid. He remembers things. He tells Cakes about the woman who told him it gets harder to sleep the older you get. It is all so long ago now, that one night in an apartment house in a little town in Virginia, with the woman, then seventy-something, his last lover.

It was a bad time, really. The memories are not pleasant. His wife, Angela, whom he called, for the twenty-eight years, Angel, had been dead almost fifteen years. He was living in a corner room, in a boarding house on Granville Avenue in Point Royal, Virginia; he had retired from almost thirty years of teaching high-school English to take up his own small business, a repair call service, for which he used an old beat-up Ford truck and a big box of tools Angel had bought for him years ago, when he was forty, and thinking, among other things, of quitting his job to do the one sort of work he had always loved—the work, he would have said back then, of his two good hands. It had taken him the rest of his working life to make that decision, and having made it, he went all out: he borrowed two thousand dollars to buy the truck, and he had an ad put in the local paper offering his services. The trouble was that his health had begun to give him trouble, and he went for a long time without being able to do much work at all; the payments piled up. He was almost seventy, he lived alone in the small room, and every envelope in the mail had a window in it; everyone wanted him to pay up or else. His pension and the Social Security were not nearly enough to cover the wild growth of the cost of things, and what money he could get went through his fingers like water. To add to things, someone had complained about him to the real estate company that he did most of his repair calls for, and the company had stopped calling him. There had been a complaint, someone told him over the phone, there had been quite a few complaints, as a matter of fact: Arthur talked too much; he was too friendly with the women, and frightened some of them.

He wanted to know who these women were.

No one seemed to know. Times were worse every day. He stayed in the room a lot, and drank a bit more whiskey than he should have, and the bank he'd borrowed the money from began to call him about the payments—he was way behind. He owed two hundred fifty dollars on the loan, and they wanted the full amount. The loan officer of this bank was a man named Crowder, and Crowder called him three or four times a day claiming he wanted to work things out; he was sure there was a way to work it all out to everyone's advantage.

"I'm flat broke," Arthur told him. It was the second time in his life he had decided, pretty much, to give up.

"If you can come up with ten dollars," Crowder said, "I'll see what I can do."

"Feed me next month."

"Max," the loan officer said.

"Look," said Arthur, "I get home from the hospital, from being sick with an ulcerated stomach, and I get beat up by some punk in the street. The punk takes my last two dollars and a Social Security check. That's what's happened so far this month."

"That's not what you told us yesterday."

This was true. Arthur had taken to making things up over the phone when creditors called; he had decided that someone on the other end of the line had to listen to these explanations for a living, and he might as well make it interesting; it was hard to care about anything anymore. The truth was, you couldn't get blood out of a stone. "What did I tell you yesterday?" he asked the loan officer.

"I have it right here, Max. You wrecked your truck."

"I was coming to that," Arthur said.

"Max, a person can have a thing taken away if it's not paid for."

This angered him. It wasn't as if they were talking about a million dollars. He said this to the loan officer, and then before he knew it, he was shouting at the loan officer for calling him Max. "I'm old enough to be your goddamn grandfather," he said. "Call me Mr. Hagood."

"Are you finished?" the loan officer asked.

Arthur said he was. His knees started to shake a little; he was trembling. It was as if he could feel the tremendous power of the bank marshaling itself against him.

"I want to inform you of the bank's next step."

He tried a joke. "Make it quick," he said, "they'll be coming in here to take the phone out any minute."

"The bank will have at least twenty dollars by this afternoon. By two o'clock."

"I'm sorry," Arthur said. "I'm trying." He spoke sincerely; he was sincerely afraid now.

"Look," said the loan officer, "there must be somebody you can borrow twenty dollars from."

But Arthur had borrowed money from everyone, and even so he thought of asking the loan officer for a personal loan of twenty dollars.

"Have the money to us this afternoon, Mr. Hagood, or we'll take the necessary action."

"I can't make any money without the truck," Arthur told him. But the loan officer had hung up. Arthur stood there for a minute or two hearing the dial tone. Then he hung the phone up and went into the bathroom and washed his mouth out; there was a taste in his mouth, like copper. He ran the tap and wet his face, thinking he might shave, clean himself up, get himself presentable. The bank was coming. When the phone rang, he was startled into a cry of alarm. It was Maxine Sandusky. At the time, he only knew her last name. She wanted to know where he had been, why he hadn't stopped over to see her in such a long time. He stood listening to her voice, and that taste, like old nails, blossoming on his tongue. It was strange; he had worked honorably all his life, and he had come to this, standing with a threat climbing his spine, the bank getting ready to seize his property. "I thought you might've died off," she was saying, and he came to himself.

"I'm still here," he said.

"Where've you been?"

"Don't get much work anymore."

"Well, you get on over here sometime soon and pay me a visit." She was cheerful, and he remembered that the last time he had been at her place, she had asked him to leave. For a moment he was ready to entertain the idea that she was one of those who had complained about him. "I bet you're surprised to hear from me," she went on. "I bet you're just shocked to death."

"I'm surprised," he said.

The conversation became quiet, and sort of awkward, and though they said a friendly goodbye, he thought there was something a little desperate in her voice. He did not think of going over to see her; the call had been, in fact, an irritation, since he had been unable to think what he should say to her. He did not know what he should say to anyone, and he went out on his little porch to wait for the bank to come take his truck. He sat there and remembered Angel, remembered that, even now, after the fifteen years, he still found himself speaking to her, forgetting that she was not in the next room. It was a soft Virginia morning, and there were cars in the street, people walking by him, birds singing. He was going to lose the truck, and then there would be nothing but to go north, to beg on his daughter's doorstep. And then it struck him that he could take the truck and run somewhere; he could simply not be here when the people from the bank arrived. In the next moment he had made up his mind to pay that visit to Mrs. Sandusky. Why not? There was nothing holding him here. Except that he didn't really know the woman, didn't really like her very much, either. He had never called her anything but Mrs. Sandusky; she had never called him anything but Mr. Hagood. It had been an odd sort of friendship. All he knew about her was that she had lived in foreign cities for a long time and then come back to Virginia to live, and that she liked jigsaw puzzles. She had a large cutting board where she did the puzzles, some of them with more than five thousand pieces. She told Arthur that she was afraid of ever doing the same one twice, and so whenever she finished one she immediately destroyed it. Arthur thought this was a bit silly in a harmless, small way, and he thought she was a little strange: a skinny woman who moved around very well for her age, but didn't own any transportation and walked to the grocery store two blocks from her apartment pulling a wagon. The first time Arthur had met her was on a repair call for the real estate company; his call on her was perhaps the fourth call he had been sent on to the apartment complex where she lived. That time, she answered the door in a housecoat and took Arthur into the kitchen and talked to him while he worked. It was in November, and Kennedy had been dead a year. She talked about the assassination, told him about herself and her puzzles and coming back to Virginia, which she hadn't seen since she was twenty-two. She was a widow. She knew how poor Mrs. Kennedy felt. Her husband, she said, poor man, had quit smoking on a Saturday, and died in a flash fire the following Monday. She smoked excessively, telling him this. She didn't seem to him much different than a lot of people he saw on those repair calls: they all wanted to talk, it seemed, and they were all inclined to tell you things they wouldn't tell anyone else. He was always content to listen, or pretend to listen, depending on how interesting the person was, and he thought Mrs. Sandusky interesting enough. Truth was, he had begun his own talk, had noticed some of the books she kept and was asking about them. Even so, things might not have gone a step further if he hadn't hurt his thumb trying to get the reset button on her garbage disposal to work. She put a Band-Aid on it, and they wound up having a cigarette, really talking about the books. It was very odd and awkward at first, because both of them knew this was a change, somehow; they were connected by the wound, the bleeding, her efforts to dress and bandage the thumb. She seemed embarrassed, but they had discovered mutual interests; in fact, she had taught English for a while in a school in Kenya, back in the late forties.

By the time he left, that first time, she had invited him back, had asked that he stop in any time a repair call brought him to those apartments. And so he had done that; he went back four or five times. She would pour him a touch of whiskey and ask him what sort of a day it had been. It was like a game in some ways; it was as though they were playing at being married. There was a married feel about being asked what kind of day he'd had and whether or not he wanted a sandwich, something more to drink. But the last time he had been to see her, they had a rather unpleasant misunderstanding.

It happened like this.

They were sitting in her kitchen, sipping whiskey, and he had got the idea that perhaps he might make love to her. He said, "I'm not going to play games anymore. I'd like to go to bed with you."

She drank her whiskey in a gulp, and he knew he had said the wrong thing. "Men," she said.

"I understand," Arthur said. "I won't mention it again."

"Were you ever unfaithful to your wife?" she asked.

He told her he had never done any such thing.

"Do you think I'm attractive?" she said.

"No," Arthur told her. "Neither one of us is much fun to look at, I guess." He wanted to be truthful with her.

"Get out," she said.

"I was teasing," he said.

"You were not," she said.

"Come on," Arthur said. "How old are you?"

"Seventy-something."

"You don't look a day over fifty."

"Fifty," she said. "Fifty."

"Not one single day."

"I'm seventy-one," she said.

He told her he thought that was a shocker.

"Please," she said, "just get out—get out." She sat there waving her hand across her face, as if something were flying around her eyes. "You ever been to Syracuse?" she asked.

He said, "Yes—once, long ago."

"Do you remember it?"

"Not much."

"My daughter lives in Syracuse," she said.

He told her he thought that was fine.

"It's cold up there in the winters, isn't it."

"Gets cold," he said, "sure."

And then she stopped talking, stopped everything, it seemed; she just sat there, not looking at him for the longest time, and so at last he got up, begged her pardon, and left her there, certain that this was the last time he would ever see her.

And then had come the late May morning when the loan officer told him he would lose the truck, and Mrs. Sandusky, like a saving angel out of the blue, had called to tell him he was welcome any time.

On days when Edward Cakes does not come to see him, and the television is too banal and empty for him to be able to stand it, and he can't read for the way it hurts his eyes, he makes his way down the hall to the lounge, to sit in the bright sun of its wide windows and gaze at the world, and think about a certain night twenty years ago, when he was by all definitions already an old man; there is something in the animation that comes to Edward Cakes's eyes when he talks about his flapper, the mountain cabin —it invigorates Arthur, somehow, makes the blood move in his temples and along his thighs. Yet when he thinks about that, he sees the rooms of Mrs. Sandusky's apartment, and the girl is a woman past seventy—or rather, she is, somehow, both women:

the girl in the photograph on Edward Cakes's wall, and the memory of Maxine Sandusky in a night that yielded, finally, a kind of forgiveness for Arthur Hagood, who, then, did not feel as though forgiveness would ever come to a man like him.

The apartments Mrs. Sandusky lived in were all in a row, as most apartments are; they looked like barracks buildings. There were signs about how this was the future everyone was dreaming of; on a summer day you could hear a hundred different kinds of music coming from a hundred different windows; there were always the several odors of the several dinners or meals being prepared. There was a swimming pool and a tennis court and a little play park for children. There were fir trees looking, in the hot noon, parched, somehow breathless, like someone wearing too many layers of clothing. Arthur pulled into the lot and got out, and here was Mrs. Sandusky in front of her door, down on her knees with a trowel in her hand, digging in the dirt beside the stoop. She had a blue bandanna on, and for a second she looked like a girl. He walked up the sidewalk, and she glanced at him and kept on digging.

"I thought you were the daughter," he said.

"I don't want to talk about her." She kept digging.

"Well, I came to visit you," Arthur said.

"Marry me," she said.

"Pardon?"

"You heard me," she said.

"I guess I did."

"Marry me."

"That's rough," he said. "I can't."

She stood up and wiped her face with the back of her arm. The trowel was aluminum and the sun leapt from it and blinded him. "You know what my daughter has decided?" she said.

"It's very hot out here," he told her. "Can we go inside? In the air-conditioning?"

"My daughter thinks I'm unable to take care of myself." She turned, walked to the door, opened it and left it that way, going down the hall away from him. He followed. They sat in the kitchen and she poured them some whiskey. There was a window at his elbow and he looked out at her clothesline, clothes hanging from it in disarray, as if someone had just flung a handful of them at the line: some were lying on the grass, and in one corner of the yard a cat was rolling around in what looked like a nightgown or undergarment.

"I'll tell you what she's really worried about—money."

"Tell you the truth," Arthur said, "I'm a little worried about that myself." He took a big swallow of the whiskey. He was tremendously unhappy, and he thought she would be no good company; it was a mistake to have come here in the first place, he supposed.

"Marry me," she said. Her face twisted suddenly and she moaned. It came quickly, and then, whatever it was, she stopped it. She pulled the bandanna off carefully, and bunched it up over her eyes, then put it down and lighted a cigarette; there was something disjointed and almost spastic about her movements as if she were not in control of the signals her brain was sending to her body. "My daughter wants me to move in with her."

"In Syracuse?" he said, and was proud of himself for remembering.

She nodded.

"That's rough."

"Don't tell me it's rough," she said. "I know that already. In two weeks I'll be crazy-demented, living in her house. They'll put me in a home."

"I don't have any money," Arthur said.

"Rob a bank."

"Ha."

"I mean it."

"I'm sorry," he said.

"Everybody's sorry," she said. "You know I didn't mean to spring this on you." She poured more of the whiskey, and there was an unsettling look in her eye, as if she might tell him something insane. "I called every man I know and said stop by. Any time, I said. And the first one, I was going to make him a fat dinner and be sweet and see if I could seduce him. And you're the first one. And now I've gone and ruined everything."

He didn't know what to tell her, except that he wished she had gone ahead with the seduction plan. He remembered that he had liked those old visits, when she would pour him a whiskey and ask if he didn't want something to eat.

"I'll make you a good wife," she said.

He couldn't look at her. "This is very flattering and all—"

"Don't say no. Okay? Just—don't say anything."

He was silent.

"It wouldn't work, anyway," she said.

"I'm sorry," he said.

"My husband died," she said, "damn him."

"I guess if he had a choice, he'd still be around."

She had poured more of the whiskey and had drunk it all down, and now she poured more, started to drink it, too. She looked at him and nodded at the bottle.

He poured himself some more.

"I'd rather be dead than have to live with my daughter—like another one of her babies. I just don't want to be in Syracuse."

"I have a daughter," said Arthur. "Lives up north, too."

"Would you live with her?"

"No."

"See?"

"Well," he said, "she's got a family of her own."

"There."

"Why do you have to live with your daughter?" he asked.

"I don't have any choice in the matter."

He took the rest of the whiskey and felt a small ache under the heart. "I know what I'm waiting for, I'll tell you," he said, "and you're waiting for it, too, and it's a hell of a wait, isn't it."

"What has that got to do with anything?"

He shrugged. "Seems like I've been waiting a long time."

She looked out the window at the clothes on the ground. "We ought to get big money for making it this far."

"That would be all right."

They drank most of the bottle, then, without saying a word. She began to miss the glass, and the ashes dropped from her cigarettes onto the front of her blouse.

"You want some sex?" she asked finally.

This caused him to swallow the whiskey in the wrong way, and for a while she was patting his back as he coughed and sputtered and tried to breathe. Then he sat back and took her hand. It was very soft and dry, and there were dark blotches in the skin.

"Well?" she said.

"You're very nice," he said.

"Then we might as well go into the bedroom."

He didn't speak, and she didn't move.

"Ah," she said finally, "you want any more whiskey?"

"No thank you," he said.

"You're drunk?"

He said he thought he was all right.

"You sure you don't want a little to go?" she asked.

"Whiskey?" he said.

She smiled. "No."

He was thinking she must have done this for a living at some time in her life. "I guess I am drunk," he said.

"You shouldn't drive."

"Maybe not."

"I ought to try and keep you here."

"Got to get back," he said. It was all very friendly, and they shook hands at the door, and she sighed out something about staying drunk in Syracuse.

"Syracuse," he said.

"That's where my daughter lives," she said.

He told her he hated the winters up north.

"So does my daughter," she said.

He was beginning to feel strange, because there wasn't anything else to say and because, really, he had no place he wanted to go. She stood blocking the door, holding his left hand, turning it over and looking at the back of it. He had not come here to see her: he had come here to hide. He did not look at her, stood letting her turn his hand in her own soft hands, hating himself with an old fierce hatred.

"It's been nice knowing you," she said.

"A pleasure," he said.

"Nice," she said.

"You take care of yourself," he said.

"Yes, you too." She was smiling, nodding, but her eyes were welling up. "You realize we almost got married."

"I'm very sorry," he said.

"We could've been man and wife—we were friends, almost lovers. We could've been husband and wife and not moved to Syracuse, and now you're going off to God knows where and I'll never see you again. And you're the best of my gentleman friends."

"Don't talk like that," he said.

"I'm telling the truth—if we were twenty or thirty or even fifty—I mean if there was life ahead of us, well that would be one thing. But life's behind us. We have to do what we're told now. We don't have any time left—goodbye is goodbye. I can't tell my daughter to leave me alone—this is her apartment. She's paying the rent. I have to go to Syracuse and die when I wanted to die in Virginia where I was born." She put her head down on his chest. They were in her doorway. He looked out at the parking lot, which was just a blind glare of sunlight reflected off the cars; it got in his eyes, and he saw fireballs everywhere. When he glanced down to where she had been digging, it was like light floating up out of the ground. He patted her shoulder blades.

"God," she said.

"Come on," he said, "Tell me why you were digging."

"A garden." She backed away from him, wiping her eyes. There were little blue lines along her wrists. "You go on, now," she said. "I'm stupid to bother you."

"Goodness," he told her, "we were almost married, remember?"

She tried to smile.

"What were you planting?"

"I don't know. I haven't even bought the seeds yet."

"If you don't want to go to Syracuse, I don't think you should go." He walked her into the kitchen; he just seemed to see himself doing it, and then he was doing it. They sat down again;

the door was open down the hall, and then a sudden draft slammed it shut, startling them both.

He poured more whiskey for them both. "Now take me, for instance," he said. "I'm in all kinds of trouble right now, with—you know, payments, money troubles—those payments come like a tribe of Indians, every month. I don't have the money to pay anyone. And I just tell them they'll have to wait."

"I don't understand," she said.

"Why don't you tell your daughter you're not coming. Let her do what she wants about the rent here—this is not such a wonderful place."

"It's been home for nine years. I don't like new places—they frighten me."

"But you could do it." He poured still more of the whiskey, held the bottle toward her. She nodded. He filled her glass. "You could adjust. You don't have to go to Syracuse if you don't want to—all you might have to do is move out of here."

"No, it's not like that. You don't understand. I never worked—I don't have anything. My husband left me with nothing."

"You could find something," he said. It was just talk, and he knew it. He would get very drunk.

"No, there's nothing." She took a good long drink of what was left of the whiskey now, and he did too. "I raised my daughter. Period."

"You type?"

"No."

He took another sip. "Ever sell anything?"

"No," she said. Then she leaned forward. "I'm like your wife—remember? You told me once that she wasn't good at very much but making you happy. Your—what's the name?"

"Angel," he said.

"Right. She never worked. If you had died and left her without anything, she'd be at the mercy of your daughter. Except I don't mean it that way—not 'at the mercy' of her. But she would—she would have to depend on her."

"I never said that about my wife."

"What?"

"That she couldn't do anything. She could. She could sing. She used to sing all the time in the house."

They drank. The whiskey was almost gone. He knocked over the sugar bowl, somehow, and they both watched it run out on the table. It made him think of avalanches, landslides—things falling apart, mountains crumbling. He thought it was funny in the bitterest sort of way.

"I used to want to sing," she said.

"I don't want to talk about my wife."

"You loved her so, I know."

"I told you," he said. "I told you how I loved her."

"What's the matter?" she asked him.

"Nothing."

"I just said I used to want to sing."

"Then why don't you sing."

"I sang at a wedding once."

"See? I bet you were a hit."

"Five or six people—a small wedding in Chicago when I went to visit with my husband's family."

"You didn't sing at your daughter's wedding."

"My daughter was married without my knowledge—I wasn't invited to the wedding. I could've sung there."

"Let me hear you sing."

"No."

"Come on."

She was taking the last drop of whiskey out of the bottom of her glass, her tongue down at the bottom of it, her eyes crossed; there were tears in the corners of her eyes. He pushed the whiskey bottle over so she could pour the trickle that was left, but she ignored it. She stood up, tottered, straightened herself, and folded her hands in at her waist, locking the fingers. She took a deep breath, and started to sing, but it came out as a cough; it burst up out of her like a gust of wind. She coughed for a while, then straightened herself again. "Ready?" she said.

He said, "Ready."

She sat down, suddenly, held her fingers over her mouth. "Oh."

"Quite all right," he said.

"I'm dizzy." She closed her eyes, opened them. "I'm very dizzy all of a sudden."

"Keep your feet planted."

She laughed. "That's a hell of a note." And she slapped his arm. "Get it? A hell of a note. I'll tell you what I'm drunk."

"Me, too," Arthur told her.

She slapped his arm again. "You know what I hate?"

"What."

"Syracuse and Mother's Day." She threw her head back and laughed. "What do you hate?"

"Myself," he said.

"Aha. Himself. What else. That doesn't count. What else."

"Banks," he said.

This made her almost helpless. They were both laughing now. He had his head on his arms, laughing. "Banks," she was saying, "banks, he hates banks."

"I do," he said.

"So do I. Let's drink to hating banks."

There wasn't enough. They held the glasses to their lips and waited for the residue to come down, laughing about that.

"What's all that stuff about hating yourself?" she asked. "I hate that kind of talk."

"I talk like that when I'm drunk," he said, staring at the table.

"You get blue."

"Some," he said.

"You get to feeling sorry for yourself."

"I guess." He smiled weakly.

"Poor thing."

"I miss my wife," he said.

"Come on," she said, "let's talk about what else we hate. You know what I hate?"

"No," he said.

"I hate people who think little old ladies are cute."

This struck him as very original and funny. He nodded.

"Do you think little old ladies are cute?"

"Not even when I was young did I think that," Arthur said.

She laughed very hard. "You know what I say to people like that?"

"What."

"Well, I can't repeat it in front of a gentleman."

"That's right," he said, "good for you."

"Good for you," she said.

"Right," he said. "Little old ladies are not cute."

"You know what else I hate?"

"No."

"Syracuse."

"Right," Arthur said, "you already told me that one."

"Too cold. Too cold in the winter. I'll tell you it's fucking cold in Syracuse."

"Right."

"You know," she said, "actually I have a dirty mouth. I'm being very polite."

"Me, too."

"You have a dirty mouth?"

"Right," he said, "me, too."

"I never would say anything bad in public," she said. "Not really. But when I was alone. Well, let me tell you." She stared into her glass, turning it a little. "When I'd get up in the morning, I'd be all alone because Robley would be out being religious, going to churches. I tell you about Robley? Tried them all. Every one, I bet, once at least. Kept looking and looking for the right church. The right—oh, how did he used to say it?" She frowned, put the glass down. "I can't even think straight. Avenue? The right alley or conduit or whatever—something like that. A highway to the Lord. A railroad track to God." She laughed again, throwing her head back again. "That's a good one. Highway to the Lord. Anyway—Robley was religious, very devout—so it came out of *my* ears. And I used to get up and he would be gone to one of his churches, and I'd stand in front of the bathroom mirror and say every blasphemy I could think of. Isn't that evil." She folded her hands in her lap, looking at Arthur as though he would be able to tell her how evil it was. But then she went on. "I loved him, too.

Isn't that the strangest thing of all? I'd cuss and I'd scream foul names in the mirror because of him, watching myself curse and pretending I was him, watching me. And—and then he'd come home and I was always so surprised at how glad I was—deep down glad to see him. Glad like it had been a long, long time and I'd been a thousand miles away. Isn't that the strangest thing?"

He told her Angela used to sing when she was angry, to calm herself down.

"That's right. And I was going to sing for you, wasn't I."

"You don't have to."

"I will."

"I'm so drunk," he said.

"You can't drive that old truck now."

"I have to. I've got to come up with some money. I'll lose my truck if I don't come up with some money."

"If you don't want to lose it, you ought to tell them to wait." She smiled.

He patted her wrist. "I owe you the truth about it—why I came here—"

"Oh," she said, "I believe I am going to be ill."

"Try not to think about it."

She held the tips of her fingers up to her lips. Then, quite without warning, she reached into her mouth and brought her teeth out. "Excuse me," she said.

"Quite all right."

"Oh," she said. Her eyes were wide.

"Better go in the bathroom."

She breathed deeply, her fingers over her mouth. She swallowed once, twice. "I just hate to be ill."

"It'll be okay," he said. "I've seen it before."

"There," she said, folding her hands in her lap again. "I'm fine."

"Guess I ought to be going." He looked for her reaction.

"No. Not in this condition. You stay here with me." She took a deep breath and reached over and touched his face. "I don't care why you came to see me. You stay here with me."

Her mouth looked odd without the teeth, and he tried not to

look at it, tried simply to be glad of the fact that she wanted him to stay, and he was staying, but then she had seen him staring at her, and she picked the teeth up and clapped them back in.

"Sorry," she said, and ran her hands lightly over her thighs. "You should see what else is removable on me. I come with replaceable parts, you know."

"You have a parts list," Arthur said. "I guess I do, too."

She was laughing loud. "A parts list—oh, that's great. A parts list. I love it. I got a parts list."

"I guess I do, too," he said again.

"Teeth?"

"Uh, partially. I still have my bottom ones and a few of my top ones." He was sorry for this, almost as he said it. He thought he saw the disappointment in her face, as if he had told her he was fifteen years younger than she was.

"You don't have a lot of hair," she said.

"No."

"Well?"

"Well what?"

"Your parts list." She seemed a little impatient about it now.

"Well," he said, "I've got a piece of metal in my leg, up near the hip bone."

"That's all?"

"That's about it." He was sorry he didn't have more.

"That's nothing," she said, and then she lifted her hair up, like a cap. He was sitting there looking at the curve of her scalp, and it shone like something polished. "No teeth," she said, "no hair—I got fake nails on my fingers and my toes."

"What happened?" he said. It was out before he could think to stop it. She looked at him for a long time, and then she laughed.

"I'm a leper," she said, laughing. "We're all lepers, on the way to the colony." She put her hair back, rested her elbows on the table, still laughing, or he thought at first that it was laughing. But it was something else—not crying, quite, but a kind of hysterical, garrulous tic that seemed to take hold of her. Finally she gained control of it, smiled weakly at him and said, "Spend the night?"

"Looks like I have to," he told her.

"You're too drunk to drive."

"I'm glad," he said.

It was a love affair. She looked off into space. "You know, I feel so far from home. And *this* is home." She wiped her eyes with the bandanna; she had crushed it in her fist, and she looked out the window. The light made her cheeks look waxed. "Why, I don't believe I know your first name, Mr. Hagood." She spoke so delicately, her voice trembling over the vowels and consonants.

He told her his name, and then said, "But people call me Max, sometimes."

She smiled. "I'm Maxine."

He couldn't believe it. He let go a laugh, sent it, wild, at the ceiling.

And then they began to make love. They got to know each other a little better; they laughed and they were drunk. Sometime near eleven o'clock he went out and got a six-pack of beer. She gave him the money, and he walked all the way down to the end of the road, to the 7-Eleven store, and all the way back; it took him the better part of an hour, and he was singing all the way. There he was, walking along the sidewalk, a summer night, and he had the paper bag with the six-pack of cold beer in it, just like so many summer nights long ago, when he wore a tie, and summer was his favorite time of year. There was a bright moon following him in and out from behind the houses, and the smell of honeysuckle was everywhere. A beautiful night, like a gift. He had forgot how it felt to be carrying something home to somebody. It felt very good; it was an easy familiar summer feeling. She was standing in the doorway waiting for him; she kissed him on the cheek as he passed through. They played old records and danced, and he held her lightly, quite gently. Then they took a shower together until there wasn't any hot water left: she washed him and he washed her, and they teased about how old and wrinkled they were. He was beginning to get a headache, and twice she excused herself to go fight off being ill. She said it was a little upset stomach. Finally, all humble accommodations made to age and circumstance and the liquor they had drunk, they snuggled deep in the bed and she was asleep right away, and he lay there with his headache and a feeling like grief, though that was not exactly what it was. He was not thinking about his dead wife because when he did go to sleep at last he dreamed about her, and as always it was like running into her on a street corner, with everything he had ever done to hurt her, or that would have hurt her, grafted to him like scar tissue. But then he was awake, and something had gone out of him, had let go inside, and he turned to the breathing woman next to him, put one arm over her thin shoulder, and went back to sleep.

15

▲

Arthur's daughter came rustling into the room in a new dress, she said, and she modeled it for them; she called Arthur "Max." She stood at their table, knocking ashes from her cigarette into their empty ashtray. She was a tall, nervous-looking woman with cold black eyes and a strange long nose that made her appear always about to sneeze; she was wearing a lot of makeup, especially around the eyes, and, looking at her, it was hard for Edward Cakes to believe she was Arthur's daughter. She had driven into town in a new car—she was proud of that—and she wanted Arthur to see it.

"I was talking to Cakes here about Maxine Sandusky," Arthur told her.

"You never change," she said, bending down to kiss him on the cheek.

"So where's the rest of them?" Arthur wanted to know.

But she was looking at Cakes. "Do I know you, sir?"

"An old friend," Arthur said. "I see him more often than I

see my family." He nodded at Cakes. "Edward, you remember Linda. My one daughter."

"I nearly had a heart attack coming through all that traffic," she said. She opened her purse and was searching in it for something. Then she closed it and sat down next to her father.

"Well, so where's the rest of them?" Arthur said.

"They're all gone, Papa. You know that. They're all over the country—I get letters once in a blue moon. They call their father when they need money. When they worry. They send us cards. We get to go to their weddings if we're especially nice and don't say anything about their divorces or the ways they've thrown out everything we taught them. Agh, I feel old."

"She feels old," Arthur said.

"So," she said to Cakes, "you live here?"

"He visits me. He comes to see me two, three times a week."

"Well," she said, "That's nice."

"So that means you can stay home more if you want to." Arthur stared at the table.

"I will if I have to listen to talk about old flames," she said. "All those old stories about ladies you spent the night with—who begged you to marry them." She looked at Cakes. "He was telling you that story, right? The lady at the apartment complex. She begs him to marry her—but they're coming to take away his truck, he has no money. Right? She gets him drunk and together they have a great passionate love affair. Am I getting it right, Papa?"

"It happened," Arthur said.

His daughter looked at Cakes and shook her head.

"It happened. Just like I say it happened," Arthur said.

"Okay, Papa. If you say so."

"Where were you? Where were you that you can say with such authority it never happened? Am I a genius, to make it all up in my head, every last detail?"

She was still looking at Cakes. "He has time on his hands, and his imagination. He's such an exaggerator. He starts to believe these things. How long have you known him?"

"Go home," Arthur said. "Just leave us alone."

"I'm sorry, Papa. But you have to admit I know you like a book, now don't you?"

"Get away from me. You don't know anything. It happened. It happened just as I say it happened and you will not rob me of my own history."

"Max, I'm only teasing you."

Arthur raised his arm high above his head and brought his fist down hard on the table. *"Just* as I say it happened."

"All right," she said.

He did it again. "JUST as I say it happened."

She stood. She was about to break into tears. "I said all right."

Cakes took her wrist. It was bony and surprisingly supple. "Sit down."

She did so. They sat quietly for a few moments while she again opened her purse and searched through it. Again she simply closed it and sat gazing at her father.

"So where's the rest of them?" Arthur said.

She said nothing.

"How did you get here?"

"I told you. I have a new car. I drove."

"Must be expensive."

"I can manage." She seemed just now to be noticing the condition of Edward's face.

"He got in a fight—with a cabbie."

"Oh."

"We're a tough bunch—right, Cakes?"

"Right," Cakes said.

" 'Cakes'?" said the daughter.

"That's his name. He's sleeping with a young girl."

"Please, Papa."

"Ask him."

"I will not ask him." She moved, seemed about to get up, but she had only drawn in a breath. "Look. I'm not here to talk about sleeping with girls. I'm not going to put up with that kind of talk."

"She's religious," said Arthur.

"You might remember that you raised me that way."

"Excuse me," Edward Cakes said, rising.

They both reached for him, and they spoke almost in unison. "Don't go," Arthur said.

"Please stay," said his daughter.

Cakes sat down.

They were all silent for a time, as if to adjust themselves to the new situation: Edward Cakes remaining for whatever they would say to one another. Cakes had the odd suspicion that if he were to get up again, they would let him go. He held still. Arthur's daughter lighted another cigarette, and Arthur stared at his own folded arms on the table.

"Well," Linda said at last, "so—how are things."

"Beautiful," Arthur said.

"You're all right."

"Beautiful."

"That's good."

"You?"

"Beautiful."

"Wonderful," Arthur said.

There was another silence.

"Do they have any kind of Thanksgiving here?" Linda asked.

"You want me to stay here for Thanksgiving, I'll stay here for Thanksgiving."

"I didn't say that. I was expressing interest in this place. I thought you might know." She turned to Cakes. "Did I say anything?"

Cakes said, "She just asked a question, Max."

"In Alaska," Arthur muttered, "they just leave them on a floating block of ice. They just move on and leave them. It's expected."

"What are you talking about," Linda said.

"It's all right. You're getting to be an old woman. You'll know. Your children leave you, they stop obeying the commandments—"

"Daddy, I tried to get you to move in with us. You wouldn't do it. Do you remember that you wouldn't do it?"

"I wouldn't do it. That's *just* the way it happened." Again Arthur brought his fist down on the table.

"Will you stop it?" Linda said.

Arthur looked at Cakes. "Will you tell her to leave me alone, please. I don't need this. Tell her."

Linda put her face into her hands.

"Arthur," Cakes said.

"She comes in here," said Arthur, "and tells you I'm lying about something I remember as clear as you remember that cabin in the mountains in the snow. I remember it like my own name, everything. The sounds of the voices and the smells and everything. And she tells you it's a lie. A fantasy." He gestured toward his daughter. "Go ahead. Tell him. You come all this way to do that to me. Tell him how everything is a lie."

"I'm sorry," she said, the hands pressing into the eyes. "I'm sorry. I came to see you—"

"You came to see me once in six months. For you," Arthur said, raising his arm again. "For *you*. You. For your little conscience."

"Stop it, Daddy. Stop it."

"You want to know about Maxine Sandusky? That woman was in the bombing of London. She was there. You think I'd make a thing like that up?"

"*Okay,* Daddy."

"Don't come to see me anymore. Do me a favor and don't bother yourself. You got a family of your own. Stay with them—give them what they want. I absolve you, understand? I release you."

She stood. "You wonder why I don't come here—"

"Get out," Arthur was saying, "get out, get out."

She whirled, almost knocked her chair over, then did knock two others down as she made her way to the door and out.

Arthur turned to Cakes and bowed his head slightly. "Thank you for staying until my daughter arrived."

16

▲

It snowed seven inches. All night long it swept against the window in a whisper. The kitten mewed in the chair, and the girl only wanted to snuggle, to be kept warm, lying with her back to his stomach. Then she grew uncomfortable and moved away from him, shifting her weight with the impatience of someone unable to sleep.

He said, "Can't sleep?"

And she moaned. "Quiet."

He was wide awake. She jerked, tossed, moaned, snored. Her neck and the side of her face were moist with sweat. He lay watching her in the faint light, hearing the music upstairs, the kitten mewling and complaining. The music was not loud, but it was part of everything that, along with his swollen mouth and aching bones, kept him sleepless.

"Will you stop sighing?" she said.

He had not been aware of any sighing. He turned to the wall and closed his eyes, heard her breathing become regular again.

In the morning she tried to get the kitten to drink from the saucer again, and Cakes started breakfast. He had watched the sun rise, he was exhausted, yet this felt good, putting bacon in a pan, hearing the girl's voice in the room, softly insistent: "Come on, kitty, kitty, kitty. Drink up, drink up."

Paula and Denise were banging around in the hallway, complaining about the snow. Paula came to the door to tell how the storm had damaged the trees, and they all looked out his window at the street, which had not yet been plowed. The trees had not quite shed their leaves, and the weight of the snow on the branches had broken some of them; one old pin oak looked as though it had been struck by lightning: it had split down the left side where a big branch had sheered off and left a yellow, splintery gash.

"Ain't that something?" Paula said. She had her uniform on, and her hair was arranged in a pile on top of her head. She walked around the room, talking about early snowfall, and one storm she had seen as a little girl, a storm just like this one, only in Texas, in a part of Texas you never thought you'd ever see snow. "Yes, sir," she said, "busted up every dang tree for a hundred miles, and knocked out all the power lines, too."

Denise stood in the doorway. "Come on, Paula. We'll be late."

"I'll tell you, I hate the day shift."

Cakes realized that Paula was curious, wanted to know about him and the girl. When she and Denise were gone, he said, "I suppose you know they're very interested in us."

The girl was sitting on the bed with some clothes in her lap, the canvas bag of her things at her feet. "I got to get to a Laundromat."

"We'll go together."

She bent down and picked the kitten up. "Why would they be interested in us?"

He went on with making breakfast.

"Why would they be interested in us?"

"Ask them," he said.

"I guess I should."

The eggs were ready, the bacon. She lay on the bed, stroking the kitten, murmuring to it, twirling one finger in the tufts of fur around the ears. "I can't decide if he's going to be gray or black."

"Breakfast," he said.

She got up, shuffled to the table, sat down, not looking at him. They ate without speaking. Very early in the morning he had gone downstairs and got the newspaper, and now he sat reading it, looking up from time to time to see her pushing the eggs around the plate. She seemed rather listless and uninterested in the food, yet she ate it all, then got up and went back to the bed.

"You ever felt—trapped?" she asked.

"Of course," he said.

"Tell me."

He thought a moment, wiping his mouth with a napkin. "When my son was just a baby, I remember once—I was opening the front door of this house we lived in, to take the garbage out to the curb. It was winter, I remember; there was snow on the ground, like now. And—and just for a second there, as I opened the door, I had this strange sense of being able to breathe—this feeling of release, I guess you'd call it. And then when I thought about going back inside—you know, I stood out on the sidewalk and breathed. It was almost dark out, and I stood there and saw the lights in the windows, and for just a second I didn't want to go back in there. It lasted just a second. But it shot right through me —this feeling of being—well, trapped."

"Did that happen a lot?"

He shook his head. "But every time I opened that door, from then on, I thought about it. It passed through my mind."

"Where do you think you would've gone if you'd run away?"

"Oh, I never would've run away."

She looked at him. "I bet."

"No," he said.

She sighed. "I wish I knew what to do."

He began to clear away the dishes.

"I don't want to be a mother at all."

He had just been thinking about her with a baby. Now she arranged the kitten in the crook of her arm.

"I'm afraid kitty's sick."

"He won't eat, will he."

She shrugged this off. "Poor old kitty."

"It needs its mother."

"Maybe."

Presently she said, "Boy, we're having a high old time."

"Would you like to watch television?" he said.

She didn't answer.

"Where did you go yesterday?" he said.

"Seeing the sights." She smiled at him.

"All alone?"

"Sure."

"You shouldn't go around the city all alone."

She looked away, and he felt the sore places in his mouth like taunts, mockeries.

"You can stay as long as you like," he said.

"That's sweet of you."

"I'll help you in any way I can."

"That's sweet." She was not looking at him.

"Anything you need, you just let me know."

"Look, not now," she said. "Okay? I don't feel like it. Maybe tonight."

He washed the dishes while she took a bath. His face and neck burned with embarrassment. When he was finished with the dishes, he turned the television on, but there was nothing very good to watch, and so he switched it off, sat in his chair and waited for her to come out of the bathroom. She emerged fully dressed and started pulling her jacket on.

"You're going out in this?" he said.

"It's not snowing now."

"You don't have any boots—that jacket's so light—"

"I'm warm enough."

"Where will you go?"

She shrugged. "The college."

"What's at the college?"

"Do me a favor," she said crisply. "Don't worry about me." She picked up the canvas bag of her things and put it in his closet.

"Would you like me to come with you?"

"I'm meeting a guy," she said. "Okay? A friend of Terry-and-the-Pirates Dillard, believe it or not. He's married and all, but he's—he's a sort of friend. His name is Mort and he's a med student and he's going to help me out. Okay?"

"Sure," Cakes said.

"Anything else?" she said.

"He'll get you a job?"

She hesitated slightly, seemed for an instant to peer at him as if across a great distance. "Right," she said. "A job. Right."

"But—but you're going to have a—" The look in her face stopped him.

"I told you I don't want to be a mother at all."

"What about your family?" he said.

"What *about* them?"

"They could help you."

"Get an abortion?"

"No."

"You mean have the baby?"

He was silent.

"Is that what you mean?"

He got up from the chair and moved to the sink to pour himself some water. "I don't understand. I don't understand this world."

"That sounds funny coming from somebody your age."

"Age has nothing to do with it."

"You'd think it would."

He drank the water, not looking at her. There was just the sound of his swallowing; he had never been able to gulp things, and so when he drank he would swallow, breathe, then swallow again.

"Look," she said, "I don't like it—I don't know what I'm going to do about it. But it's my business, okay? It's my problem."

He poured the rest of the water in the sink, turned to face her. She opened the door to go out. "Be careful," he said, "they haven't plowed the streets yet."

"You'll never see anybody careful as me from now on," she said. Then she had closed the door and was gone. He went to his chair, let himself down in it, looking for her in the snowy scene below, and quite suddenly the quiet seemed wrong. He remembered the kitten. "Here, kitty, kitty, kitty," he called, getting out of the chair, looking gingerly through the folds of blanket on the bed, and then, on hands and knees, crawling from bed to bureau to chair, calling. At last he found the poor creature in the bathroom, curled up in a shivering ball in the corner opposite the toilet bowl. "Oh," he said, lifting it gently in his cupped palms. "Poor thing, kitty, kitty, kitty." He walked with it back to the bed and laid it down on his pillow. It shivered and breathed and its eyes stared at him. The mouth opened and closed. He stroked the gray, emaciated back gently until the eyes closed. The kitten breathed in little shuddering gasps as though each breath were the last one.

"Kitty," he murmured, kneeling down next to the bed, his hands, with infinite care, coming to rest on either side of the smoky little body.

17
▲

He spent much of the day worrying about the kitten, which wouldn't eat, or play, or drink, or do much of anything except sleep and tremble. Finally he could only hope that the sleep was restorative, and so he tried to put it out of his mind. He cleaned the apartment, made the bed and fixed himself a light lunch, and then he took a bath, lay back in the water, thinking about the girl, wondering where she might be at that moment, with whom, saying what, doing what. He must try not to sound like her father, he told himself. Then he sat up and spoke aloud. "Welcome back." He liked the rich sound of his voice, echoing slightly in the room; the bathroom was the best place for listening to one's self. "I'm glad you're back," he said. He was a baritone. He said, "I am a baritone." When he got out of the tub, he looked at himself in the mirror and winked, smiled and turned his head a little to the side, studying himself. "Yes," he said, "Edward Cakes, lover."

He watched television for a while, dozed, and woke up during the afternoon movie—two women pulling a mule along a dusty, red-clouded road in twilight. He sat up straight, remembering the kitten again; it was where he had left it on the bed, still asleep, its body still shaking with each breath. He lay down next to it, lay dreaming about the girl, her long, lithe body in the night, and, for the first time in many years, he found himself masturbating. When it was over, he was ashamed, and he took another bath, sitting quietly in the water with his hands resting on the edges of the tub.

Toward evening he got the kitten to stir a little, to take a little water and then some milk. The tiny pink tongue fascinated him as it touched and disturbed the trembling surface of milk in the saucer. "That's it," he said, "nourishment. Good kitty."

By the first hours of dark he had a new worry: the girl had not returned. He put the kitten in the chair, wrapped in an old shirt, and went out and down to the street entrance, stood on the small porch and looked up and down the street. It was very cold, and windy, and the snow blew like a long cloud over the tops of the buildings beyond the square. The city had been totally unprepared for the storm, and so the street was still not plowed. At the end of the block, in front of the old boarded-up drug store, a single wooden sign rattled in the wind.

He went back up to the apartment and closed the door. The kitten was where he had left it, still breathing in that odd, spasmodic way. He lay down on the bed, closed his eyes and tried not to think. Again, above him, the music began, and he heard the soft shuffling sound, the dancing. He lay there a long time listening to it.

Near midnight, he got the kitten to take a little more milk. It crawled under the chair, and when he brought it out and put it, in the old shirt, on his pillow, it only waited for him to doze before it hopped down to crawl under the chair again. So he let it remain there. He lay down and folded his hands behind his head and waited, and began to be frightened that something had happened to the girl: the wind shook and blustered at the window, and he could not imagine that she could be safe, warm: she was out there in the cold, and the dark. Twice more he went down to the porch to look for her shape in the cloudy desolation of the street, and at last, when he could no longer keep his eyes open, he simply fell off to a sort of wakeful stupor in the chair.

He awoke when the music stopped.

The window was a pale gray rectangle, it was morning, and he knew suddenly that it was not the music from the apartment above him that had just ceased, it was Paula's stereo. The other music, apparently, had stopped hours ago. He sat up and knew this, hearing Paula and Denise in the hallway, one of them saying something to the other through a yawn. He went to his door and opened it, and Denise, seeing him, said, "Oh." Her eyes were red, and she had put her makeup on too thickly, so that it caked at the hairline. Paula, wearing a scarf over curlers, put both hands up as if to hide this fact.

"Cakes," she said, "what're you doing up at this hour."

"Have you seen my friend?" he said.

She let her hands drop. "Who—that girl?"

"Yes."

She looked at Denise, then back at Cakes. "Not lately."

"She didn't come home last night."

"Yeah, well what makes you think I might've seen her."

"Nothing," Cakes said, "I just heard you out here. I thought I'd—see."

Paula's expression was not quite a smile. "Poor old Cakes," she said. "I wouldn't worry about her too much. I think she can take care of herself, don't you, Denise?"

"I sure do," Denise said.

"Yes, sir," said Paula, "I believe she can take care of herself just fine."

They started away, and then Denise came back, put her hand on his wrist, patted the bone gently, gazing into his eyes. "You're a nice man, Mr. Cakes. Don't mind Paula's rough talk. She was raised on the prairie and never learned any manners."

He nodded dumbly, watched her go on down the stairs, closed his door and turned to see the kitten lying on the floor between the chair and the wall by the bed; it lay on its stomach, the head down on the paws in an odd, straight-ahead way as if something were weighing it down. He knew immediately that it was dead. He let his back come against the door and stared at the half-open animal eyes, which reflected light now opaquely, like marbles; above him the music began, faint and scratchy and sad. He went to the table and sat down slowly, not looking at the kitten now. He must decide what to do about it—he would have to wrap it in something; it would have to be buried. He saw himself digging in the snow behind the house, working through the seven inches, trying to find ground—and how deep in the ground did one bury a kitten that could be held in one's cupped palms? Did one dig a hole six feet deep? In any case, it was too much for an aging man to do, so he would think of something else. And then, as he sat there trying to decide about it, the stillness in the room grew frightening. He looked at the kitten, and something damp blew through him, sent an impulse along his nerves to get up and bolt out of the room.

Once more the music upstairs had ceased.

He went out into the hall, into the shadows there, and down the stairs to the street again, where he stood in his stocking feet, in the wind and the blowing dust of snow, looking first one way and then the other for the girl. There was no sun; the sky was a pale screen of gray, like one covering cloud, yet the brightness hurt his eyes. People were in the street, children throwing snowballs, a man digging snow off the sidewalk; in the park a single policeman sat atop a tall chestnut horse that had paused to urinate in the snow.

He went back inside, back up the stairs, and then on up to the third floor, the attic room. It was quiet, for some reason he had felt he should use stealth, and now that he had come to stand here at this door he wondered if he shouldn't cough or clear his throat before he knocked. He could not hear the music now, and he was listening for it, or, really, for any sound. Perhaps this person, whoever she was, slept during the days. Just as he coughed into his fist, took in a breath and used the fist to knock on the door, he felt the absurdity of his position—it was all one thought, one action, and then he was standing horrified that he had actually knocked on the door, and was now going to have to go through with whatever this would be: could he just say, "Excuse me, I've got a dead kitten in my room and I can't look at the eyes"? The whole thing was ludicrous. He was waiting here with his hands folded at his belt, and there wasn't a single word in his mind to say beyond the stupid admission that he was unable to bring himself to go near a dead kitten. He waited one second longer and then snuck away from the door and had started down the stairs when the door opened. From where he was, he could see only the blade of light that the opening made.

"Never mind," he said. But then he was curious, wanting to see this person who played Paul Whiteman records and danced alone at night. "Excuse me," he said. "Wait."

The door closed.

He knocked. "Excuse me." Perhaps a minute went by. Again he knocked. "Miss? Excuse me."

The door opened, and he saw an old woman in a bright, multicolored bathrobe. "It's been a long time since anyone called me *miss.*"

He said, "Hello."

She gave a slight bow of her head. Her hair was jet black, arranged in tight curls, like a bathing cap, around her face, which was deep-eyed, almost gaunt, the bones visible just under the skin. "You live downstairs."

"Yes."

"Does my music keep you awake?"

He stammered. "I—the music—"

"I'll turn it down."

He said, "It's nothing. Never mind," offering his hand. "I'm Edward Cakes."

She took the ends of his fingers, then let go; it was just a touch, dry and cool. He saw that one finger of her left hand was bent and blue. "Yes?" she said, and again gave the little bow of her head, never taking her eyes from him. "I'm hard of hearing, so you'll have to speak up. Is my music too loud?"

"I have a problem—a dead cat—"

She looked at him.

"Never mind," he said, "I like the music. It's a bit loud sometimes—I live in the apartment just below you." He spoke loud, yet he did not want to shout at her; he didn't know what the right balance would be, and so he fumbled the words, couldn't quite get them spoken clearly. "Just wanted to welcome—a girl— a girl and me—" He was backing toward the stairs. "Just wanted to say welcome, you know and all—all that."

"I can't understand you." She had come out on the landing,

clutching the collar of the robe, her deep eyes fixed on his as though she were trying to look through him. "What did you say about a cat?"

"Nothing," he said, "never mind—thank you. Nice to meet you. Welcome."

Well, what kind of man was he, anyway? Back in the room he got a plastic garbage bag from under the sink—the only one left in the box. He sat at the table for a long time with the bag folded over one knee, trying to get his courage up for what he had to do. Finally, using a folded section of newspaper like a scoop, he got the stiffening little body into the bag, tied the top tight, hurrying now, finishing it off with a shudder. It was done. He carried the bag downstairs and put it into one of the trash cans in the alley alongside the house. Above him the building loomed in its brown, snow-daubed height, casting down its winter shadow. He breathed the cold air, glad of the sting of it in his lungs.

18

▲

The girl returned that evening as a cold sun was breaking through the clouds low in the west. He saw her come walking up the snowy street and almost opened the window to shout her name. The room, he realized with horror, was a clutter of his solitude—books strewn on the bed and dishes on the table, dirty clothes draped over a chair. How could he have let it get this way? Frantically he went about putting it in order, and it was mostly done before she knocked on the door. He combed through his hair with his fingers, tucked his shirt in, stood straight and opened the door.

"It's me," she said.

There was something very wrong. She stepped into the light, going past him, and there was something the matter. When she turned, he saw a bruise, like a smear, on her cheek.

"For the love of God," he said.

She sat on the bed, kicked her shoes off and lay down.

"What happened?" He closed the door. "Who did this to you?"

"Leave me alone."

Standing over her, he felt outnumbered somehow, by his own shadow there on the bed; absurdly, he thought of the cabbie who had hit him. "You've got a bad bruise." His own voice sounded strange.

"I'm cold," she said, wrapping her arms over her chest.

"What happened—tell me what happened."

"Nothing. Somebody didn't like me, okay?"

"Who? Who did this."

"I didn't bother to ask." She closed her eyes. "I don't want to talk about it. I stepped in where I shouldn't have. Just please— I'm sorry—you've been nice. But leave me alone about it."

He sat on the edge of the bed; she had turned to the wall and lay breathing, shivering. He took the blanket from the chair and put it over her. "It was that young man, wasn't it—that Terry fellow."

"Terry. Yeah."

"I'll kill him." Having said this, he felt ridiculous. He patted her shoulder and stood, hands on his hips, in the center of the room.

"It wasn't Terry," she muttered.

He sat down at the table, and for a while there was nothing but the sound of her quiet sniffling and sighing. "I don't know what to do," he said. "Mary, I haven't the faintest idea."

She said nothing.

"Tell me what to do."

"Where's the cat," she said, sitting up, moving the blanket.

"The cat's gone."

She looked at him. "Gone where?"

He told her.

There was no expression at all on her face. "I guess I shouldn't be surprised."

"I'm sorry," he said.

"It was just a stray cat."

He went over to her, got into the bed, and she turned from him, curling up in the blanket as if hiding. They lay very still, the light passed through all the gray stages of dusk, and at last he knew that she was asleep. He stared into the dark; he was past seventy and this was happening to him. He heard someone come in downstairs and labor up the steps; it was Paula or Denise. There was the jangle of keys out in the hallway, and then he heard Paula's voice. Others arrived—four or five people clattering up the stairs. More followed; it became a full-blown party, Paula's stereo beating in the walls.

The girl stirred and sat up suddenly. "I think I'm going to be sick."

"Here," he said, trying to get out of the bed to help her.

"Goddamnit," she said, "Oh." Then she was moving beyond him in the dark; she had made her way into the bathroom, and the light was on there, the door ajar. She stood sighing and breathing over the toilet. He turned the room light on, ran water in the sink, trying to seem busy, and when she came out, he offered her a glass of milk. He would make something to soothe her stomach.

"I haven't had anything to eat," she said. "I can't get anything to come up."

"Do you feel up to eating?"

"I can't stay here." She was rubbing her upper arms as if her skin crawled.

"We'll go out," Cakes said. "Can you eat?"

"Yes, I can eat. I haven't had anything to eat."

"We'll go to the café. I'll buy you something."

She had moved to the bed, and now she turned and came back, not looking at him. "I'm scared."

"Here," he said, and reached for her. But she shied away.

"No."

"Do you want me to call someone—"

"Everything's all fucked up," she said.

"I wish you would let me help you."

"Fucking Dillard," she said savagely.

"He hit you."

"No, he ran off. He ran off and left me—here. And I don't care anymore. The son of a bitch."

"Where were you all night? Were you with Dillard?"

"Come on," she said, "take me to eat. Fuck it."

"We don't have to do anything if you don't want to."

"I'm going to *scream* if we don't get out of here."

He took her arm and led her out of the room. The door to Paula and Denise's apartment was partly open, and there were the shifting motions of people dancing. The girl gave no sign that she had seen or heard anything, but descended the stairs ahead of Cakes, who had paused, momentarily entertaining the notion that he might ask the nurses for help, have them look at the bruise on the girl's face: there was the possibility of concussion, or of some delayed reaction—internal bleeding, cracks in the bones. Were there other bruises? How badly had she been beaten? He knew, really, nothing more than he had known in the first moments of her return. Yet somehow he understood as he watched her descend that she would not stop, would not allow herself to be questioned, examined or treated, and so he hurried to catch up with her; and when they were out in the street, she said, "I want to go somewhere."

"I'll take you somewhere."

She let him lead her, leaning on his arm, still shivering. There were patches of packed-down snow that had hardened and built up a glassy coating of ice, and where the sidewalk had been cleared, the melting snow at its edges had formed a sheen. It was very unsteady going, and more than once they nearly fell. Cakes thought of broken bones, and of the fierceness of a winter that could already be so cold.

The People's Café was nearly empty. Two elderly women sat in one booth near the back wall, and the waitress was talking to them, standing with arms folded, all her weight on one foot. Cakes and the girl sat in the booth nearest the door, and the waitress walked over to set menus before them. She was tall and gray-looking and rather humorless, but very efficient, and she knew that Cakes liked black coffee before a meal. She never wrote orders down, no matter how complex or how many people were ordering, and she never forgot anything or mixed things up. Cakes told the girl about all this, trying simply to make conversation. The girl seemed beset, her eyes wide and frightened and quick; she let Cakes order the food—two hot roast beef sandwiches with mashed potatoes and gravy—and when it was brought to them, she seemed uninterested in it.

"Is your stomach still upset?" he asked.

She shook her head, looking around the room.

"Why don't you eat?" he said gently.

"How come you're so nice to me?" she said.

He could only shrug; the question was embarrassing.

"I know why."

"Why," he said.

She was silent.

Looking at her, he felt suddenly as though his questions had badgered her, and he was sorry. "You don't have to tell me anything."

"Kind sir." This was said with an edge of irony. It baffled him.

"Try to eat something. It'll make you feel better."

"My cheekbone hurts." She touched the bruise gingerly.

"Why can't you tell me, in simple language, what happened —who did this to you. Were you just—was it a—a mugger or something? I still have no idea what happened to you, and I want to help you."

"It was a mugger or something," she said.

"All right," said Cakes.

"Look—you don't know him."

"It was somebody you know."

"It wasn't anybody. It was a guy. Okay? It was somebody I never saw before."

Presently she said, "I went to see Mort. You remember I told you about Mort. Well, I stayed with him and his wife, and we had a nice time and then I started back—in the—after the day. We spent the day at the college, and had lunch. And then I started back and this—guy jumped out of the bushes and socked me one, and I woke up and came here. I guess he wanted to rob me—only I didn't have anything to rob."

"It's not safe to walk around alone," he said. He didn't want to talk about it anymore, wouldn't pursue it, though he was by now fairly certain that she was lying. Or she was bending the truth to make it seem other than it was; he began to wonder how much of all that she had told him was true. He ate the rest of his meal in a sort of placid quiet, nodding at her as she muttered that she was tired, headachy, unhappy with the food. When the meal was done, he paid for it, and the two of them walked back over the treacherous, iced streets to the house. Paula was on the front stoop waving goodbye to someone who was climbing into a taxi; the taxi pulled away, and she stood with her hands on her hips, looking at Cakes and the girl.

"By God, you're invited to a party," she said, too loud. Then she leaned toward them slightly, narrowing her eyes at them as they came up the stairs. "What happened to your face, honey."

"Nothing."

"Here, let me look at you."

"I'm all right."

Paula held her there in the light of the doorway, turning her small chin to the side and gazing at the bruised cheek. "That's a nasty one. Who the hell hit you?"

"It was no one—I'm all right."

"You ran into a door." Paula nodded, smiling. "Right?"

"It's just a bruise. I'm all right."

"Did you do this, Cakes?" Paula's face was stern, the eyes fixed on him, though they were glazed over with what she had drunk.

"She came back like this," Cakes said.

Paula looked at her. "Boyfriend?"

"I'm going inside," the girl said, and shouldered her way past Paula. Cakes followed her up the stairs, where she stood facing the wall, waiting for him to get the key in the door. The party across the hall was still going on, and the door there was wide open. Cakes hurried, his fingers fumbling with the keys, and by the time he was able to slip the latch, four drunken people were trying to get him and the girl to join them. Then Paula was there, too, and Denise—and finally the commotion began to be about the girl's bruised face. One of the men was a doctor, and insisted with a lubricious sneer that he must examine the patient. He was thin, and dark, with a long, acne-scarred face and an overbite of very white teeth that seemed false until one realized, with a shock, that they were real, and that this person was in fact rather absurdly ugly as if somehow he were uglier than necessary to make the point. His behavior was no less ugly. He took the girl by the shoulders and buried his snoutlike face in her breasts, slobbering about listening to her heartbeat. The others, his companions, were too drunk to do anything about him, though Paula tried to pull on his shoulder. The girl simply stood there, arms at her sides, while everyone tottered and shouted and laughed around her, and the man kept his face against her chest. Cakes was pressed against the frame of his door, and he saw it all, but there was nothing he could do about it; he couldn't even hear his own voice shouting at them to leave her alone. The drunken man slid down the girl's body like someone collapsing face first against a wall. And then it was over: the others had lifted him, carried him back into Paula's apartment, the door was closed, and Paula stood there, facing Edward Cakes and the girl. "I guess you don't feel like a party now, either one of you," she said. She was obviously trying to speak clearly, to ungarble her tongue. She wavered slightly, stifled a belch. "Sorry—all in fun."

The girl gathered herself, not looking at anything, standing there in the shadows of the hallway as if unable to decide what she should do next. She did not speak. Cakes opened the door for her and she went in and lay down on the bed; he remained in the hallway with Paula, who seemed uneasy now, even a little frightened, the noise beginning to increase on the other side of her door.

"Things get out of hand sometimes," she said.

"I'd appreciate it if you'd keep the noise down," said Cakes.

"I'll kick their asses out the door."

"Just please, let us have some quiet."

"Look," she said. "It's not my fault."

"Just please see to it." Cakes turned from her, went into the apartment and closed the door.

The girl lay on the bed, one arm up behind her head. She only glanced at him as he crossed the room to stand at her side.

"There wasn't anything I could do," he said.

"Forget it."

"It all happened so fast."

"I said forget it—it's nothing."

He sat down on the bed. Again it struck him with a kind of shock that she was pregnant. "I'll take care of you."

She looked at him. "Will you." There was nothing at all in her face.

"Yes," he said into that look.

"Well."

"You'll see," he said.

"And what'll I do for you?" She smiled out of one side of her mouth. Then she looked away. "I don't need you to take care of me. I don't want you to take care of me."

He was silent.

"Look at you," she said, turning that smile on him again. "It's amazing. You're—you're—ancient. And believe me, the total weight of what you don't know—"

He was still silent, looking down at his hands, the good bones there, the ropelike veins in the skin.

"I'm sorry," she said.

"If you tell me, Mary, I'll know, won't I?"

She stared at him a moment, drew in a breath, then seemed to catch herself. "Ah, forget it. It's not worth it. I just want to go to sleep."

"Tell me," he said.

She had turned in the bed so that her back was to him. "It's nobody's business—it's my business. Please."

A moment later he said, "Do you want me to sleep in the chair?"

"You can sleep where you want to."

He undressed and got in next to her but kept his body from touching hers.

"Thank you for letting me stay here," she said.

"I wanted you to stay."

"I know you did—thank you."

"I'd like you to stay as long as you want to."

"Do you want to screw now?" she said.

He sighed. "No."

"Good. Maybe in the morning."

He said nothing.

"Good night," she said.

After a time he got up, put his robe on and went to the door. The party was over at last, and people were leaving. There was a lot of confusion, Paula shouting for everyone to be quiet, someone else howling with laughter. Cakes opened the door to tell them all to get out and came face to face with the woman from upstairs. She was wrapped in a thick black imitation fur coat with enormous padded shoulders, and she had apparently stumbled to his doorway to avoid the staggering mob as it went roiling down the stairs.

"Aren't they having a good time," she said.

He did not answer her.

"My, my, I'll bet the noise kept you up."

They stood there as the noise receded, and Cakes began to think about stepping back inside; but the woman did not move, seemed to be waiting for him to speak.

"You said something about a cat," she said.

"Oh—" He straightened; he could think of nothing whatever to say. "Yes."

"I love cats."

Paula came back up the stairs alone. "Denise got sick."

"You look like you will be, too," said the woman.

"I never get sick from drinking."

"You know how to control it."

"No, I just never get sick," Paula said.

"I wonder if that means you're lucky."

"It means I don't get sick."

"Well, it's certainly lucky not to get sick."

Paula went into her apartment and slammed the door.

"She's drunk, isn't she."

"Yes," Cakes said.

"Notice how everything's so emphatic when people get drunk. Have you ever noticed that?"

"I guess I have."

"I don't drink."

He said nothing.

"Well," she said, smiling, "good night."

He watched her go up the stairs, and in his mind he was already hearing the frayed old records spinning out their antique tunes. He went back inside the apartment, moved carefully in the dark to the side of the bed, dropped the robe and got in. The girl was asleep; he lay listening to the small sounds she made, waiting for the music to begin. But there was no music, and at last he was asleep.

He woke to the sound of the girl getting back into the bed. It was still dark. "Is everything all right?" he asked.

"I just went to the bathroom."

He could feel her shivering next to him, and he realized that, in the first seconds of waking to know she was there, he had thought she was Ellen—he had been gone, years away, a younger man in a room at night, and someone who lived and slept with him was getting into the bed. "Do you want me to hold you?" he said through the trembling of his voice.

"I'm fine," she told him.

In the morning she bathed, dressed—jeans and sweatshirt and tennis shoes—and sat at the table brushing her hair. He fixed toast and coffee, but she wanted nothing.

"It's sunny out today," he said.

"Right."

When she was through with her hair, she tossed the canvas bag of her things into the closet and turned to face him. The bruise on her cheek was darker, and in its angry discoloration it seemed to have drained all the softness out of her features. "I've got to go take care of a few things."

"Where are you going?"

"Out."

"You're going to see that Dillard fellow, aren't you."

"Not quite."

"Well, then—*where?*" He was a little tired of all the mystery, and his voice gave him away.

"Look," she said, "what are you, my father? I said I had to take care of a few things, and for the rest of it you can just mind your own business."

He got up and carried his cup and saucer over to the sink and ran water over them.

She had moved to the door. "You told me it was okay if I stayed here. I don't remember agreeing to anything else."

He nodded, not looking at her.

"Just don't worry about me," she said. "I can take care of myself."

"Should I expect you back tonight?" he asked.

"I've already learned not to expect anything. Maybe when I get older I'll unlearn it."

There was nothing else to say to her.

She walked over to him and kissed him—a light, daughterly kiss—then turned and went out, closing the door quietly behind her. At the window, he stood with his hands shoved down into his pockets and followed her progress down the melting street.

19
▲

She returned that afternoon, with a half gallon of cheap wine. She had been drinking from it, and wanted him to join her. The sun had come out; there was reason to celebrate. "Come look," she said, standing at the window. "It's a gorgeous sunny snowy day."

He humored her. He even had some of the wine.

"Love wine," she said, spilling it as she poured it. She got into the bed and put her legs under the blanket, propped herself against the headboard, holding the bottle with both hands in her lap. He pulled the chair around to the side of the bed, and let her fill his glass again.

"I'm a little tipsy," she said.

He was silent.

"I get romantic when I'm tipsy."

The wine was too sweet, but drinking it relieved him of the necessity of saying anything.

"Don't you want me to get real tipsy?"

"You seem so unhappy, Mary—"

She interrupted him. "Agh. Don't call me that. Mary. What a name."

"It's a lovely name."

She made a face. "A lovely name—right."

"Well," he said.

"You're such a sweetie."

He sipped the wine.

"You got a sense of chivalry, don't you."

"I'm sorry if I seem silly to you."

"Oh, Jesus." She drank, swallowed. "Why don't you get pissed or something?"

He shook his head, looked at the glass of wine in his hand; it was a Chablis but its color was stale gold.

"Love the big city, I'll tell you. You meet all kinds. Some people are nice to you and some people are mean. Same thing in the end. Everybody gets what he wants."

"Since you won't tell me anything," he said, "I can't understand what you mean."

"But you know."

"I'm afraid I don't."

"It's all a lie," she said.

"What's a lie."

She stared at him.

"Your despair is adolescent," he said.

"What despair?"

"Calling everything a lie."

"No," she said. "Not that. I mean everything I told you. It's all a lie."

He waited.

"Almost all of it, anyway." She took a long pull from the bottle, then wiped her mouth with the back of her hand. "What if I told you my name's not Mary?"

"I don't know," he said.

She laughed. "It is. You don't have to worry about names."

"Mary—" he began.

"Listen," she broke in, "want to tell you something. I'm no dummy. I know how it all works. And you know what? The secret to everything is organization. Everything's organized. From the time you get born on. It's organized—who your parents are, your brothers and sisters, what sicknesses everybody will have. School, church, all of it. Everybody's organized, and one thing you can't do—can't get away with—is being outside the, you know, the organization. No. No free agents allowed. I learned that. I know that. I got that straight now. And you know what my professor father would say I should do now? I should act on it. He's real big on acting on what you know. Oh, he used to drum that into me, Edward. Because I was too loud, I messed things— made my mother nervous. So he'd *teach* me. And then I'd learned it. I was supposed to act on it. Simple as pie. The simple secret to everything." She was beginning to cry; but then she took more of the wine; seemed to draw it all down inside herself. "Boy, I gave them hell before it was over."

"Who," Cakes said. It was almost reflexive.

She seemed momentarily confused. "Them. My parents."

"How long has it been since you left them?" he asked.

"I'm twenty-four."

"Well?"

"I got out as soon as I was of age."

"Eighteen?"

"Right. Eighteen."

"That's six years, Mary."

"So?"

"And you haven't seen them since?"

She smiled. "You're so cute."

"Well, have you?"

She shrugged. "I don't want to talk about it."

A moment later, she said, "Tell me, do you think a person is made into what she is by her parents?"

"I don't quite understand—"

"Do you think—" She was exasperated now, and she rolled her eyes at the ceiling. "Do you think a person has any choice about who she is."

"Of course," he said.

"What about skin color, hair. What about the color of the eyes?"

"Well." He hesitated. "Those things—"

"What if all the rest of it is the same way. Like pigmentation. What if personality and all that—what if it's like pigmentation, that you can't help."

"Yes?" he said.

"Well, what do you think?"

"The question makes an absurdity," he said.

"How?"

"It's like saying—like saying what if water were stone. It—it makes no sense. What *if* water were stone."

"The ocean would be hard as a rock." She laughed. It was almost a hysterical laugh. "God. The ocean would be hard as a rock."

Presently she said, "You're not drinking."

"No."

"Want to get romantic?"

He made no answer.

"Want to fuck?"

At this he rose from the chair, walked to the sink and poured out what was left of his wine. "Please try to take a nap or something."

"I upset you," she said.

He had turned, was leaning against the sink, looking at her. "I'm sorry, Edward."

"Look, why do you say these things. Is it because you want to sound tough?"

"It's because I *am* tough."

"You don't have to convince me of that."

"Are you going to tell me you're in love with me now?"

He could not look at her.

"I told you I was tough."

"Yes," he said.

"You're taking a beating, Edward."

"Yes."

"It's because I'm drunk. I'm mean as shit when I drink."

"I wish you wouldn't talk like that."

"I'll talk any way I goddamn well please."

He busied himself with the lunch dishes.

"Edward," she said.

"What do you want."

"Come here."

"No, thank you."

"I was just going to give you a kiss."

He went to her. She had put the wine bottle down on the floor next to the bed. She locked her arms around his neck and kissed him, open-mouthed. Her tongue tasted of wine, of the unsubtle alcohol in the wine. She pulled him down on the bed, reached for his belt buckle.

"I know what you want," she said. "I know just what you want."

There was something brutal in her voice, and it made him take her by the upper arms and push her, gently, back from him.

"What's wrong?"

"Mary," he said, "This won't do. Not when you're—not when it's like this."

"Not romantic enough, is that it?"

"No."

She rolled over on her side, pulled the blanket up over her shoulder.

He lay down, not touching her. "Mary, I don't know what to think."

"I'll tell you," she said. "You know what? There isn't any character in a name."

"I don't understand."

"That's because you don't know me."

"I want to know you."

She got out of the bed, went to the television and turned it on, stood there waiting for it to warm up, her arms folded tightly across her chest.

"Mary?" he said.

"Never mind me, okay? Just pretend I'm not here."

"I can't do that."

She faced him. "Well then what do you want to do? You just tell me and, man, we'll do it. Anything you want."

"I'd like to talk," he said, putting his feet down on the floor. "And make love."

"Okay."

"You seem so—angry."

"I'm drunk."

"Well, I was saying. You seem so angry, so hurt."

"Don't make it into something it isn't."

"I only know what you've told me."

"About what?"

"You—your family."

"Oh, that. Yes. It was tough. Real tough all the time. It made me what I am today. It molded me into the girl you see standing before you this minute."

"Why do you have to deride everything?"

"Jesus," she said.

"No, really, Mary."

"Cakes," she said, "I wish I could've picked you out of a line or something. I wish I'd had a choice back before I was born."

"What would you have chosen me for?"

She smiled at him; it was only a little sardonic. "Oh, yes," she said, weaving slightly, moving back to the bed. "That." She shed her clothes and climbed in. He lay on his side, facing her, and when she moved to take him into her body he let himself be led. He kissed her hair, her neck. She lay caught beneath him, somewhere off in herself, nowhere near. Her eyes swam, and she would not look at him.

"Mary," he said.

"Go on," she murmured. "Good."

When it was over, she slept. The light began to fade at the window, and Cakes got carefully out of the bed, dressed quietly; he would go out and buy a few things for dinner. He would try to get her to help him make something, would try to distract her.

Outside, the snow had melted further, and was freezing again in the dusk. Far off, he could hear the immense roar and whine of the city, its sirens, engines, cries. But here it seemed rather peaceful, deserted—a ghost town. It was that hour of twilight when everything appears insubstantial, as though it is fading along with the light. Cakes walked through pools of shadow, careful of the ice, concentrating on keeping his weight balanced, his knees flexed slightly. Even so, at the corner, the ground slipped from beneath him and he fell, hard, on his back. For a moment he lay there feeling the cold all along his spine, and then he heard voices, someone saying his name.

It was Denise and Paula. They had seen him fall, and were struggling to reach him without falling themselves.

"Stay still," Paula said. "You might have broken something."

"I'll call an ambulance," said Denise.

"No," Cakes said, trying to rise.

"Stay still." Paula held him down.

"Let me up, please. The ground is cold."

They assured themselves that he was not seriously injured, and then helped him get to his feet. He felt a hot blade of pain in the middle of his back, and they supported him.

"Can you walk?" Paula said.

He could walk. Denise said it was a miracle. He took a step; they held their arms out to catch him if he started to fall. "It's a miracle you don't have a broken hip," Denise said. "You must be built strong as an ox."

"He's strong as an ox," said Paula.

They walked with him up to his room, and all the while Paula admonished him about going out alone in such weather. It had been the wildest luck that she and Denise had happened along when they did, or Cakes might have been in serious danger of freezing to death. It was a wonder he didn't break his hip. It was an outright miracle, in fact.

At his door he thanked them for their help, and after Paula cautioned him yet again about taking chances at his age, he went inside, closed the door gently so as not to wake the girl.

But the girl was gone.

Perhaps she had awakened and, finding herself alone, become frightened. It was so hard to guess what she might do, or might have done. The bag containing her belongings was still in the closet. Perhaps she had simply gone out for a breath of fresh air. Except that it was cold, and getting colder, and the ice could only be getting more treacherous.

On the floor next to his night stand he found a small piece of newspaper with the words *You've been* scribbled on it. Evidently she had started to write him a note. She had been drinking. She had seemed so unhappy.

And now he was frightened for her. He phoned the police, and of course they could tell him nothing. He left his name, his number; the hours of the night dragged by. He sat in the chair by the window and watched the street, and dozed against his will, and in the morning he walked the five blocks to the police station, where again he found that no one could tell him anything. They were dubious: the girl had only been gone a few hours. He wasn't even her father. The city was a big place and one could go where one wanted to in it, even in the cold and even in the middle of the night. Cakes went back to the room, half hoped to find her there. Denise and Paula were cleaning their apartment; their door was open. He looked in, and Paula smiled at him, wiped her forehead with the back of her hand. She was wearing a robe and had a dust rag in her fist. "How do you feel?"

"Sore," he said.

"I bet."

"Where's your lady friend?" Denise asked.

"I don't know."

"You guys have a fight?"

"No."

"Poor Cakes."

He unlocked his door, shuffled into the room and turned the television on. Someone started up the steps and he hurried to see who it was. Ida Warren came laboring up, carrying a bag of groceries in one hand and an umbrella in the other.

20

▲

Arthur wants to tell his friend about the two sons he has, in California somewhere, both in their sixties by now. My family is scattered all over the globe, Edward. All of them descendents of my grandfather and his brother, who migrated from the Ukraine years before I was a gleam in my father's eye, as they say. Hagood is not the actual name, which I do not remember but which was an unpronounceable clump of consonants ending, I think, in s-k-y. My father changed the name in 1908. He was anxious that I not grow up with the attitudes and speech of the immigrant generations that preceded me; there was no one more proud, more patriotic, than my father, but you know, he never did learn to be at home, and I'm afraid he transferred this to me in spite of himself: I still feel temporary, as if in my closet there should be a suitcase, packed and ready to go whenever the time comes. I never had a sense of place, Edward. And even so, I might have stayed in Virginia and married Maxine Sandusky.

"Cakes?"

"I was trying to tell you about the girl," Cakes says.

Arthur tries to frown at him. He knows he has managed a scowl.

"It's been two days now," Cakes says.

Cakes, I was talking to you.

"I don't think she's coming back."

"I was telling you something," Arthur says.

"You were sitting here staring into space."

"I'm tired, Edward."

"She left her things in my closet. But I'm sure she's not coming back."

Arthur moves to the bed, lets himself down, closes his eyes for a moment; things swim, he is a little nauseous, but then he opens his eyes and stares at the ceiling, fixing his attention on it as though it is some mooring to anchor himself to. Cakes is somewhere in the room, talking about the girl, and Arthur pretends for a moment to listen. But it bores him, he wakes to the realization that he is bored and mutters, "Give me the flapper."

Cakes is reciting it. Vermont, the cabin, the snow. The animation is not there, and it hardly matters. Arthur feels sick. He simply can't pay any attention. Last night he woke up and knew he was wetting the bed, hauled himself to his feet, feeling it, warm on his legs, breathing the acrid odor of it. He washed the sheets and the wet pajamas himself, kneeling painfully over the bathtub. There was no laundry detergent, so he used his own bath soap, lathering it up in his hands and then dipping his hands into the water. The whole business took most of the night, and he had hung the clothes in the bathroom with the window open and a fan blowing on them to dry them. The mattress he had rubbed hard with a soapy rag, then tried to dry with a bath towel; it still smelled faintly urinous, and it had made a damp spot in the fresh sheets he had made the bed with. Now he is lying here breathing the odor while Cakes talks, and he remembers that the last time he wet the bed he was twelve years old. Thinking this, he feels a small tremor run through his blood, and somewhere in himself, something cold and amazed looks at the fact that it was seventy-seven years ago. He sees the room, the old wood-smelling room with its leaded windows, his schoolroom, one of three rooms in a schoolhouse on a flat black plain in Indiana.

"Nineteen fourteen."

"What?" Cakes says to him.

Nothing.

Nineteen fourteen, and a war starting off across the world.

Arthur remembers a morning seventy-seven years ago. A boy looking out a window and praying that he will never wet the bed again.

Well, seventy-seven years is a good long time.

There were twenty-eight years in there, when I was with Angela. But, you know, Cakes, I wasn't much of a husband. I thought things were one way, and they were another.

"When Angela's legs began to go, it started with this little twinge behind the knee. She was fixing Linda's hair for her, and she felt this twinge behind the knee."

"I was going to leave. You went to sleep on me," says Cakes.

"Let me finish," Arthur says.

"Are you all right?" Cakes asks.

"Just be quiet. I was telling you. Angela—when her legs started to go."

She went into the hospital with a twinge behind the knee, and she stayed in the hospital for three months and every day the news was worse than the day before, until one night past one o'clock they called me and woke me out of a sound sleep to tell me I better get down to the hospital because there was infection and it was spreading and they were going to have to take her legs. They were going to have to take her legs, Edward. From a twinge behind the knee. They took one leg at the knee, and the other leg at the hip. They told me she would have to stay in the hospital for another six, seven months. She was going to go through therapy— all that. All that, Cakes. All that. All that.

"All that."

"Go ahead," Cakes says. "I'm listening."

"I told you."

"Her legs began to go," Cakes says, coaxing.

"Never mind."

"What's wrong."

"Nothing. I'm tired. I'm eighty-nine years old."

"I'm sorry," Cakes says.

"They took her legs, Edward—"

They said it would be traumatic for her, of all things to say that's what they said. I had been at the hospital for a day and a night and another day, and I got home and walked around the house, looking at things—her garden, her roses, and it was a sunny day and for twenty-eight years we had got up together and done our various business and made friends and had the babies and got possessions. She was my friend, and I couldn't do anything to save her and I couldn't do anything to keep her from hurt. There was a young man in the yard next to mine and I stood there leaning on my fence and talked to him about Angela, and then I told him how I used to change my name when I traveled and met other women because they wouldn't be able to find out who I was and it was safer that way when you wanted to cheat and I cheated, I cheated more than once, and Angela was dying and I was telling this kid how to cheat, how I had cheated. I was anxious to be thought of as a real man, that knew what was what, and this kid was full of himself, only thirty. I could see he thought I was past it, and felt sorry for me—the old man with the sick wife. I was fifty-six years old and it was summer but very, very cool, and I stood there leaning on my fence and began to sweat for what I had said. My sons were off in the army, and Linda was married, having trouble with her husband. I told the kid I had to get to work and build a ramp for when Angela came home, and over the next couple of days I just tried to work myself to death, building that thing. I cut every piece of wood for it and nailed every nail and sanded every surface myself, and when it was done I stood out in the front yard and felt proud of myself until I remembered what it was for. . . .

"Arthur?" says Cakes.

"I made a ramp."

"I think I should go."

Arthur blinks, peers at his friend, whose face seems elongated somehow, as if about to dissolve. But then it comes clear, and he knows he has drifted again. "I didn't sleep last night, Edward."

"I'll go."

"You know how I met Angela?"

"I believe you told me once."

"Her brother. Red. Old Red. You know how he died?"

"No."

"Died of a heart attack, on the Golden Gate Bridge—he was sixty-nine. When we were young boys, he brought me home from the Army to meet his sister. Did I tell you that?"

"I think you did," Cakes says.

"Agh." Arthur tries to scowl at him again. "You'd remember if I told you that."

"My memory is fading," says Cakes.

"Don't make patronizing jokes."

"I wasn't joking."

"My memory gets better every day," Arthur says.

"Good."

"No," Arthur says, "not good."

21

▲

Two orderlies came in, then, to vacuum the floor and to dust the furniture. Arthur got up and went into the bathroom, moving with a kind of deliberation, as if each step had to be planned, thought out to the last nerve. Cakes saw that his ankles were blue, the veins forked over the bone, the lower legs unbelievably thin.

Both orderlies were blond, very tanned and muscular—they might have been members of another species, or a pair of Nordic angels, they were so smooth and flawless and young. They spoke only to each other as they worked, and they worked very quickly and efficiently. Arthur came out of the bathroom as they finished, and the taller one asked if he wanted his sheets changed.

"I can take care of my own bed, thank you," Arthur said.

"How old are you, Mr. Hagood?"

"I could've fathered your grandfather, young man."

The tall one nudged his companion. "See?" Then he saluted Arthur, who saluted him back with an exaggerated stiffness, an obvious attempt to render an exact military salute. The two younger men exchanged a look, which Arthur did not see, of derision. It was derision; Cakes saw it, and now he saw his friend's face registering the pride and pleasure of having mistaken this exchange, of thinking he had shown the younger men how a man behaves. "Nice boys," Arthur said when they were gone. He had let himself down in the bed again.

"Maybe I could get an apartment downtown and you could move in with me," Cakes said.

"What about your girlfriend?"

Cakes was silent. He sat watching the other begin to doze off again, and the thought of leaving, of going back to the room alone, raked through him like fear. He had come here, had risked a fall on the still slippery streets to get here, because he couldn't stand the room. He had been sitting by the window looking out at the patches of unmelted snow, thinking of the girl, and quite suddenly he felt himself to be angular, odd, somehow sick. He made a face at the ghost of his reflection in the window, and then something else began to happen, something more complex: he had, over the years, managed his life, arranged it; he was aware of this —he was proud of it, proud of the tidiness of it, its symmetry and shape; it was a simple, orderly existence, and in it there had been room for a kind of easy mockery of himself: he was anyone's idea of the quiet little man. Except that now he seemed to see everything in a glaring new light: he was outside himself now, looking in, and what he saw was this wintry soul on a thousand afternoons at a window in a barren room, watching the progression of people and traffic in the street. He saw this bitter old man who had steadily emptied his life of everything. The room became, then, a manifestation—a portrait of him. This artless, this mean little place. He went from it, strode across the park to the library, where he stood in the great arched doorway and saw himself, some solitary figure still wearing coat and hat, drowsing over a book at one of the tables: nodding, nearsighted, faintly ridiculous. It was appalling. It sent him fumbling out into the street, in a gray, bone-cold dusk, to make his way here, to his one friend.

"You're still here," Arthur said.

"Want to watch television?" Cakes asked.

"What's the matter with you?"

"Nothing."

Arthur looked at him. "You look like a funeral."

Cakes said nothing.

"Cheer up. She'll come back."

He hadn't been thinking about the girl.

"You're afraid, aren't you," Arthur said.

"What makes you say that?"

"Fear is general, Edward."

"I can't explain it," Cakes said. Then he almost laughed. "I had to see you."

"Ask yourself what you're afraid of, why don't you."

"I don't really know. The worst things have happened to me, Arthur. They happened before I was fifty."

"You don't know worse," Arthur said. "You don't know anything. You want me to show you worse? You know what I was doing when you came in? I was trying to figure out if I had to piss. I wet the bed last night, Edward. Good God—me, Arthur Hagood. I wet the goddamn bed. I got a kid sixty-some years old living ten miles from here, and the one time I see her, she accuses me of lying. Instead of coming to see me more than once a year, she goes to the supermarket and spends all her time shopping for nice cards to send me, like she lives in California. But she's sixty; she feels old, Edward. She's backing up from things, scared, you know, thinks everything's behind her. You can tell it from just looking at her. And so I get these—these cards—" He reached over and opened the nightstand, brought out a handful of fancy, embroidered-looking, padded cloth cards, and dropped them on the bed at his side. "You see this? Get-well cards when I can't get out of bed, how-are-you cards, I-owe-you-a-visit cards—all of them made to order like this. That's what I get. She makes her husband sign them. She makes her husband that hasn't read a real book in his entire life sign them, and I bet he can't read the cards. I can't have anything to do with the girls, can't drink, smoke, eat a goddamn egg. I would like to eat a scrambled egg. I would like very much to drink one shooter of nice American Bourbon, and chase it with a cold glass of beer. And here—see—here I am. This becomes the story, see. This is the story of the end of my life. I got a friend who comes to see me on his two hind legs because he doesn't have anyone else to see or anything else to do or because he likes to think about how he can come and go as he pleases. Look at *me,* Edward. I'm not a character in your story. I got my own story."

Cakes stared at his own freckled hands.

"I'm not yelling at you," Arthur said. "At least you do come to see me."

There seemed nothing left to say.

"Let's change the subject," Arthur said. But he closed his eyes again, seemed, again, to be dozing off. Perhaps two minutes passed, and then he moved, rolled over on his side, facing the other man, eyes still closed. "Did I tell you Maxine Sandusky was in the bombing of London?"

"I think so."

Presently Cakes said, "You were telling me you almost married her." But Arthur had gone to sleep, lay curled, knees up, looking terribly small and weak, a sack of bones under the sheet, and one bony hand dangling over the side of the bed.

22
▲

He sat in the chair and drifted in and out of sleep; sirens wailed beyond the shadows of the buildings up the street, and he watched the clouds trail past the moon. Then there were no clouds. In the morning it was sunny, balmy; a southerly wind was blowing. He went out and walked to the library, and, standing at the foot of the marble steps that led up to the entrance, changed his mind, turned and went back the way he had come. He stopped at the People's Café and sat in a booth by the window, drinking coffee, watching the street. The sun was blinding, and the last patches of snow were almost gone.

It was almost November.

He thought about how the girl was one of those people who could just go off and leave everything. It was amazing.

In the People's Café there were two other customers, and they both knew the waitresses. Edward's waitress was a familiar face, and he had never spoken to her as a person, out of the context of a meal and her job. "How are you?" he said.

She looked at him. "Fine. You?"

"Fine."

Now she smiled. "Can I get you anything?"

"I'm going," said the other waitress to the one Edward was speaking to. "Wish me luck."

"Good luck."

"I'm going to need all the luck I can get."

"You'll do just fine."

"It's been years since I did any typing, though."

"You'll do all right."

"You know what I'm afraid of, I'm afraid I'll go blank."

Edward paid for his coffee and went out. The waitress was still talking about the typing test she would have to take, still standing in the doorway, as if only the gestures of leave-taking were ever accomplished. These people would never walk out of a place and, abandoning everything, never return.

Back in the room he found himself going through the girl's things: two blouses, a skirt that matched neither of them, three or four pairs of jeans, some undergarments, a black turtleneck sweater. He did not know what he might find, or what he was looking for: he would know it when he came upon it—and then, quite clearly as if in a way he *had* come upon something, he understood himself, and this prying through a girl's few possessions: he was looking for the one thing he could believe she would not leave behind; she had left family, friends and home to come here. He remembered, too, how diffident she had been about going to the train station to pick up these few items of clothing.

As he was putting everything back in the bag, there was a

soft tapping at the door. He froze. And then he hurried; he was a man frantically trying to hide wrongdoing. The tapping continued, without pause, right up to the moment when, out of breath, sweating with effort, and trying to compose himself, he opened the door.

It was the woman from upstairs. She had put on makeup, wore a dress that was strangely recognizable: it was swept low across her hips, and there was a bow very near the hem. He stood staring at it.

"Hi," she said.

"Hello." He was not sure he had spoken it loud enough to be heard. He said again, "Hello."

She did a slight curtsy. "Like it?"

He thought he recognized it. He went to the picture on the wall to be sure; it was almost the same—almost, in fact, exactly the same. He turned again and saw that she had come into the room.

"I thought I'd come down and make friends." She looked at the room, seemed to be looking *for* something: she was not merely taking it in. Her face showed something like surprise. "You're alone here?"

"Yes," he said.

"Do you want me to come back another time?"

"I'm Edward Cakes," he said.

She said, "What?"

"I said I'm Edward Cakes."

"Oh. Nice to meet you." She gave her hand to him. It was a completely peremptory gesture and she withdrew it almost immediately. "I'm Ida Warren." Then she went to the door. "I'll come back another time."

"No," he said.

She stopped. "I hope my music hasn't disturbed you too much."

"No."

"You seem upset."

"I'm a little tired."

"You seemed so upset before. Well, you know, you're positively white." She came back to him, reached out and touched his forehead. "No fever."

It was absurd. They were standing in the center of his room, and she had the back of her hand on his forehead as if waiting for something to move there.

"No," she said, bringing her hand down. "No fever."

"I'm fine," he said.

"I thought you looked pale the other day." She went to the door again, he thought, this time, to close it. "Do you have any tea? Tea is just the thing when you feel a little under the weather."

"Really, I'm all right," he said.

"Wait right here and I'll get some tea. I have plenty of it upstairs."

"I have tea," he said.

"I bet you don't have herb tea."

"No."

"I'll be right back."

He sat on the bed and waited for her. It was quiet; it took her a long time. There was the soft sound of water dropping from the eaves outside his window. Lately everything seemed to glide past him somehow, as if his eyes could catch things only as they had just happened—his mind able to read the significance of an event only after it was already in motion: he did not want tea. He was suddenly very tired; it had been days since he had been able to sleep undisturbed. He lay down, folded his hands over his chest and closed his eyes; they burned, were salty, and there was a sound in the room.

She had returned and was making the tea. "Don't go to sleep yet," she said, moving before him in that dress. There was no shape to her; she was all skin and bones. He sat up, rubbed his eyes, tried to shake the sleep off, and then he knew that time had passed, hours. The woman had gone back upstairs. Paula and Denise were arguing about something across the hall; they had their music on, loud: drums and guitars and screams. He would ask them to turn their sound down, turn it off, be quiet, please.

When he opened his eyes again it was morning—late morning, in fact, and he had slept deeply. He got out of the bed, put a

robe over his shoulders and padded over to the sink. Ida Warren
had left the makings for her herb tea, and so he fixed himself a
cup. The girl had simply gone. It was almost impossible to understand how a person could just leave everything. When he heard
someone on the stairs he allowed himself no hope. Rising from the
table, still feeling the aches and the soreness of what he had been
through, he moved to the bed, thinking to lie down, rest. The
someone on the stairs was outside his door. He waited for the
knock, and even so it startled him.

"Yes?" he called.

"Hello?" A man's voice.

Cakes opened the door. A dark-faced man with puffed,
rounded features and round black eyes stood there. "Yes?" Cakes
said.

"I'm Howard Bellini," said the man. "Can I speak to you
please?"

In the first confusing moments—the handshake, the offer of a
chair, some refreshment, tea—Cakes tried to remember everything the girl had said about her father, and could recall only that
she had spoken with bitterness about him. The rest was a blur. He
could not call up a single detail that would help him know how to
act, what to tell this stranger who sat with his legs crossed and
stared at the backs of his smooth brown hands moving restlessly
along one wide thigh. Mr. Bellini had a sleek, well-fed look about
him, a groomed look.

"I spoke to my daughter on the telephone. She gave me this
address to send money to."

"I'm afraid she's not here," Cakes said. "She hasn't been here
for two days."

"She hasn't."

"I don't know where she is."

The backs of Howard Bellini's hands were youthful; his nails
were manicured; the wide, flat fingers looked polished. The hands
kept moving along the crossed thigh. "I have money."

Cakes only nodded.

"She called me and asked for money."

"I'm sorry," Cakes said.

The other man shifted in his seat, brought a handkerchief out of his pocket and blew his nose, then folded the handkerchief and put it back. "I'm at the end of my rope."

This took a second to register with Cakes: the words seemed to have no connection to the man's calm demeanor.

"What has she said about me?"

"Nothing," Cakes said too quickly.

"She was born late. My wife and I—we had her late in life. Well, I'm seventy years of age."

After a moment Cakes said, "I'm seventy-five."

"You have children?"

"No."

"We have Mary. That's it."

"She—" Edward began.

"Yes?"

"She—she said there were—that she had brothers and sisters."

The other man shook his head.

"She said her mother had nervous breakdowns."

"Yes."

They were quiet for a moment.

"One more since all this started."

"Excuse me," Cakes said, "but I wish you'd explain."

"She and Dillard."

"Yes."

"Dillard's no good. No damn good. I know she's pregnant." Cakes nodded.

"I don't want her to abort it."

Again, all Cakes could do was nod.

"Dillard is involved with drugs, too."

"He lived in the room above this one," Cakes said. "He spent all his time studying."

"I'm sure he's involved in some way. There have been people —you know, coming by the house, asking for him. Asking for both of them. I guess they figure if they can find her, they'll find him."

"*She* can't find him."

"Is that what she's telling you?"

"He ran out on her—yes."

"I don't know," Mr. Bellini said. "I don't believe her."

"He—he was a student," said Cakes. "He was worried about keeping it quiet so he could study. He was always threatening to call the police."

Bellini was staring at his hands. "These people who have come looking for him—for—for *them*. These people say he owes them a lot of money. They're—not what you'd call average citizens. Mary's involved with drugs. I know it. I'm sure of it."

"What drugs," Cakes said.

"I don't know. Cocaine, maybe."

"Your daughter is on cocaine?"

"Her husband is."

"Her husband."

The other man looked at him. "Dillard."

"Dillard is her husband?"

"I thought you knew that."

"Your daughter told me she came north to marry him because she was pregnant."

"They separated last year. After two years of hell for her mother and me."

Cakes was speechless.

"She was going to start school," Bellini said, and brought out the handkerchief again. This time he wiped his eyes. "Then she started talking to Dillard on the phone. And they—they saw each other on the sly. He came down to see her. They were sneaking it, and they were involved with these people—the drugs. I'm sure of it."

Cakes just sat there shaking his head.

"You know what Dillard made her do?"

"Dillard is her husband," Cakes muttered.

"Yeah. You know what he made her do? He had some—there were some friends of his that found her attractive."

"Please," Cakes said.

Mr. Bellini wiped his eyes again, cleared his throat, staring at his own hands folding the handkerchief. "If I were a different man I'd have killed him a long time ago."

"I wish I could help you," Cakes said.

"She stayed with you." Bellini's eyes changed now, and he took in the room. "Where did she stay?"

"I slept in the chair by the window." Cakes felt the color rushing to his face, and he looked away.

"And she's been gone two days?"

"Yes."

"God knows we weren't much good to her."

"No, we weren't."

"I meant my wife and I."

"Yes. Forgive me."

"What did you mean?"

"I meant I wasn't—wasn't able to be much of a friend."

Mr. Bellini nodded, took the handkerchief out once more. "I made my mistakes, God knows. Not that I didn't love her. I loved her as much as a father ever loves a child. But I just—maybe I just didn't know how to be what she needed."

"Why would she tell me she had brothers and sisters?"

"She's always making up lies. Ever since she was a baby, really." There was a kind of brutal impatience in Bellini's voice now. "You can't ever believe her. What she does, see, she twists the truth. I mean there's always an element of the truth in her lies —so you just can't tell where the truth leaves off and the lie begins. She's very good at it."

"She said you were a professor."

"She did."

"Well, are you?"

"I do geological surveys for the government."

"But you don't teach."

"Never."

A moment later Mr. Bellini said, "See?"

"Yes but why. Why would she tell me that."

"I wish I could tell you," Mr. Bellini said.

"She said you traveled a lot."

"No."

They were quiet. It was as if they were both going over in their minds what Mary had told them.

"What did she tell you about Dillard?"

"That they went to high school together."

"That's true. She got mixed up with him then."

"She said Dillard asked her to come north."

"That's probably true."

"She said he was still over at City College. She said she saw him there."

"I hope that's true. Because if it is, I'll find him." Mr. Bellini straightened a little, then let his broad shoulders droop. "Then what. I keep asking myself—then what. She's twenty-four years old, and I'm at the end of my rope." He wiped his forehead with the handkerchief, folded it and put it back again. "If I could just talk to her—face to face."

"She mentioned someone named Mort," Cakes said.

The other sat forward, reached into the pocket of his coat and brought out a pen and scratch pad. "Mort," he said.

"I believe she said he was a medical student at City College."

Bellini wrote this down. "Anything else?"

"I'm afraid not."

He tore the page from the pad, shoved the page into his pocket; then, after writing something else on the succeeding page, tore that off and folded it. "Here," he said, rising. "If she comes back here will you—can I trust you to give her this."

Cakes took the folded piece of paper from him.

"You've been very helpful, sir." Bellini now offered his hand. It was all suddenly very awkward and unpleasant as if somehow Edward's real relation to the girl had been made visible on the walls of the room. There was also the guilty fact that Cakes had not mentioned the girl's things in his closet. He sought for an opening, a way to say it out into the other man's departing words of polite gratitude, and the opportunity was gone before he could gracefully take advantage of it. Mr. Bellini's last words to him, called up from halfway down the stairs, were almost a challenge. "All she's ever known from men," he said, "is suffering."

The note he'd written was short, and he had crossed part of it out:

> Mary,
>
> ~~I forgive you~~
> We love you.
>
> Your father.

23

▲

Later, Edward walked down to the park. Boys were tossing a football around, and he asked if he might throw them a couple. He was too stiff. The ball fell short, and the boys grew kind: they ran slowly; they tried to stay within range. Impatience and frustration showed in their faces. Cakes thanked them, remained for a while at the edge of the field, watching them. Strangely, he caught himself thinking of them as males, of a species. It was chilly. The wind blew. When he walked he had to hold his lower back with one hand, for the bruise there: he was everyone's idea of an old decrepit man, walking along cramped in his age. All he lacked was the cane. He went back to the room and rested for a time, then gathered all the Fitzgerald novels into his arms and made his way to the library, where he spent his afternoon. It was quiet; you could drowse in it. There wasn't anything he felt like doing. He hadn't eaten all day, so he stopped at the café on the way home. He would not let himself think about the fact that he was keeping a girl's few things in his closet, and that there was something quite wrong about everything he had done and said concerning that girl. Yet he couldn't put it together in his mind, couldn't straighten it and look at it, this sense of wrongdoing, of complicity. He had not sought her. He had only done what she apparently wanted to do, and she was a grown woman. And she was gone.

It was as he ate his meal of chicken and rice that he decided he could not go home yet. Not now, just at early winter dusk. Dusk, the worst time of day always. The time of shadows, Arthur used to say. Our time. Cakes would not go home, then. Perhaps he would go to a movie. He had finished eating and had left the café when the idea struck him that he should take a bottle of whiskey to Arthur. He went straight to the liquor store, bought a six-pack of cold beer as well, and a box of rum-soaked cigars.

"Every day now," Arthur said, "you come to see me. You know something I don't know?" They had hooked him up to an I.V. and a catheter. He could not leave the bed, now. "My appetite," he said to Edward. "They're worried about my appetite."

Edward closed the door and turned and lifted the bottle of Bourbon out of the bag.

Arthur stared at it.

"I got beer, too," Cakes said, putting it all down on the nightstand. When he looked at his friend, he saw that he was trying to keep tears back. "And—and cigars."

"You stupid son of a bitch," Arthur said, and, taking hold of his wrist, squeezed it tight. "You damn fool."

"Here," Cakes said, breaking the seal on the bottle.

Arthur tried to reach into the drawer of the nightstand, but the I.V. hindered him.

"Let me," said Cakes. There were glasses in the drawer. He got two of them out, poured the whiskey, then opened two beers.

"A toast," Arthur said.

"To us," said Edward.

They drank. Edward sat in the chair by his friend's bed and watched him sip the whiskey, then the beer. Arthur's eyes were closed, and his lips trembled on the lip of the glass.

"Good?" Cakes said.

"Ah."

They drank slowly, without talking now. Edward traced the

line of the I.V. from its plastic bottle to the taped place in the back of Arthur's skinny, discolored hand.

"It bruises," Arthur said.

"What?"

"The hand. Where they put the needle." Then Arthur laughed. "Everything, old friend. Everything bruises."

"More?" Cakes asked, holding up the bottle.

"Throw the cap away," Arthur said.

Edward poured more for him, and for himself. They drank again for a while, without speaking.

"Edward, I'm going to tell you something I never told anybody before. And I hope you don't mind it if I do."

"No," said Cakes, "I don't mind."

"This happened the year before Angela got sick—1950, I guess. I was fifty-five years old, I'd been married for twenty-seven years—I'd been teaching high school almost twenty-five years. I'd been making a little extra money as a carpenter on weekends. My boys lived close, then, and they'd help out. We'd have Sunday dinner together, the whole family. And—well, I don't know. One day I looked up and realized I was tired of it. I got quiet. It's amazing how little everybody else talks, Edward. When you're a talker, like me, you get used to hearing your own voice, you don't notice how quiet everybody else really is. I got quiet, and suddenly my house is like a tomb. These people sit at the dinner table and stare. Angela walked around making sure there was enough food on everybody's plate. Nobody said anything. And maybe there was never anything really to say. Who knows. But I was tired. I was tired of talking. Let somebody else do the talking for a change." Arthur took a long drink of his beer, then put it on the nightstand and held his hand out. "Light me one of those cigars, would you?"

Edward did so and gave it to him. He took a deep puff, inhaled it and blew the smoke at the ceiling.

"Good?" Edward said.

Arthur's expression answered the question. He sat up, pushing his pillow behind him, nearly disconnecting himself from the I.V. "Where was I? Oh, I remember." He took another puff of the cigar and talked the smoke out. "So I got quiet and of course it's not that simple. What I did was change, and they noticed it, and so they began to wait to see what it would mean. Except Angela, of course, who wouldn't take any of it and kept telling me to come out of whatever it was that was bothering me. Now I'm sure you know, Edward, that there is more than one kind of quiet—and for about a week we had *my* kind, the kind I've just been telling you about, and then we had the *other* kind. The kind that sulks, and poisons. Angela wouldn't have anything at all to do with me, and I guess everybody started worrying about the two of us, and not just me. But then one day she just started talking to me like nothing had happened, and we had one of those Sunday dinners, everybody acting like nothing at all had happened, and nobody ever said another word about it, and still I felt like I'd lost something. Or given it up to Angela. I'd sit with one hand on each knee and look at them all, my family, and I felt like somebody from outer space. Angela—well, she looked bad. She was just beginning to get sick, I guess, although none of us knew it at the time. She had just let herself—she was—I mean she was ready to be old, sort of. She'd made herself ready, and so she was. One day I looked at her and saw an old woman, without shape at all, wearing stockings rolled down below her knees. It was like a blow to the stomach, looking at her across the table. And so I decided I was going to have myself a little fling. A regular orgy if I could arrange it."

"Is this when you met Maxine Sandusky?"

Arthur frowned. "I was seventy when I met her."

"Oh, that's right."

"This is years before Maxine." He drank his beer, and puffed and blew on his cigar. When he began again, there was something almost declamatory about his voice, as if he were performing: an actor saying a monologue. Yet he seemed to relax, too, somehow, to settle into this recitative like someone who had performed it many times and knew every nuance, every shade of it. He said he had started with the simple accession to the idea of infidelity. He would cheat on Angela exactly as he had cheated on her when he was younger, and drank rather more than he should. Except that this time there would be no element of a slip, or of the failures of will involved in drunkenness and flirtation: no, this would be something done coldly; and, having decided upon it, he felt as though he were breathing new air; it excited him in ways he had forgotten. He was like a boy again, wondering what sex would be like, and with what luscious companion it would first take place. He began to daydream of his soon-to-be-committed adultery, and then one day it dawned on him that it was only that: a daydream. He had been settled into the pattern of his life so long that, indeed, the chance for the sort of fling he had been imagining had passed him by: he didn't have a lot of money in the first place, and his days were such that no opportunities could present themselves. He was a high-school teacher, a part-time carpenter, a man nearing sixty, and this all carried with it certain attitudes, responsibilities, expectations; he was neither attractive nor particularly distinguished. He had nothing, really, to offer a partner in adultery, except his hunger for it, his lust. And then he seemed to turn inside of himself, and he saw the absurdity, the banality, of his own dearest daydream. It was as if he were standing in a room where people once lived, and he saw the whole of himself—this sordid, shameful clutch of desires. It was simply ridiculous. It seemed to him then, realizing this, that all his joy in things went out of him. He grew strange. He felt, from then on, like someone quite sick in spirit, someone secretly worse than everyone else. His own daughter, coming to the house to have her mother fix her hair, made him feel craven, hooved; when Angela said good night to him, complaining about the twinge in her leg, behind the knee, he wanted to tear her nightgown from her, bury his face in her flesh, rooting, not with love but with the plain hunger for contact, the simple bodily need, that was enough like anger to frighten him, to recoil from it as if it were a temptation to do harm, to hurt her.

It made him want to die. In a sense, he realized, he was already dead. He no longer felt anything with anyone except his difference, his isolation. He lay in the bed next to Angela, and he could not find anything in himself that he would have said he was not ashamed of, or that was human. It was truly as if he had been set down in that house from some far planet with, in his chest, an alien heart.

He wanted to die.

And then Angela began to die. It all went so fast, and on many nights while she slept in her hospital room, he wandered the house, recognizing everything, her touch everywhere. The house was so quiet, and he thought about how quiet love was, like a breath in sleep, the smallest arrangement of things, every day, and he stared at himself in the mirror in the upstairs bathroom, thinking about how he could not go on without Angela. Thinking about her, seeing in his mind her face—about which he knew, really, almost nothing; knew only its aging, and a few of its moods. He could not go on.

And then Angela was dead, the family had buried her. They had all gone off to their own lives; his daughter to the city, the two boys to the Army. He was alone, and gradually, over that year, he decided that he would kill himself.

"Did you ever think about suicide?" he asked Edward Cakes.

"I guess," Cakes said.

"I mean—really."

"I don't know. I mean I don't think I ever *wanted* to."

They poured more whiskey and opened two more beers, and again Arthur offered a toast. His voice had grown slightly higher, and his eyes looked jaundiced.

"Why're you telling me all this," Cakes said. "I mean I'm flattered, but I don't understand."

Arthur sighed. "Because it's such a funny thing. To have wanted, all those years ago, to die. I was—young, really. I could get around. I had no reason to want to quit except this thing I'd done—to—you know—to take my wife's dignity away."

"How is that taking it away?" Cakes asked.

Again Arthur sighed. "Not to see it is to take it away. I know that now. It's the truth. Everything else comes from that."

"Well," Cakes said, holding up his glass of whiskey, "you didn't die and I'm glad of it."

"Thank you," Arthur said.

They drank. Cakes said, "Imagine if you'd done it."

"I was unsuccessful," Arthur said. "But I tried it, Edward."
Cakes waited.

"I did."

"You tried to kill yourself."

Arthur explained how, over a period of seven months, he had come to the conclusion that his life was no longer bearable. He began to look for a neat way to end it. The problem was that in spite of his personal and spiritual ugliness he was a man of intense privacy and dignity; he could not imagine simply leaving himself for someone else to find. He wanted to cancel everything, without notes or fireworks or remains, and of course there was no way to do this short of finding a volcano to jump into, or taking an ocean voyage and slipping over the side somewhere in the North Atlantic. It was a problem he would carry with him, like a secret condition. And, well—it was just that. A condition. He grew to like the feeling of his mysterious difference from everyone else, his visiting status as a man from another world—or at least as a man who was about to leave this one. And one afternoon, while he was visiting his daughter and her new family, he went into her bathroom and got the sleeping pills from her cabinet and took most of what was left in the bottle. He had gone beyond worrying about how he would be found, or what would be the result, because he had looked upon his own grandchildren and felt nothing, nothing. So he made his attempt, left no note, just walked into the bathroom and got the pills and sat there on her toilet and swallowed what there was in the bottle, dropping a few on the floor between his feet. When he was done, he lay down on the floor and waited for sleep. The whole thing had been done on impulse, finally. He had thought about what sort of medicines his daughter might keep in that cabinet and had opened it and, seeing the pills, decided it was time. He didn't know how many he took, but he had thought it was enough. Of course it wasn't. In fact, he hadn't even gone to sleep. Instead, he grew cold, shivered, coughed, and vomited into the sink. He was dizzy, sick, utterly awake. In the end, nothing happened but this seizure of chills, nausea and headache.

"I didn't even see a doctor," he said. "I just got sick. And stayed in her guest room for three days."

"Didn't she know you took the pills?"

"She was ashamed of it. She didn't want it getting out that her old man had tried something like that."

"No."

Arthur lay his head back. "Who knows. It was a long time ago. I'm here. I made it this far." The room was hazy with his cigar smoke. He blew small puffs at the ceiling, then he sat up and took a sip of the whiskey. "Ah."

"Did you ever try it again?"

"No."

"You got some sense scared into you."

"No," Arthur said. "The whole thing looked so—absurd. I just never tried it again. I figured I deserved to live, like a punishment for all the selfish things I did."

The door opened, now, and a young nurse came into the room waving her arms and coughing. She went to the window and opened that, turned, and with her hands on her hips began to scold the two men. "Shame on you, Mr. Cakes," she said, "for bringing this stuff in here. Do you know this could kill him? Do you know this could kill you, Mr. Hagood?"

Arthur took a deep puff of the cigar and blew the smoke at her. "Honey, the language is going to get rough in here in a minute, and I suggest you take your little ass right out."

"You don't scare me," she said. "Now put that cigar out and stop this—"

Cakes stood.

"Sit down, Edward."

"I'll just go get an orderly and we'll see about this," the girl said. She was very thin, with very soft features and large, watery gray eyes, and when she spoke, her eyeteeth showed.

"Why don't you sit down and have a little whiskey and shut up," Arthur said.

She turned abruptly and went charging out of the room, and Arthur, blowing smoke from the cigar, looked at Cakes and said, "Snot-nosed kid talking to me like that." He held out his glass. "Let me have a little more of that whiskey."

As Cakes leaned forward to oblige him, the two blond orderlies came into the room and stood over the bed.

"Let's put the cigar out, old buddy," one of them said.

"When I'm through with it." Arthur stared at him. "You boys want a touch of whiskey?"

They let Arthur finish the cigar; they understood that they would've had to fight him for it. But they confiscated the whiskey and the beer, telling Cakes he could pick it up when he left the hospital. The fact that they used the word hospital upset Arthur, who shouted at them that it was a *home,* that it was his *home,* and they were invading his privacy: he would just see about it, he said, shouting, and the veins stood out on his thin neck. When the orderlies were gone, Edward stood.

"Where are you going?"

"I thought you'd want me to go."

"Why?"

Cakes didn't know.

"Sit down. They'll never take us alive."

"Calm down," Cakes said gently, "there's no use having a fit about it."

"Shit." Arthur lay his head back again and seemed to have to gasp for air for a moment, his small, bony chest heaving. He coughed, sat up and spit into the palm of his hand. Edward got him a napkin from the nightstand, and when Arthur was finished with it, dropped it into the trash can beside the bed.

"Sit down," Arthur said. "Don't leave yet. Do you feel drunk?"

"A little."

"I feel drunk."

"We had quite a bit."

"We did, didn't we. We had enough to get drunk."

"More than enough," Cakes said.

"Do you feel good?"

"I feel good," Cakes said.

"Yeah—me, too. Me, too."

"I guess we're a little drunk."

"Last time I was drunk," Arthur said, "was that time with Maxine Sandusky—I told you about that."

"Yes."

"Did I tell you what happened when I woke up?"

"I'm sorry?" Cakes said.

Arthur lay back again. "Never mind."

"No, tell me."

"I'd rather just sit here and enjoy this, Edward."

They were quiet.

"Forgot how good it feels to be drunk," Arthur said.

24

▲

In the middle of the night, just as a nurse shuts the door going out, Arthur wakes, feels the headache, the sourness in his stomach. He is thirsty. The bed is dry, and this is a relief to him. He gets up and makes his way, pulling the I.V. apparatus along with him, to the bathroom. The light blinds him, and he stands just inside the door, holding onto the sink. When his eyes grow accustomed to the change, he moves to the toilet bowl and tries to urinate. Nothing comes. He waits a long time, and finally, with a low curse, gives up. The light from the bathroom falls on the carpet near his bed, and shows him the shadow of himself, with the tube and the gibbetlike aluminum rack from which the I.V. bottle hangs. He tries not to look at it, making his way to the bed, and as he lets himself down, there is a little tremor of dizziness, which is somehow pleasant.

"I'm still drunk," he says.

Maxine, I thought I'd never meet anybody.

He stares into the light at the bathroom door. It is all right to sleep in light; he must wake himself all night, and the light will help. He keeps his eyes fixed on the shadowless white room beyond the open door and remembers the summer night in Virginia, so long ago, when he had already thought himself old, his life over. There is the sweet memory of the moon ducking in and out behind the neighborhood houses, the honeysuckle smell in the air.

He remembers how it felt to wake next to Maxine Sandusky, and to know somehow that this was a sort of truce with himself. He hopes Maxine is still alive somewhere, that she is not a casualty yet; he hopes she remembers him with the same fondness he feels now and that she does not regret him.

He remembers himself as being young and strong, then. Waking next to Maxine, and then going back to sleep, and then waking again, this time with a headache and a parched throat.

He plays it all back in his mind, the last love of his life, and is not sad. It is as if he is only an observer now, of this amorous old pair, waking to stare at each other and smile in the middle of this night.

"I have a headache," she says.

"You want an aspirin?" he asks.

"Not supposed to use it," she says. Then she reaches up and pinches his ear. "I'm not allowed to have whiskey or cigarettes, either."

"Got any?" he says. "Aspirin, I mean."

"No."

He puts his arm over her rounded shoulder. "It's a pretty night."

"Beautiful night," she murmurs.

"Know what I was thinking when I was coming back here with the beer?" he asks.

"Tell me what you were thinking," she says.

"I was thinking how good it felt to be coming home to somebody."

She snuggles.

"Let's do get married," he says.

"How nice." She begins to cry.

"Don't cry," he says.

"I'm so happy."

"We'll be happy," he says.

A moment later she says, "Max?"

"Yeah?" he says.

But then they are quiet. They sleep again, and he wakes first, hours later; there is light coming into the room. He walks quietly out to the living room, looks out the picture window at the Virginia countryside—out beyond the row of buildings in the lot. It is green, shimmering with dew under the new sun, and there are splashes of oxblood earth. He feels invincible somehow, and he starts to go back into the bedroom—but then he lies down on the sofa, wanting to extend this peaceful sense of strength and well-being. And he sleeps again, dreams he is getting up and wakes to see that he has not moved, that the sun has climbed above the window ledge, is blazing through the glass onto his face. He smells bacon. There is a blanket over him. And there is a bell. He sits up, Maxine comes out of the kitchen drying her hands on a towel, and she looks at Arthur and says, "My God, that's Carol!"

He says, "Who?"

"My daughter," she says.

Arthur doesn't understand. "Well?" he says.

"God," says Maxine. "Get up."

He does what she wants, and she hurries him into the bedroom and closes the door. He waits there; he presses his ear to the cool surface of the wood, listening. Maxine says hello to her daughter. And then Arthur hears the daughter's voice. It is a pleasant voice; there is nothing hard or unfeeling about it. It is a kind, even a loving voice, concerned, a little tired, and very unhappy with worry. "Mother," she is saying, "don't you see how impossible it is, with me in Syracuse and you down here?"

"I'm sorry," Maxine says.

And Arthur hears the change in Maxine's voice.

"How can I be calm, Mother? Do you know what this is like for me?"

"I'm so sorry, dear."

Arthur puts his shirt on slowly—it is as if he has bruises on his arms and back. Maxine is talking the daughter into driving her into town. The daughter will go pull the car up. In everything the daughter says there is love, devotion. It is like musical notes in her anxious, worried voice, and Arthur wishes he could see what they are doing, how they are standing, because the image he has of them is of the daughter holding Maxine the way you would a baby. He hears the front door close, then, and Maxine comes into the bedroom and closes the door.

"I was going to give you breakfast," she whispers. "Sorry."

Arthur says nothing.

"I left bacon warming in the oven for you."

"Thanks," he says.

"That's my daughter—Carol."

"She sounds very nice," he says. Then he draws a breath and says, "Marry me."

"Sweet," she says.

He looks at her.

"I can't live on joy, Max."

She dresses fast, and when the daughter knocks on the door, she says, "I'll be right out, dear."

They listen, he and Maxine, as the daughter opens and closes the front door.

"She'll wait in the car," Maxine says.

He is tying his shoes. He says nothing. She looks out the window, holds the curtain an inch to the side and peeks out.

"You can sneak away after we go."

"They'll never take us alive," he says.

"Just please—take the whiskey and beer bottles with you. They're in the trash can under the sink."

"Did you know your daughter was coming?" he asks her.

She stares at him as if he has accused her of something.

"Did you?"

"Of course not."

"I want you to know something," he says. "I don't care if you did. Do you understand me? I don't care. I'm thankful for the good time."

"It was nice to dream awhile," she says. Then she walks over and sits next to him on the bed and kisses his cheek. At the door she dabs her eyes with a handkerchief.

"I had a good time," he says.

She smiles. "Yes."

Then she is gone. He watches out the window and sees the car, a long white Lincoln, go by, with Maxine Sandusky in the front seat staring straight ahead.

I didn't take the whiskey or the beer bottles with me, Edward. When the car drove out of sight, I just let myself out, not sneaking, either—walking straight. I walked straight, Edward. With my hands in my pockets. I whistled, like I belonged there. And went down the row to where I had parked my truck. It had started raining, I remember. I just seemed to look up and notice that it had begun to rain—this slow, warm wall of water out in the parking lot. I stood in it. I hadn't loved anybody enough and maybe I never could, Edward. But I felt all right, then, standing there in the rain. You could see the sun out beyond the road, the sun of every day of this life, like always, headed west. It was bright out there beyond the clouds.

I got in that old truck of mine and drove on home. When I pulled up in the drive, there was this boy sitting on the step at the end of the sidewalk. He was wet, like I was wet. The rain had come and gone so fast, but here this boy was, soaking wet and doing nothing about it. I said to him, You have to get in out of the rain, boy. My voice was in the bottom of my throat. It had all the experience of my whole life in it, Edward.

Not raining now, the boy said to me.

Yeah, I told him, You're a smart kid. I said, All you kids are smart. It had the knowledge of my whole damn life in it, Edward. Then I went inside and lay down on the sofa and calmed myself. I waited, calmly, for the phone to ring, or the mail to come, more rain, visitors, heartbreak, the troubles I was used to.

Edward.

"Mr. Hagood?"

It is the nurse. It is light, and he is being moved on the bed.

"Mr. Hagood."

He looks at a round, smooth, rouged face.

"You had a little episode, Mr. Hagood. Can you sit up?"

The bed is wet. He says, "Oh." Then he stiffens. Her hands are on his back, pushing, someone else is leaning over him now, two of them, and he comes to a sitting position, his feet on the cold floor. "Oh," he says. They are already pulling at the sheet, and he looks back at what he has done.

"There we are," says the nurse, lifting his arm. "We'll just get this I.V. out for a minute."

"Oh," he says. He can feel his own heart beating in his forehead, his neck. He stands. They are supporting him now, and the bed is stripped. Someone throws the pile of sheets into a canvas bin on wheels. Someone else laughs, but perhaps that is out in the hallway.

"Edward," he says.

"Just relax, now," says the nurse. "You had a little episode. We're going to have the doctor look at you."

I was talking to my friend.

"Hold still, please, Mr. Hagood."

They are all around him, and the door to the room, he sees, is open. He wants to tell them to close it, but now he is being led to the bathroom. He finds himself standing over the toilet bowl, the nurse holding his arms at his sides.

"It's going to be fine," the nurse says.

"Call me Max," says Arthur.

"Fine. Max. That's very nice—is that your nickname?"

"It's my name."

"Very nice. It's a very nice name."

"Do you know anybody named Max," he says.

"I can't say I do."

"No," Max Hagood says. "Right. You don't know anybody named Max."

25

▲

When Cakes returned that early evening, he found the woman from upstairs sitting on the ratty sofa in the downstairs parlor, her arms slack at her sides, her legs spread slightly. She wore the multicolored housecoat and a pair of furry slippers. At first he thought she was asleep, but when he stood over her, she looked at him.

"Hello."

He said, "Are you all right?"

"I couldn't make the stairs," she said.

"Can I help you?"

"I'm fine. I couldn't make those stairs. I'm fine now. I was out for a walk. It's ridiculous."

"You've been sitting here—"

"Just a while. Just sitting here thinking about the stairs." She laughed. "Could you not stand over me like that—I'm getting a crick in my neck." She patted the cushion next to her, and he sat down. As he did so, he thought about how her laugh was like a cackle. It unnerved him to have this in his mind, sitting so close to her—as if she would be able to discern it somehow.

"Well," she said, "here we are. Doesn't this remind you of the old days? You know, when a gentleman would come calling, and sit in the parlor with a young lady? All we need is a piano."

"I can help you upstairs," he said.

"I don't need any help now. I'm quite happy just to sit here."

"It's a little dusty."

"I like the padding." She shifted her weight. "Isn't it soft?"

He said it was. He didn't know how he would take his leave, now.

She said, "You conked out on me the other night."

"I'm sorry."

"I got quite a jolt today," she said, again shifting her weight. It was as if something hurt in her lower back. But she smiled, turning to him. "My grandson came to see me. Walked right in here and up those stairs and knocked on my door. I almost fell over."

"Does he live far away?"

"Miles and miles," the woman said. She was staring happily off into space now. "We had a nice talk. I fixed him a sandwich. I cut the bread into these little squares, and shaved the crust, so it was very light. A little lean ham, a little cheese and lettuce. Some mustard. He always loved to eat my sandwiches. Of course, he's on a diet now, and so I had to eat most of it. I fixed him some tea."

"How many grandchildren do you have?" Cakes asked.

"I've seven." She patted him on the knee. "How about you?"

"No," he said.

"You don't have any?"

"None."

"Oh, I'm sorry."

There was a silence.

She said, "There's four boys and three girls, and one of the girls is expecting, and you know what that means."

He stood. "Well, excuse me."

But she extended her hand, and so he wound up helping her climb the stairs. She thanked him, asked if he wouldn't like some tea.

"Some other time," he said.

"You don't really mean that, do you." She smiled.

"I certainly mean it."

"No, you're just saying that to be polite."

He couldn't look at her.

"I don't mind—"

"Why don't you tell me when—" he said. They had both spoken at the same time.

"Pardon?" she said.

"Tell me when you want me to have tea with you."

"Now." She smiled at him again. But then she put her hand on his chest. "Just kidding—you go on."

He said, "Thank you." He might have given her a slight bow, he felt so awkward, backing away from her. In his room he leaned against the door, and, abruptly, he knew he could not stand to be here just now—it seemed so dreadful; such a poor, bare little place. When he opened the door again, he was surprised to see that she had started back down the stairs.

"Going out?" she said.

He nodded.

She was standing just below him, one hand on the banister. "Where to?"

"I was going for a—walk."

"Mind if I go, too?"

"You said you were so tired—you couldn't climb the stairs."

She waved this away. "Oh, that. I'm rested now. I have a lot of energy. My son says I'm a regular dynamo."

He did not want company. Yet he couldn't find the words to evade her without being rude. "Well," he said, "if you feel up to it."

"Fine." She took his elbow as they descended. "Isn't this going to be nice?"

On the front stairs they were met by Paula, who put her hands on her hips and made a great show of looking them over. "Well, well, look at you two. You got old Baby Cakes on your arm, huh, Ida?"

"Come, Edward," Ida said.

"Great," said Paula. "Great to see it. Love to see old folks making it, I'll tell you. Makes my heart sing."

"Good evening," Ida said haughtily.

"You know he's a married man, Ida."

Edward said, "I'm a widower," and felt immediately that he had made a mistake in speaking at all. Ida's grip tightened on his elbow.

It was a long evening, and she talked through it. She was not interesting, he decided, yet she was keenly aware of whether or not she was being attended to: one couldn't simply pretend to listen. Periodically she would pause to quiz him as to where she was, and he began to see that these intermittent questionings were rather perversely aimed at the least attentive moments, those times when he was, in fact, most absent; it was intentional, it was a clear exercise of her will, and he grew more certain of this as the evening wore on. She accompanied him to the People's Café, and then through the park on a long, rambling walk; whatever had kept her from climbing the stairs was no problem now. It was more than two hours, and the whole time she talked. It was all about her wonderful grandchildren—their little sayings and do-ings—and about her son, who was stalwart and prosperous and kind, and who reminded her of her poor dead husband. Poor Howard had died of a heart attack, as so many men did. Poor Howard died happy, though, she said. He'd knocked a golf ball two hundred yards and then dropped over dead. It was the best hit of his life, and he was just ecstatic about it, according to the poor dears who were with him. He hit the ball, it sailed away and before it landed, he was dead. She went on, a garrulous, birdlike old woman, talking along as if the world wanted to know all this about her family and her life and all the small day-to-day things that, apparently, she found fascinating enough to recite: how she liked her bath water, and the three-way switch on her reading lamp; the way her father liked to read the newspaper from back to front, and how many times she stroked her hair with a brush each night. Once or twice he tried to interrupt her, to say something, anything, and the one time he was able to break through—telling her he'd stopped reading newspapers, meaning to say the obitua-ries, where everything was heart attack, heart attack, heart attack —he'd regretted it almost immediately, for it launched her into another monologue about her father and the newspapers. Her father, she said, not only read the newspapers from back to front, he also read only certain parts of it: the financial page, the sports page, the front page. She explained his reasons for these prefer-ences, and then listed the preferences of everyone else in the house, in 1919, of her girlhood. The house was in Illinois, by the Mississippi River. A beautiful place, she told him, sighing.

He had learned by now to say nothing.

But then she was asking him about himself—she wanted to know everything. Where had he come from, his family, who were his parents. He had not thought about any of these things in so many years, and he did not want to think about them, so he evaded the questions. He was vague. His parents were like everyone else's parents. This was true enough. At any rate, it was all the truth he wanted to give her.

But she persisted. "Where were they from?"

He said, "Here."

She squeezed his arm. "Something tells me you're hiding a deep, dark secret."

He was harboring no secret. "They were from Ohio. I was born in Ohio."

"What year?"

"Nineteen eleven."

"Yes. And your father?"

He gave a little frustrated sigh. "He was a banker. A bank teller. He was born in 1878. His father was a captain in the Union forces in the War Between the States."

"Oh," she said, "think of it. My grandfather was a Confederate."

He said nothing. He was exhausted.

"You come from people who live long lives."

"My father died in 1920, of the black flu epidemic."

"Oh."

"I was nine years old."

"I'm sorry."

There was nothing to say to this.

"And your mother?"

"She died in 1950. She was sixty-nine."

"What was she like?"

He thought a moment. His mother had been strong-willed, shrewd about people, rather phlegmatic. He remembered how, once, while sitting before him in the living room of the house on

Pickapple Road in Granger, Ohio, she had suddenly begun to cough up blood. She put a handkerchief to her lips, spit the blood into it, sitting there in the sun of that room, 1936, and said, "Don't worry, son, it's just this ulcer of mine. It's nothing at all to worry about."

"She was strong," he said to Ida Warren.

"I bet."

"She was, in fact, brave."

"I'm glad," Ida Warren said. "Mine wasn't, you know. Mine was just afraid of everything that moved."

He thought she would go on to tell about this woman, her mother, but she stopped and said nothing at all for, he thought, a blessed moment. Then she squeezed his arm again.

"What about your wife?"

"She died in 1953."

"Ah," she said, "That's the trouble. If you get old enough, everybody dies."

"Yes," he said.

"All your friends die. And your loved ones. Did you love your wife?"

"Not enough," he said.

"It's never enough, is it."

He guided her back to the house and faked a deep yawn that, before it was done, was real. They climbed the stairs. At his door she shook his hand vigorously and then reached up and kissed him, clumsily, on the cheek.

"I guess I talk too much," she said, smiling. She did not wait for him to answer her, and he was grateful for this. As it was, their parting was awkward. She shook his hand again and started to kiss him again; they bumped and turned and missed each other, and then she was going up the stairs to her room.

He went into his own and closed the door. Before he was quite aware of himself, he had brought the canvas bag out of the closet and was looking through the things in it again, bending over the bed, each scrap of clothing a mystery—how could she just throw things off and leave, like some creature shedding a skin?

26

▲

In the morning Ida Warren was at his door early. She had played her music all night and danced, shuffling—all night. He had been unable to sleep, he was groggy and unhappy and faintly nauseous, and he had thought her knocking might be the girl. He had been dreaming about her; and he had rushed to the door only to find Ida Warren, already talking, coming past him to stand before the photograph, one hand to her chin, studying it.

"I've been thinking about it all night. I've been going over and over it in my mind, and I'm sure I knew this person. Was she a dancer?"

"Yes," Edward said, surprised.

"I knew it. Was she ever in New Orleans?"

"No," he said. And for some reason felt a little rush of disappointment; it was almost like loss.

"You're sure of that."

"Positive."

"How about Washington, D.C."

"She never danced there."

"Where did she dance, then?"

"Here," he said.

Ida Warren shook her head. "I didn't come up here until after the war. This was before the war. Back when we dressed like that. I have a dress just like that."

"I know," Cakes said.

"Well—so where else did she dance?"

"She never danced anywhere but here."

"Well, that just can't be. I'm just certain that I knew her. Her name was Marie, right? No, not Marie."

"It was Ellen," he said after a pause.

"That's not it."

"That was her *name*," he said.

"I mean she was calling herself something else. Marie or Maggie or Marya—I can't—it's right on the tip of my tongue."

"You have the wrong person."

"Well," she said, "I could just swear." She stared at the picture, shaking her head slightly. "The spitting image. Like twins."

He said nothing.

"You must've loved her very much." She was wearing the housecoat, and now she brought a handkerchief out of one of the pockets and wiped her nose, then took a sort of gulping breath as if the air were cold and bracing. "Well, you must have my cheese omelet. You simply have to come upstairs and try it." She took him by the wrist. "Come on, it takes just a couple of minutes to make—and you can finally have some of my herb tea."

There was no denying her. He had to break her grip merely to get his door closed and locked. It was as if she hurried frantically through everything against the chance that, if she paused, even for breath, he might beg off. Finally he couldn't: he didn't have the heart to: she was so frenetic, so anxious to please him. She sat him down on her red velvet sofa and put Paul Whiteman on the phonograph, then began to prepare the breakfast, talking all the while. One of her grandchildren had speculated once that it took a Chinaman hours to eat a bowl of rice; the poor dear had pictured those people picking up one grain at a time with the chopsticks. She asked Edward if he had ever eaten with chopsticks, and as he said he had, she asked if he liked bacon mixed in with the cheese and egg, and before he could answer that question, she went on about how her father had liked his crushed fine, like the bacon bits they made for salads.

"He was a fine man," she said. "My father. Very precise about things—always kept his watch handy, and he'd take it out of his pocket and look at it. Like a—like a nervous tic or something. I used to love to watch him shave in the morning."

The record ended, and she put on another. She brought out a photograph album and set it in his lap. In it were pictures of her mother—a woman of strange, soft, sad features, who stared won-

deringly out at some studio photographer or other—and her father, whose face was obscured by a walrus mustache and thick
glasses, but who wore a tight white collar and a vest with a watch
chain. There were Polaroid shots of a woman with wiry gray hair
and a hard, faintly alcoholic face, with apparently her children,
two in their late teens, one with, apparently, a child of her own.
"My youngest sister," Ida said. "I haven't seen her in almost five
years. She lives in Florida. Sends these pictures, you know."

The sister smiled from some affluent living room. Her children looked happy, if slightly dull—perhaps bored. There was
something quite lost about the sister's eyes, he thought.

Ida turned the page. "My boy," she said.

The son, who was bald and very paunchy, was evidently fanatical about his automobile and his camper: in numerous photographs he and the grandson were shown polishing or working on
one vehicle or the other. In one shot they all stood—the son, *his*
four boys and three girls, the son's wife, whose eyes had something of the forlorn look of Ida's mother—all of them, arm in
arm, in front of the camper; there were fleecy clouds in a rich blue
sky behind them.

"This is the house," Ida Warren said, and put her finger on a
picture of the same group of people standing before a large colo-
nial brick house in a treeless yard. Behind them was the same blue
sky, it seemed, the same fleecy clouds, but they were all wearing
different clothing. Ida pointed to one of them, a tall boy, long-
faced, with unruly hair, and lanky, big-boned limbs. "That's the
one who came to see me yesterday."

"Nice-looking boy," Cakes said.

"They all want me to come live with them," said Ida, "but I
told them I'd rather have my own place."

He thought to ask where she had lived before, but he didn't
have to: she was already telling him, moving across the room to
continue preparing breakfast, talking about her Aunt Ruth, who
was really only a year older than she was; how the two of them
had lived together in a condo in the heart of the city, not far at all
from the theaters and the good restaurants. But Aunt Ruth became ill and had to be hospitalized, and so Ida had been forced to

leave the condo and look for another place. She had promised herself she would not take her son up on the offer of a room in his house.

The breakfast was light and surprisingly good, considering that her attention had never quite been on it. She had so much to tell him. She would ask him to remind her sometime to tell him a thing, and then she would go on and tell it; this happened over and over. And when the food was gone, the last of the herb tea drunk, when the polite cigarette was smoked and the table cleared, she kept right on talking, still eyeing him, still making certain of his wandering attention, still calling it back—the morning passed this way.

"Well," he said at last.

She did not even pause, did not even hear him.

"Well." He cleared his throat.

She said, "Ah."

He thanked her for the fine breakfast, excused himself and, before she could begin again, made his escape. But she followed him. She came down and knocked once, lightly on his door, and when he opened it, she came around him into the room, begging his pardon, almost suppliant, her hands clasped near her mouth. She just needed to keep talking a while, because it was a little lonely upstairs. She sat at his table and ran the palm of one hand over the surface as if to smooth it out, or dust it. He went to his bed and lay down.

"Please forgive me," she said.

"There's nothing to forgive," he answered.

"You're a very kind gentleman," she said.

"Thank you."

"I know if you have somewhere to go—"

"Not really," he said.

Then they were quiet. She moved in the chair, and the wood made a small, muted cracking sound.

"You really are very kind," she said.

He was waiting for her to begin to talk again, begin another storm of words; he would simply lie very still and listen to it, and then he would go to sleep.

"Did the young—did your young friend go away?" she asked.

"I still have her things."

"You've been very patient to listen to me."

"Thank you."

"Is your young friend coming back?"

"No."

"I should mind my own business—but, you know. In a small building like this everybody knows everybody else's business."

Presently she said, "Seems strange."

"What seems strange?"

"That she would leave her things."

"Yes," he said, "I thought it was strange."

A moment later she said, "I have a dress just like that."

"I know. I saw it."

"You know what I think sometimes?" she asked. "I think somewhere in space, maybe, on some other planet, there's another bunch of humans, except they don't get old and die, and when they find out about us, you know, about this—world, they're appalled. They probably would not be able to see how we do it."

"Do what," he said.

"Get through."

"Get old and die?"

"Just—get through. Get on—from day to day."

He was silent.

"What's your fondest memory?"

"I never really thought about it," he lied.

"Mine is kind of silly. It's a summer night, and I'm—oh, twenty-four. It's July, and hot, and there's a breeze beginning to get up, and I'm standing on a porch, looking out over a cornfield. I'm married, and my husband and I rent this house across from a cornfield. And there I am, watching it get dark, and suddenly I'm aware that I've never been happier in my life." She sat there, lightly caressing the double folds of skin below her neck. "A little music playing on a scratchy old RCA in the house behind me. I love summer, you know. A summer night is just—is something so —special."

"I like winter," he said.

"Oh, I do too."

"The first snow," he said. "I always liked the first snow."

"Oh, I'd want it to snow so deep we didn't even want to burrow out. I loved the deep snow when everyone stayed inside."

"Yes," he said.

"You know what I do, sometimes?" she said. "I dress up—you know, and dance. I put the old music on and—and—" She seemed momentarily confused. "Well, of course. You've heard the music. I know I play it too loud."

"No harm done," he said. He could not keep the weariness out of his voice.

"You're such a quiet man," she said. "I never got a word in edgewise with Howard, or those children of mine."

"How many children did you have?" he asked.

"Why, I had four. I thought I told you that."

"I don't believe you did."

"I didn't, I guess."

"Where are they?" he asked.

She seemed distracted. "Mmmm?"

"Where are they?"

"All over."

He waited, but she said no more.

"Where?" he said.

"Oh—Michigan. Texas. Iowa."

"I had one son," he said. "I lost him in Korea."

"I'm so sorry."

"It was a long time ago."

"Isn't this an appalling place?" she said.

"It's just a room."

"No, I mean this—the world."

He was silent.

"Mr. Cakes," she said, "why don't you tell me about yourself?"

"I'm tired," he said.

"Do you want to sleep?"

"Yes."

She was quiet.

He lay with his eyes closed, listening for her, waiting for her to get up and go out of the room; but there was no sound at all, not even of breathing, or of the rustling of clothing, and he thought he might have slept.

She was sitting there staring at him. "Would you like some herb tea?" she said.

They spent the day together—or, rather, she hung onto him through the day. They went to the library, and to the People's Café for lunch, and in the afternoon they watched a movie on his television. It was an old movie, and she spoke to the characters in it as though they could hear her. "Bless your heart," she said as a cowboy tried unsuccessfully to stay astride a bucking horse. "You're trying so hard." He turned the volume up.

"Bless your heart," she said to the shifting figures on the screen.

When the movie ended, he got up and turned the television off.

"What shall we do for dinner?" she said.

"I have an appointment."

"Oh."

He thought she would get up to leave. She had shifted her weight forward, fumbling with the folds of her dress where it bunched in her thin lap, seeming to gather herself. But then she stopped, sat there with her hands tightly folded over her knees, and began to cry. "Look at me," she said, "I swear I have no idea why I'm doing this. Do you have a napkin by any chance?"

He was astonished. He got her a Kleenex, stood at his window and looked out at the street while she sniffled and blew her nose behind him.

"It gets so a person can't control her emotions anymore."

He said nothing. Outside it was clouding over and a raw wind was blowing the bare branches of the trees that lined the street. He wished she would go now; it would be an awful embarrassment to have to turn and look at her.

"Well." She sniffled again. "You'd think I just lost my best friend or something."

"What about your grandson," he said as evenly as he could.

"Yes. I certainly want you to meet him." She hadn't moved, was still sitting there with her weight shifted forward as if she were about to rise, the hands folded so tightly the color had left them.

"When is your grandson coming to see you again?" he said.

"Oh, yes." She was crying. "Won't that be wonderful."

He told her about Arthur on the way over to the Homestead. By now it seemed almost natural that she would be with him, and that he would be in this state of agitated, half-blind exhaustion. The walk to the Homestead had never seemed so long to him. Ida Warren talked about the nice walk and the chill in the air and how the leaves were all gone from the trees. How all her life she never seemed to see the leaves begin to go: each fall it seemed to happen in secret, once they turned colors. You looked up and they were gone. She went on talking, she was impressed to learn that Arthur had been a teacher—and then she was saying something about the high schools, and Cakes lost the thread; he kept nodding, pretending to listen, even trying to. She had been with Howard almost fifty years. She never got used to something. Too many people in the same house. They were younger, lives of their own. The phrases reached him as if through static, and he couldn't connect them. Finally she was telling him about how her grandson had come to see her, how her grandson had walked up the stairs and knocked on her door, and how she fixed him some sandwiches and tea. "He took me shopping," she said.

When they arrived at the Homestead, she slowed, hesitated in the doorway.

"Are you sure he won't mind having me come barging in?"

"He won't mind."

"Are you tired?" she said. "You seem tired."

"I'm fine."

"I won't make him uneasy, will I? I don't want to make him uneasy."

"You won't make him uneasy."

"Are you sure?"

"I'm sure."

"Are you all right?"

"I'm fine."

"You seem tired."

As they were getting on the elevator she said, "I hate elevators. Much as I hate stairs, I hate elevators more."

"They scare you."

"They terrify me." She reached for his hand, clasped it tight. "Absolutely terrify me."

A moment later she said, "How old did you say he was?"

Edward told her.

"My, my."

The elevator climbed, and they were quiet until it stopped. "Made it," she said, starting out before the doors quite opened. She had let go of Edward's hand—but then, as they stepped across the little open space between the elevator and the floor, she reached for him again. "I'm always afraid I'll fall through somehow."

In the corridor she paused, looking at him. "You know, you ought to take vitamin C. It'll do wonders for you. Give you all sorts of energy. I take one vitamin C tablet every morning."

"This way," Cakes said, leading her toward Arthur's room.

Arthur was sitting up in his bed, still hooked to an I.V. The cover sheet was tight against his chest, and Edward Cakes looked at the blue place on the back of his hand where the needle was.

"Arthur," he said.

"You're the only one who can call me *Max,*" Arthur said.

Edward nodded. "Max, this is Ida Warren."

"Sit down." Arthur lifted his free hand to indicate the chairs on the other side of the room.

Cakes pulled them up close to the bed, stood behind the one as Ida Warren settled into it, then took the other. For an awkward few seconds no one said anything. Cakes cleared his throat.

"Ida lives in your old room, Max."

"It was a lovely day," Arthur said.

"Did you go out today?"

"I looked out the window."

"Edward tells me you're his oldest and dearest friend," Ida said.

"You're not so young," said Arthur. He looked at Cakes. "You said she was a young girl."

Ida laughed nervously. "I'm no spring chicken."

"Ida lives upstairs in your old room, Max."

"Oh," said Arthur.

"So," Cakes said after a pause, "how do you feel?"

"I feel okay."

"Good," Ida Warren said.

Arthur looked at her. "To tell you the truth, I'm a little sick."

"You—you want us to leave you alone?" Cakes said.

"I'm okay. Stay a while."

"We'll stay as long as you want," Ida said.

Arthur now seemed to study Cakes. "Did you tell her I was your dearest friend?"

"He sure did," said Ida. "Isn't friendship a wonderful thing?"

Arthur nodded. "Friendship is a wonderful thing."

"That's what I always said."

"It's true."

"It certainly is."

"It's a goddamn cliché, but it's true."

Ida put her hand over her mouth and laughed.

"You live in my old room, huh," Arthur said to her.

"Yes, sir. That I do."

"I wish I lived there with you."

"Why, Mr. Hagood, that's scandalous." Ida laughed again.

"You bet," Arthur said. "You bet."

There was a pause, then. Ida was composing herself. Cakes cleared his throat, shifted his weight in the chair.

"I couldn't get up the stairs anymore," Arthur said.

"I had that same problem recently, didn't I, Edward?"

"She did," Cakes said.

"I'm tired," said Arthur. "It was a lovely day today."

"Beautiful," Ida said.

"I'm sorry. I should have been a better host."

"You were wonderful."

"Maybe you'll come back tomorrow."

"I think that would be wonderful."

Arthur looked at Cakes. "I thought she was a young girl."

"This is Ida," Cakes said, "from your old room."

"The one with the music."

"That's me," Ida said.

"You like to dance," said Arthur.

"Well I—I guess I do, yes." She looked at Cakes, then at her hands.

"I used to like to dance," Arthur went on. "I was never any good at it."

"I bet you were wonderful at it."

"No."

"You're being modest, I'll bet."

"I'm too sick to be modest."

Cakes said, "We'd better let you get some rest," then started to stand.

"Don't leave."

"We don't want to tire you out," Ida said.

"What's your name again?" Arthur asked her.

"I'm Ida."

"I never liked that name."

"You know," Ida said, "I never did either."

Arthur turned his gaze to Cakes. "She has a sense of humor."

"At your service," Ida said.

"Cakes here, he's got no sense of humor."

"Oh, he's all right, though, don't you think?"

"Isn't that right, Cakes. You have no sense of humor."

"Edward tells me you'll be ninety," Ida said.

"Ninety. Yes. How old are you?"

"Never ask a lady her age. Anyway, I'm much too old."

"You have a nice way about you," Arthur said.

"Why, thank you, sir." Ida was pleased. "You know I was very nervous about coming to see you."

"Maybe you'll come back tomorrow."

"I'd love to," she said. And then she began to tell Arthur about how her grandson had come walking up to knock on her door. Cakes, having heard it all twice before, sat gazing at his friend's face. The skin was surprisingly gray. The bones of the skull were visible above the old eyes. It struck Cakes with a strange jolt that his friend was skin draped on bone, and he looked away, tried to find something to concentrate on in the shadows by the bedstand.

"Maybe you'll come back tomorrow," Arthur said suddenly, and it was a moment before Cakes realized that this had been an interruption—that his friend had broken into Ida Warren's talk. There was silence now, and the silence was quickly becoming awkward.

"Well," he said, "we'll let you get some rest."

"I'm sorry," Ida said. "Running my mouth like that. Sometimes I don't believe myself."

"Don't go," said Arthur.

". . . never know when to shut up," Ida was saying.

There was another pause. When the nurse came in to take Arthur's temperature, it was as if they had all been waiting for her to arrive. She was new, apparently, and took great care not to get in anyone's way. Arthur asked her if she was a married lady, and she said in a mild Slavic accent, "Yes, I am very happy married lady."

"Where are you from?" Arthur asked her.

"Czechoslovakia."

"How long have you been here?"

"Nineteen sixty-eight I come here. My husband, he is American boy."

"Do I have fever?"

She studied the thermometer, which was one of the new electronic ones. "Yes. A little."

"I'm dying."

They were all quiet.

"Make love to me before I die," Arthur said, smiling.

The nurse laughed, and then they were all laughing; it was not very loud or hysterical but there was, nevertheless, something helpless about it. The nurse patted Arthur's forehead, nodded at the others and went out, still laughing.

"You never change," Cakes said to his friend.

"Maybe you'll come back tomorrow."

Again, they were quiet.

"Hello," Arthur said to Ida. "I don't remember your name again."

She told him.

"That's a good strong name."

"I always liked it," Ida said.

"Very good name."

"Thank you, sir."

"I think I'll go to sleep now."

"Maybe we'll come back tomorrow," Ida said.

In the elevator, she took Edward's hand again, and when they stepped out into the first-floor corridor, she still held onto him. She did not let go until they had traversed the shining, empty lobby, and were out in the slow drizzle that had begun. It was past sunset.

"We're going to get rained on," she said.

"Do you want me to call a cab?"

"Heavens, no."

They walked down the street, and she hooked her arm in his.

"I think your friend is wonderful."

He thanked her. It felt odd, thanking her like that, and he thought he should say something else, but nothing came.

"I talked too much, didn't I."

"No," he said.

"Yes, I did. I started right in. I'd no more than been introduced and I started right in."

"You shouldn't worry so much about it."

"It's my worst fault. I swear I open my mouth and it's like a flood. I can't talk it all out fast enough, and the whole time I'm worried that I'm boring people."

"It's silly to worry about such a thing."

The rain came harder now, and they sought shelter in the grotto-like entranceway to a clothing store. It was closed, the windows all dark.

"What time is it?" she asked.

Cakes looked at his watch, but couldn't read it for the bad light. When a car went by in the wet street, he turned and held the watch into the gliding-by of the headlights. "Almost seven o'clock."

"I'll make you a wonderful dinner."

"We'll see," he said.

"We'll listen to music. I have the complete everything, you know."

He thought of sitting on her sofa with the photographs. "Let's just eat at the café, why don't we."

"I don't mind cooking for you—it'll be fun."

The rain was coming very hard now, like a summer shower, except the little gusts of wind that swept it this way and that were winter-cold. Edward turned his collar up, and as she edged closer to his side, her shoulders hunched, her arms folded tight over her chest, he put his arm around her.

"Cold," she said.

He felt trapped—and yet, standing there huddled with her against the chill, it was as if the world out in the rain dissolved, emptied of everything but himself and herself. He looked at her face in profile, bowing into the hollow of his shoulder, and his heart ached.

"It doesn't look like it's going to stop," she said.

"No."

Another moment passed.

"I used to like to window shop," she said. "Especially around Christmas." She had turned slightly and was looking at the display in the window: four mannequins in the poses of happiness and certainty, graceful as dancers, wearing the fall fashions.

"When I was a girl," Ida Warren said, "I wanted to wear the latest fashions."

They were both looking at the mannequins now. Another car went by and showed them their own reflection on the glass.

"My father was very strict, though. Very religious—he thought most things new were sinful, poor dear."

"It's slackening up," Cakes said about the rain.

"I know," she answered. "Everything is. I used to be religious, too, you know. Trouble was, I was too scrupulous. I could never rest. I mean everything I did felt like a sin of some kind or other. So one day I just shed it all, like a skin."

They watched a cab go by.

"What about you?" she said.

"I never gave it much thought."

"Do you think there's an afterlife?"

"No."

"Sometimes I think there is," she said. "Mostly I hope so."

The rain had stopped, though the wind was still blowing it out of the trees of the park and off the tall eaves above them.

"I like to tell my grandchildren about my father," she said.

"What do you tell them?"

"Oh—little things. You know, how he was. The way he dressed. Some of the things he said—things like that."

A moment later she said, "They don't come to see me. I haven't seen them in a long time." She might've laughed, he couldn't tell. "I keep inviting them. They don't like to be reminded, you know."

"Shall we go?" Cakes said.

They ate in her room. She played more records for him, and she began to tell him, yet again, how her grandson had come to see her. Again, he pretended to be hearing it for the first time. And when she got the photo album out, he looked at all the pictures with the same polite interest that he had shown earlier.

"Well," she said finally, "I really am tired." She yawned and stretched, sitting next to him on the red velvet sofa. "Now I think it's time I said good night to my gentleman caller." She reached over and lightly pinched his chin, and then kissed him, softly, on the cheek. "You're such a kind man," she said, "to be humoring an old lady like me."

"Don't talk like that."

Her eyes widened; she was suddenly very excited. "You know what I have? I want to show you—close your eyes."

"I'm afraid I'd go to sleep, Ida. I'm so tired."

"Well—it's a dress. Just like the one in your picture of your wife."

"I know," he said.

"I'll have to wear it sometime." Her eyes were so bright and happy and simple. She squeezed his hand. "I'm so happy I got the chance to be with you today, Edward."

He stood, held her hands in his own. "Ida," he said, "I have enjoyed this day." As he spoke, he realized that in an odd, almost exasperating way it was true. She kissed him on the cheek and said he was her gentleman caller again, moving with him to her door. He went downstairs in the dark, let himself into his room and shuffled to his bed and lay down. He hadn't even bothered to close the door. It was very quiet. He was meaning to get up and close himself in and perhaps take a bath—wash the grime of the city from his face and neck, as his father used to tell him to do— and having remembered this, he had a brief dream that he was a boy again, in the room of the house he had grown up in until his father's death. He was in that room, lying on the bed, facing the wall, and he knew if he turned, he would see his father. He lay very still, half in, half out of this dream, and his father groaned, "Oh, God," and in the dream he knew that he should turn, should move, show his father that he was awake. He should sit up and say it's all right, it's going to be all right, and then he knew that it was all long, long ago—that nothing like this dream had ever happened, he hadn't even really known his father, and abruptly the person groaning was Ellen. He recognized her. He came out of the bed and faced her, and she turned and went out, walking slow, as in some sort of solemn procession, her head bowed, her hands at her sides; he followed, she was a ghost descending the stairs, and he awoke on the landing, sitting on the top step, his head in his hands. The dream had been so vivid and he had been so unaware of it as a dream that he shook for a long time, sitting there, and when he tried to rise, he could not do so right away; something caught in his back, his legs went away. He leaned against the wall and trembled, hearing the night sounds the house made, fearing that someone, Paula or Denise or Ida Warren or Mrs. Blackemore, would find him like this, without legs. But he was asleep. He began to know it, turned in the bed, looked at the long paleness of the open door and the faint strand of light at the bottom of the nurses' door. He got up, walked over to his own door and closed it. In the dark he made his way back to the bed, let himself down, slow, hearing, now, Ida Warren's music begin. He lay back, stared at the ceiling and wondered if he had made any noise in his nightmare.

27

▲

Early the next afternoon he heard Ida Warren's voice on the stairs, and stood stock still. She went by his door, talking, and from his window he watched her go down the sidewalk, arm in arm with a young man in a denim jacket and jeans. When they were out of sight, he sat in his chair and thought about his dream of the night before. The house was empty, Denise and Paula having left for their morning shift hours ago. He gazed at the picture on the wall. Once, during a picnic in another park, another part of the city, Ellen had smiled coquettishly at him and said, "It's the ugly people who make up all the rules for the rest of us." It was when she was still the girl of the photograph. She sat with a bright yellow dress spread around her, like a flower blossoming upside down, she said, and then she laughed, mused and came out with the phrase about ugly people making the rules.

"How do you mean?" he said.

"Bent people," she answered. "People without any loveliness."

They laughed. They were lovely; they sat in the dappled grass under a willow on a Sunday afternoon in summer, freshly married.

And there was no use thinking such things.

She would say out whatever notion her mind presented and then would look at it—you could almost see her face change as if it were in the air before her eyes—and if it pleased her, she would laugh. And then her mind would fly to something else. But no, he thought. She was not like that at all. She worried incessantly, was always brooding over something too far down for him to reach. He had never really known her at all; she had somehow never been what he needed most deeply—and once again the room, his lone place by the window, the whole pattern of his life, appalled him.

He went out, wandered over to the park and watched a group of boys playing touch football. It was another balmy day, with soft autumnal sighings of wind, and the skinny branches of the maples that flanked the pond made crossing shadows on the grass. He walked on, past the pond. What had he done with his time? What had his days been?

At one corner he stopped and bought a hot dog. Somewhere there was a fire, and the big engines roared by in the street. He made his way back to the People's Café, but saw in the window that Ida Warren was there, with the boy in the denim jacket. So he went back to the room, realizing as he climbed the stairs that he had talked himself into believing that the girl might be there. He did not even go in, but stopped when he had come partway up the stairs—when he could see that the landing was empty.

He would go visit Arthur.

He was all right, there was no reason for him to do anything in particular; it was just that he did not feel like reading or watching television or talking to Ida Warren and her grandson. He did not particularly feel like talking to Arthur, either, but it was better than staying in the room on such a day. He walked over to the home, took the elevator up to Arthur's floor, walked down the hall to his room, concentrating simply on the fact that he was coming to visit his old friend, and when he came to Arthur's room, he was astonished to discover that someone else was there —a man, any age past seventy, with a small, round face and round eyes, wearing a visor cap and sitting at a table on which some sort of gadgetry had been laid out.

"Look," the man said. "Lookee. Want to see something?"

"This is Arthur Hagood's room?" Cakes said.

The man had turned to the table. "Listen. Forty years ago."

The gadgetry, Cakes saw now, was a telegraph key. The small man tapped out something on it, and in a moment an answer came back. The man wrote it down.

"Whoopee. See?"

What he had written was illegible, but Cakes pretended to have understood it anyway, backing away from him.

"Just like New Haven," the little man said, "don't you think?"

Down the hall Cakes found the nurse with the strange eyeteeth, and she told him that Arthur Hagood had been moved downstairs, her voice taking on a quality of restraint and pity that magnified and made ominous the meaning of the word *downstairs*.

"Downstairs," Cakes said. "Where downstairs? What do you mean, 'downstairs'?"

"The first floor, where—he's very sick."

"Please, I'm his only friend in the world."

She told him the room number, and he made his way down to the lobby and moved through doctors and nurses to the corridor where Arthur would be—it was darker here, and more quiet, and the doors to the rooms were open. He saw a woman lying on her side, exposed, the front of her gray, institutional gown having come open; there was a terrible lump on the side of her face. In another room a man sat staring at his own hands in his lap while a nurse bathed his back. Arthur was asleep. He lay in a tight fold of the bed sheet and blankets, his face sagging into his neck. Edward touched his shoulder, felt the bone there, and Arthur looked at him. "Oh. It's you."

"If you want to sleep, I can come back later," Cakes said.

"Come back later." The eyes closed.

He stood there for a moment.

"Later," Arthur said.

Outside, it was growing cold. As he went down the street, a blown leaf settled between his collar and his neck with the suddenness of an attack. He tore at it furiously, thinking it was something alive, and then he stood breathing, leaning against the plate glass window of a men's clothing store while people walked by him, gazing at him with the rude curiosity of passers-by when someone in their way gyrates crazily, then stands shaking, in midday, as if he has seen a ghost. He went on, finally, staying close to the buildings, out of the wind. Before he had left the hospital, he had asked at the nurse's station about Arthur's condition; the woman there, a kindly, middle-aged volunteer, said, puzzled, "Why, his great age. He's eighty-nine, you know."

"Will he—will he be all right, though?" Cakes asked.

The woman looked at him.

Now he did not go through the park, but went around, keeping to the sidewalks, and at the People's Café he looked in the window and saw that Ida Warren had gone. He went in and ordered a bowl of soup but couldn't eat it. There were three other people in the place—two men and a woman. They sat laughing and talking in a booth; they were satisfied with each other and with everything. You could see it in their faces. They had forgiven each other of everything for now.

"Arthur," he murmured, "not now."

"Anything else?" the waitress said to him. She was new and did not know him.

Outside again, in the growing cold, he headed himself in the direction of the home. The wind blew, and he held his coat collar tight at his neck. When he drew near to the building, he slowed and began to think of scurrying away, hiding in his room. But he went in and walked down the corridor with the open doors to Arthur's new room. Arthur was still asleep.

"Max?"

Nothing.

Cakes touched his shoulder. "Max?"

The eyes opened. "They'll never take us alive, Edward."

"How do you feel?" Cakes asked.

"Sleepy."

"Do you hurt?"

"No."

"Do you want to talk a while?"

"Not now." Arthur was breathing the words out in shallow breaths.

"Do you want some whiskey?" Cakes whispered in his ear.

Arthur smiled. "Go home now."

"I'll be back tomorrow," Cakes said.

He did not go home. Instead, he walked down the street, came to a theater, paid for a ticket and entered, not thinking. He sat in back. He didn't care what movie was playing. The theater was a place to be: lives separate from him and orderly as a story. The movie was about a young couple struggling through college together. He slept through most of the complications—or drifted, really, like falling off something and then waking in horror—and came fully awake in time to see them, resplendent in graduation robes, embracing before a podium of some kind while others, in the same robes, applauded, and a scowling, heavy-jawed man looked on, grudgingly approving. The film ended. Edward Cakes sat waiting for the credits to run through, but the projector was abruptly shut off and the music garbled to a stop. The five or six other people in the theater had already left. He went out into the street and stood there looking at the buildings in either direction, all dark, quiet. He had never felt so alone. Yet there was this unfathomable resistance in him, like a wall, to the thought of going back to the room. He took the long way, around the park, and the cold bit at him, the circulation in his thighs began to falter, to feel like the beginning of frostbite.

At last he had arrived; he was standing on the sidewalk. There was nothing to do but climb the stairs, go in. Waiting for him on the sofa in the parlor was Ida Warren. She had been sitting there dozing with a magazine in her lap. She sat up, yawning, and said, "It's very late."

"Yes," he said, "and I'm very tired."

"I couldn't climb the stairs again."

"I'll help you, but then I really have to go to bed."

She didn't move. "I have terrific news. My grandson actually came to visit today. I had a wonderful afternoon."

"Yes."

"He took me to lunch. We went to an art gallery in town, and then we went browsing in the bookstores. He loves books." She went on to talk about his dream of being an actor, and how good his memory was, and what interesting stories he had to tell about all the people he knew who were struggling to be actors. She supposed that she was a little in love with the boy, if such a thing were possible. Sometime soon she wanted to take Edward Cakes with them on one of their jaunts downtown.

He was depleted; he couldn't even bring himself to be rude and walk away. He just stood there and took it, and it was she who helped him up the stairs. He was at his door, one hand on the knob, and she held his wrists.

"I was wondering if you wouldn't like some tea."

"No," he said.

"Well, some other time then."

He said nothing.

She sighed. "Ahh. What a happy day this was. I feel wonderful."

"Good night," he said.

In the room he turned the television on and felt relieved, hidden from her and from everything. He sat in the chair and lost himself in something about the sea. And then she was at the door. He knew it was her from the quick, somehow pert way she knocked.

"Oh, look," he said, "go away."

There was a pause, and the knocking continued.

He cursed, got to his feet, padded to the door. He only opened it a crack and glared out at her. "What?"

"I'm bothering you," she said. But she edged past him, anyway. "I can't hear my records. I guess I could watch with you." She put her hands up to her mouth as if to stifle a yawn, and looked at the television. "It's a nice picture, isn't it."

"You can't hear your records," he said. The television was not loud.

"Well, it's okay," she said. "I'll just watch TV."

"I'll turn it down. You can listen to your records."

"No, really."

"If you don't mind—" he began.

She turned to look at the photograph. "I swear I know this person." Before he could speak, she went on. "You know what let's do? Let's have a party. You know, I've got a dress that you'd swear was this same one—" She had taken his hands and was moving with him toward the door. "Come on," she said, "we'll have a party. All of us."

"Look." He stopped her, pulled his hands from her grasp.

"Well, all right. I suppose if we just watch television."

"What's the matter with you?" said Cakes. "Can't you see I don't want you here now?"

She looked away from him. "I—I had such a happy day, today."

"Why don't you go upstairs," he said. "The day's over. People need a little privacy."

She said nothing, stared at something beyond him, nodding slightly. Her eyes were large and shining and there were pouches of skin beneath them; she was never attractive, he saw. She had always been a little dowdy. One wisp of metal-colored hair lay across the black curls, so carefully arranged, above one ear. "You know"—she looked at him now—"I really am tired. I think I'll just go on upstairs."

"Why don't you do that," he said.

Her eyes narrowed slightly, and her chin came up. "You're such a lonely man."

This angered him, as if he were an object of someone like Ida Warren's pity. "I can stand it," he said, "if you can."

"Me," she said.

He went to the door and held it open.

"I felt sorry for you," she said.

"You felt sorry for *me?*"

"Yes. You don't have anyone."

"You're sorry for me."

She nodded almost proudly. "I am loved. I have that."

"Well," he said, near rage now, "you can forget any sorrow for me. At least I keep to myself. At least I'm not dancing around all night to a lot of old records. I don't have to talk five hundred miles an hour like some fool kid whistling in the dark—"

She walked by him and out into the hallway. "You know what's the matter with you?" she said, beginning to cry. "You don't—you don't like people. You don't have any feeling for them. You're a bitter, unkind old—you don't deserve my friendship."

He slammed the door, went over to the chair and sat in front of the television, trembling with anger, and with the old agitation that any confrontation produced in him. He watched the television—a man talking about battleships. There was the sound of movement in the hall, a knocking on the nurse's door, and then, after a long interval, on his own. It was Ida Warren, of course. She stood before him in an attitude of miserable anger and embarrassment, and mumbled something at him.

"What is it now," he said.

"I—I can't get up the stairs." She sobbed. "God—damn you. I can't get up the stairs, can't lift my leg high enough."

He helped her. She leaned heavily on his arm. They tottered in her doorway, and he walked her over to her bed, where she sat down, then lay back. "You're going to have to get a first-floor apartment," he said.

She lay staring at the ceiling.

"You'll have to get your family to find you something better."

"I'm afraid," she said. It was as if she were speaking to something in the rucked plaster of the ceiling. "Why can't I climb a simple flight of stairs. I can walk miles. I walk all the time, everywhere. But I get on stairs and I can't lift my leg high enough. It just won't go. What—what am I going to do?"

"They'll have to find you a first-floor apartment."

"It's like I can't breathe sometimes. Can't move at all."

"Get a first-floor. No stairs."

She lay quiet for a few moments. He thought she might be going to sleep; but then she moved, looked at him. "I'm empty."

"What?" he said.

"I feel like a shell—nothing but air inside."

"You're just a bit light-headed."

After a pause she said, "You were right. About the—that—the dancing. The talk. I'm sort of doing just what you said I was doing—you know, whistling in the dark. I have a little friend who comes with me no matter where I go. He's here now, in this room, waiting. I call him Romulus and Remus. I know it's two names, but that's his name—that's the name I gave him." She sat up, sagged there, sighing, gazing at him, mouth open, hands moving nervously at her sides as if she were trying to find the edges, worried about falling off. "I'm scared." She sobbed.

"Tell me," he said. "Talk about it. Who's Romulus and Remus?"

She was almost panting now, out of breath, gripping the sheet on either side of her, rocking slightly. Her legs weren't long enough for her feet to touch the floor. "Oh, Romulus and Remus is very bad. He's got very bad old scary eyes and two heads and he's—he's just very bad. Very cold and damp and bad."

"You made him up."

"He's got two very hungry heads. Very ugly." She sniffled and touched her nose with the blue back of her hand. "My father always taught me it was good to make—to use your imagination and make a thing, a specific thing out of whatever you were afraid of. They say it's the sign of a survivor, you know. To give names and personalities to such things. Do you think it's the sign of a survivor?"

"I wouldn't know," Cakes said.

"Do you have something like—like Romulus and Remus?"

"I don't think so."

"Are you scared all the time, like me?"

He muttered, "Sometimes I get scared—sure."

"What's it like—when you get scared?"

"I guess it's pretty much the same for everybody."

"Bad and cold and damp?"

He nodded. "Clammy."

"Yes," she said, and put both hands under her heart. "Right here?"

He was uncomfortable. "I guess. I don't know."

"Clutchy, kind of."

"Sure."

"You don't like to talk about it."

"No," he said.

"What do you do for it?"

"I read. Take a walk, maybe."

"Nothing much works."

"A little whiskey, sometimes."

"But nothing much really works."

"Everything works," he said, "nothing works." He had not meant to be gruff, but her insistence had annoyed him all over again. "What's the difference. I keep busy, that's all." He had tried to say this more gently, but it had come out the same.

"Do you ever talk about it with anybody?" she asked.

He shook his head.

"I wish I could be more like my father was."

Cakes said nothing.

"I wish I could think there's something out there, you know. Not just—space." She brought a handkerchief from her sleeve and wiped her eyes, her nose.

"Maybe there is something out there," he said.

"Yes," she said, "sometimes I think maybe there is."

There was a pause. Cakes realized that the door was still open; he heard Paula and Denise coming in from somewhere, talking and laughing.

"Why don't you stay with your family?" he said.

She nodded at him. "Yes—why don't I."

"Well, why don't you?"

"I have, off and on. The truth is, I have. With one or the other, here and there." She smiled at him and looked down into her lap. "You see—they all—they love me very much, they're always glad to see me. But—living—you know, day to day. The trouble is, I talk too much. I know that. I get going and—and I don't know when to stop." Her face tightened, the lips drawing down; he looked away. "So they send an ambassador over now and then"—she sobbed again—"just to be sure I'm getting along okay. They love me. My—my grandson took me to lunch today, and downtown. I felt so sorry for him, you know, trying to figure out what to say to me."

"Well," Cakes said. There was nothing he could think of to tell her.

She went on. "I guess that's why I talk like I do. I mean I can't imagine what anyone could find to say to me. I'm afraid of —pauses, you see. Pauses frighten me."

He now felt the pressure to speak, and for a moment he stammered, tried to muster an apology, sympathy, anything.

She said, "Really, it's not so awful now. I'm better now." There were tears in the pouchy hollows under her eyes.

"I never wanted to hurt your feelings," he said at last.

"It was just a little misunderstanding."

As he moved toward the open door, she said, "Would you like some tea?" She had stood, was wiping her eyes.

"Perhaps another time," he said.

"I make it very mild."

"How about tomorrow morning."

"We're friends?"

He said, "Really, Ida. Tomorrow will be fine."

"Of course," she said. "Well, good night," and she brushed the corners of her eyes.

28
▲

He considered that he had paid for his firmness with her in the sleeplessness of that night. He felt awful. She did not play her music and the quiet was like an accusation. In the morning, at the knock on his door, he resolved to be more kind, though as he moved to answer it he couldn't help seeing himself in scenes of stealth and hiding.

But it was not Ida Warren at the door.

It was the girl. "Mary," he said, gazing upon her with disbelieving eyes. She wore a tan raincoat he'd never seen, and a dark red scarf. The bruise on her cheekbone looked worse somehow, and its angry violet color startled him. He said again, "Mary."

"It's me all right."

"Come in," he said.

She did so cautiously, looking around as if she thought someone else might be in the room. "My father come to see you yet?"

"He did." Cakes closed the door.

"Did he really?"

"Why, yes."

"Well I'll be damned." She looked around the room again. Then she went to the bed and sat down. "I got drunk and called him."

Cakes said, "You never told me you were married to Terry-and-the-P—to Terry Dillard."

"What difference does it make?"

"I guess it makes no difference."

"Yes, sir," she said, "old Terry-and-the-Pirates Dillard."

A moment later, she said, "So what else did Daddy tell you?"

"That you lied about things."

"Right."

"He said you have no brothers or sisters."

"Right." She started to take the coat off, then seemed to think better of it, and pulled it back tight across her chest.

"Are you here to—stay?"

"I don't know."

"It's all right if you want to stay."

"You don't mind if I do."

He moved to the bed, sat down a little distance from her, and for a long while neither one of them spoke.

"Where did you go?" he said.

"Train station."

He waited.

"Got friends over there now. At the train station."

Cakes remembered suddenly the note her father had left for her. "I have something—" he began, rising to get the note out of his bureau drawer. When he handed it to her she gave him a look of something like suspicion, then opened the folded page and read what her father had written.

"Well," she said, folding it and shoving it into the coat pocket.

"He said he was at the end of his rope."

"Yeah," she said. "He raped me. With his hand. His finger. He's at the end of his rope."

Cakes was silent.

"But then," she said, "maybe I'm lying about that."

"I—I wish you'd let me help you," Cakes said.

She looked at him. "You're sweet. I'm twenty-four years old and I'm older than you. You don't have to do anything to help me. You already helped me. You let me stay here."

"I liked having you here."

She stood, her hands down in the coat pockets, and walked over to the window. "You're lonely, aren't you."

"Yes," he said. He didn't care.

"You missed me."

He had. "Yes."

"Want to get married?"

The question confused him.

"I didn't figure you would."

"Well," he said, "you're already—your husband—you're already married."

She shook her head as he spoke. "I don't love you, Cakes."

"No," he said. He couldn't look at her.

"I'm hungry," she said. "Let's go eat."

"I'll make you a breakfast."

She moved to the bed again. "All right," she shrugged. "Great. Make me a breakfast."

"Eggs and bacon?"

She nodded.

"Oh," he said, "your father told me that people were looking for you and Terry Dillard."

"He told me that, too."

After a pause, she said, "So he told you about my life as a pusher."

"He said that you and—that you were involved with drugs."

"I'm starving," she said.

Cakes spoke quietly. "I just wanted you to know. If there was some reason for you to—if there was some trouble you needed to keep from—"

"I'm safe. I'm safe now."

"You mean here?"

"Here, there, everywhere. I'm safe. I'm all squared away, I guess."

"So you—won't be staying here?"

"Maybe I will and maybe I won't. I'm still trying to decide."

He stood there as if something in her scrutiny of him would yield up a decision.

"How about those bacon and eggs?"

He was out of bacon. He searched the small refrigerator as though he suspected that there might be some secret compartment, containing bacon. Finally he faced her with the news: he was out of bacon. And when her face showed disappointment, he offered to go down to the grocery store and get some.

"No, you don't have to," she said.

"We could both walk down."

She had lain back on the bed, and she lifted one leg, moved the toes of that foot. "I'm tired."

"Well, I'll go then. You wait here."

"Cakes, really—you don't have to."

"Not at all," he said. "Really."

She got up and walked over to him and, putting her arms around his neck, kissed him on the mouth.

There was a lovely time, long ago, too private to tell anyone, or too ordinary. It had nothing to do with anything, really: it was almost embarrassingly humble. One December night, unable to sleep, he had glanced out the bedroom window of the house on the quiet, tree-lined street to discover that it had snowed. He woke Ellen and made her come to the window, and the surprise of it delighted her as it had delighted him. They dressed and bundled Ian up and took a walk, and watched the dawn arrive, and when they returned to the house, Edward took the day off. They played with the baby—Ian was three that winter—and when the baby napped they made love. Edward cooked dinner, and Ellen baked bread. They listened to Ian playing in his playpen, and they talked idly about anything that came into their minds, and that evening, late, after more lovemaking, they lay whispering to each other in a white bath of moonlight from the window, about what a beautiful day it had been. The warmth, the ease of it. For weeks after this there was a sort of secret shyness between them, and an exquisite unrest. She surprised him a few times, seeking him, and he went about his various tasks with the orchestra in a dazed and plentiful mood of love, a fortunate man in a good job in the middle of a happy year.

He thought about all this on his way down to the grocery store. The memory of it came through him like a breath, and then he was savoring it, basking in its warmth. It no longer pained him that it was so far gone; he would go back to the room and tell Mary something. He would explain it to her, how it was. And how he thought that this was what love really meant: this very ordinary memory. That love was easy and plentiful as grass, and as still, as calm somehow.

But when he got back to the room the girl was gone, and his thoughts seemed quite absurd and foolish. He put the bacon away. Again, she had left her things where they were, in the bag in his closet. But she was nowhere, and he went out on the landing, feeling anger now, wanting her to be somewhere, anyway, in shouting distance. He yelled her name once, then again. Ida Warren came out of her room and part way down the stairs.

"Something the matter?"

"I'm sorry, Ida," he said. "Did I wake you?" He was forcing himself to be kind.

"I've been up for hours," she said.

"Well." He started back into his room.

"Remember," she said.

"What?" In spite of everything, impatience was in his voice.

"Tea," she said gently.

"Now?"

"You said in the morning."

"Oh," he said, "I did."

"But if you don't want to." She turned.

"Ida."

She stopped.

"I'd—I'd love some tea."

"You're just saying that."

"For the love of God," he said.

"Well I don't want you just to be kind."

"I'm asking you. Will you make me some tea."

"If it's no imposition on you," she said, "if you honestly feel like having some tea, I'd be happy to make you some. And if you'd rather just have the tea and not have to talk to me, I'd be happy to bring it down to you and leave it with you. Or if you just want to come up and hear some of the records, you know, and not be bothered with a lot of conversation, that would be all right, too."

He went up to her. In the room, she began apologizing almost at once for talking too much. She poured the tea, telling him about her dead husband's problem with the bottle. Periodically, all his life, poor Howard would have these bouts of drinking; he might be quite normal for months, even years, but then something would trigger it, and one day he simply wouldn't come home from work. He would be gone two days, or more, and when he returned, he was always very contrite, and each time she forgave him, since there wasn't much else she could do. She had the children; they loved their father. She pretended his work took him out of town during these periods, and, really, children are easy enough to fool—believe, mostly, what they are told. The odd thing was the number of friends he had made while he was drunk, the tremendous loyalty of these friends, all of whom drank pretty much as he did: when he died, they had all come to his funeral—people she had never met. "They cried like little babies," she said. "I'm sorry."

"Excuse me?" he said.

"I said I'm sorry—I'm talking too much."

"I have to go out," he said.

"I know. To visit Arthur." She smiled, then seemed a little confused; her cheeks seemed to glow. "I've got so much to do. My grandson's probably coming to see me again today."

"Finish your tea," he said.

They were quiet. He looked at the small bones of her hands.

"It's very good tea, Ida."

She told him where she bought it: how each Saturday she made a special trip downtown, and as she spoke and he was looking at her hands, he remembered his anger.

"What's the matter," she said.

"Nothing."

"You can go now if you want to."

"Do you want me to go?"

"Only if you want to." She smiled. "It's all right. I'm fine in the mornings. It's the nights that get me. Will you come see me tonight?"

"I will," he said.

"Just listen to music, maybe."

"Fine."

He walked in the cold, windless sun over to see Arthur in his little room off the corridor of open rooms. Arthur was awake this morning. The hospital staff had moved his television down for him, and he was watching a movie. Edward Cakes sat down at the bedside and put his hand on Arthur's skinny, veined arm.

"Where's Ida?" Arthur asked.

"She thought it would be better if I came alone today."

"It's not better." Arthur motioned for him to turn the television off. His skin was the color of the water in the galvanized pail out in the hall. "So tell me," he said after Cakes had turned the television off. His voice rasped.

"Tell you what?"

"Anything you want. Tell me something cheerful, why don't you."

"You're looking better."

"Liar."

Edward was silent.

"I'm dying right in front of your eyes."

"Arthur."

"Right here in front of your eyes, Cakes."

"Don't talk like that."

"All right," Arthur said, "I won't talk like that. Tell me about Vermont."

"It was beautiful."

This seemed to be all Arthur needed. He lay there, smiling, eyes closed. "Beautiful," he said, "beautiful, beautiful."

Edward stayed through the afternoon. Arthur went to sleep and then woke up and then went to sleep again. They were ostensibly watching television. Nurses came in and drained the catheter and washed Arthur's face with a soft white cloth, and he woke up and played to them, acting the comedian, mumbling jokes and pretending to try to pinch them. There was something automatic about it as if he did not really hear himself, and when they were gone, he muttered to Edward about their youth and their blindness—as though it was their fate to be young, not old.

"You know what I'd like to do, Edward? I'd like to get up and go out in the street and take a cab. I'd like to ride in a taxicab again. Just once. You know what I'd do? I'd ride all the way to the train station and buy a ticket for somewhere and ride the train. I'd take the first train that was going anywhere, anywhere at all."

"They're all going somewhere," Edward said.

"So tell me," said his friend, "you and the girl. You're making love?"

"We made love every night," Edward said. "I admit it."

"Ah. Tell me."

"She just got into bed with me. I was asleep. She woke me up making love to me."

"Wonderful."

"She made me feel like a kid again."

"And she did everything to you?"

"Every night," Edward said.

"She's not so young."

"No."

"Ah." Arthur reached over and patted his wrist. "If you love her, things will work out."

They were quiet. They watched television for a time, though neither of them paid any real attention to it.

"You're a good friend, Edward."

"And so are you."

"I think my reprieve is up."

"Maybe we can get an apartment downtown."

"That would be nice—we could have girlfriends." Arthur sighed. "Ah, it's just as well." And then he lay his head back on the pillow and was gone; Edward didn't know quite when it happened: his friend said, "Ah, it's just as well," settled himself, lay his head back; Edward was looking at the television: A woman smiled and held up a can of coffee; she stood in a bright country kitchen, and then there were two men, dressed like lumberjacks, or hunters, in red-checked jackets—they were all smiling, and Edward looked over at Arthur and saw that he was gone. The eyes were half closed, the mouth open. Edward said his name and put the back of his hand against the mouth. Then he went out into the hall, down toward the nurse's station. There was a family outside one room, two young women arguing in hysterical whispers about who was to blame for something. Edward wended his way through, and found himself in the bright light of the nurse's station. He put his hands down on the counter and looked for a bell or something to ring to gain someone's attention, but there was nothing, and at last he began to say "Please," loud, over and over. He had come part way back down the corridor, moving again through the gathered, arguing family—over whose muttered recriminations there rose the sound of a woman crying—to come face to face with someone in a white smock, a man, not young, with a thin gray mustache and a wattled chin. "Please," Edward said, and led the way, he thought, to Arthur's room. But the man in the white smock had not followed him, and so he entered the room, looked at his friend. Arthur's head had lolled forward slightly. The nose ran. Something had come out of the corner of the mouth. Edward sat down on the bed and put his arm around Arthur's thin shoulders, gathered him, letting the head come to rest in the hollow of his own shoulder. Arthur was light as straw, and so thin; there wasn't anything to him at all, and Edward patted the bony point of his shoulder, as if to soothe or comfort. He could hear himself breathing, and he sobbed; the room was a blur of tears. He kept patting Arthur's shoulder as if to reassure him of something, sitting there crying, on Arthur's bed, while on the television screen, in a room whose windows looked out on a white beach, a man and woman embraced in a passionate kiss.

29

He waited for Arthur Hagood's daughter to arrive. It took her a long time. He sat in the lobby and tried to read a magazine, and then he paced the halls. They had carried Arthur down to the morgue, though it had been a few moments before they could get Edward to let him go. He knew it was what they had to do; he knew everything was what people had to do, and there wasn't anything to say about it. There wasn't anything to say once time was past, once you had done a thing, lived a certain way. He walked up and down the halls, and finally he went up to Arthur's old room and knocked on the door. There was the little man with the telegraph key, wearing, as before, the visor cap, and, as before, occupied with his telegrams. He had the thing hooked up to another room, and all day he and this friend sent telegrams back and forth to each other.

"Look," he said, showing Edward how it worked. "New Haven, see?"

Edward said he saw.

"Know Morse code?"

"No."

"See? Like this. New Haven. Listen."

He listened. The little man sat hunched over his telegraph key, waiting for the message from the room down the hall. It came. "See?" he said. He had written it down: "Christmastime is jolly." "See?" he said to Cakes. "Now I'll send one out. Let's see, what's my answer?"

A moment later Cakes said "What did you send?"

"See? New Haven."

He left him there and went back down to the lobby. He didn't know why he was waiting: he had nothing, really, to say to Arthur Hagood's daughter. And then he began to see that he did have a thing to tell her. She would want to know how Arthur died. It was what he would do, then: he would wait until she came, and he would tell her how Arthur died with his one friend in a room on the first floor of an enormous building full of strangers. Except that when she finally did come, wearing the dress he thought he had seen her in the last time and looking very pale and frightened, he couldn't say anything of the kind. He said "Yes" when she said how it was a mercy, for the best, unhappy as her father had become. Pale and ill and wasted as he had been.

"He was a wonderful man," Edward Cakes said.

"Yes," she murmured.

There didn't seem to be anything for them to do. She had looked upon the remains of her father; she would have to get in touch with all the rest of her family, and there would have to be arrangements, but none of this had anything to do with Edward.

"I'm going to have him cremated," she said now.

Edward nodded. They were standing in the lobby, and she was fumbling around in her purse for a Kleenex; it amazed him, but she was crying.

"Did he say anything?" she asked. "You know, about me?"

He shook his head.

"What did he say?"

"His last words were that—that he was happy. He said it was just—that he was happy."

"Really? Those were his exact words?"

"He said, 'It's just as well.' "

She frowned.

"He was happy."

"I wish I could believe it." She brought the Kleenex out of her purse and wiped her eyes with it. "Really," she said, "it's a triumph. Such a long, rich life. Eighty—all those years."

"Yes," he said.

"Don't you think it's a triumph?"

"Yes."

She looked at him. "I couldn't talk to him at all in the end."

"You weren't there in the end," he said.

"I mean in the last years."

He said, "Oh."

"I loved him, you know. We all loved him."

"Yes."

"No matter what anyone says."

"Yes."

"Arthur Hagood had a good life."

Edward wandered out into the street and down to the park, in what was now a gusting, icy wind. He sat on a bench for a few minutes, shivering, and then he went home. But again he felt the aversion, the sense of the appalling loneliness of the room, and so again he was out in the street. Perhaps this would be his death, too. He would wander the streets until he dropped over from heart failure, or froze to death in an alley. Above him, faintly, he could hear Ida Warren's music. Her window was the only lighted window of the house. It seemed, now, the only lighted window anywhere. He went down to the end of the block and crossed at the light; then he was heading into town. There was the wind, and the sound of trains, and traffic; he went under a bridge and on, toward the far lights. Perhaps a mile beyond the bridge he was able to flag down a cab, and as he got in and closed the door, it came to him that he had no real destination.

"Where to?" the driver said.

Cakes heard himself say "The train station." Then he sat back and watched the street. It was very late now; he was beginning to feel light-headed. Arthur had laid his head on the pillow and expired, like a breath.

"Train station," the driver said.

Edward looked at his face; it was square and friendly and young. "My best friend just died."

"Oh, I'm sorry, man."

Edward paid him.

"You want me to wait here?"

"No, thank you."

The train station was lighted up, and there were bars all up and down the street. Cakes went into one, ordered a whiskey and drank it slow, seeing himself, round-eyed, pale and frightened, in the mirror behind a forest of bottles opposite him. There were many people in the bar, and they all seemed to be arguing over the music, which was loud and somehow spiritless, mechanical, as if it had originated in the circuitry of the machine that played it. The voices, the shouts and the insistent, beating music all made a blur, and he went out, sick to his stomach now, afraid that he might begin to lose consciousness. It was getting colder, and there was a wind blowing. He stood at the edge of the street, his hands shoved deep in his pockets, and stared, crying, out at the night—the lighted windows of the buildings there, the deep shadows between them, and the blurred moving traffic. He walked down to the end of the block, and then came back, the wind biting at him, and at last he was sitting on the curb, his elbows on his knees, his face in his hands. Perhaps fifteen minutes passed, and then a policeman prodded him rudely with a nightstick.

"Get going, man."

Edward stood, wiping his eyes with the backs of his hands. "My best friend died."

"Right, move on."

"It's true."

"I don't care whether it's true or not. Move on."

"Yes." He moved slowly across the street, and the policeman followed him.

"You got some identification, gramps?"

"Yes."

"You mind if I take a look at it? I mean, I'd hate it if you were a vagrant and I had to run you in."

"No, I'm not a vagrant." Edward produced his wallet, and the cop shined a flashlight in his face.

"You're crying—are you crying?"

"Please," Edward said, "leave me alone."

The policeman handed him his wallet. "I'm sorry. Really— whatever it is."

"Please."

"You want some help?"

"No."

"Well—just don't sit there like that on the curb. It's asking for trouble."

"I won't," Edward said.

The policeman walked away, crossed the street at the end of the block and went out of sight. Edward went back to the bar and ordered another drink—a whiskey straight, to calm his nerves and to warm him a little. His hands were stinging with the cold, and he huddled in a booth away from the door, sipping the whiskey. He was a blank now, merely reacting to everything; he could not imagine himself going home. He ordered another whiskey, and in a while a young woman came over to ask him if he had ever been in the bar before.

"I seen you before, I swear."

"No," he said.

"You want to come to my room with me?" she said.

It was absurd. He almost laughed. "No thank you."

When he was finished with the drink, he went out and crossed the street. Cars honked at him. People were moving along the sidewalk now, and from a manhole cover in the middle of the intersection a shivering cone of steam rose. He moved along the sidewalk, and as a man in a long overcoat approached him, smiling, holding out a photograph, he thought he saw, in the flickers of the street beyond the man's shoulder, Mary Bellini entering a building.

"How about a little fun?"

"Excuse me," Edward said. He went around the man, walking toward the building.

"Just go in," the man said.

There was no door—only stairs, leading up. He climbed them slowly, laboring upward in his exhaustion and his wonder. The air was moist and smelled of mold; there was the faintest trace of something like perfume in it as he got nearer to the top. Then it was too sweet, and he pushed through double doors to stand before a white-shirted man at a desk. The man was balding and had combed the thin strands of hair over the bald place; he looked quite clean and orderly, like a clerk or a bank teller. He smiled at Edward and said, "Fifty dollars for a half hour. We have beautiful girls."

To the right of the desk was a doorway, obscured by a beaded curtain. A young woman pushed the curtain aside and looked at him. Then was gone.

"Well?" the man said.

Cakes stammered. "Mary—Mary Virginia Bellini."

"Who?"

He repeated the name.

"Yeah?"

"I know her. I have her things."

"Look, is this personal, bub?"

"She—I know her."

The man stood. "Why don't you come back later."

"I have her things."

"Just a minute," the man said, and went through the curtain.

Edward waited, hands in his pockets. He was probably coming down with a cold. He sniffled, swallowed, ran the back of his hand across his nose; he was aware of how bent he must look, standing here hunched over his pain, doddering and afraid. An old man. It was very quiet, and there was the thick odor of perfume; the dim red walls seemed swollen somehow, inflamed. He stepped back toward the door, trying not to gasp, and the man came out of the other room, walked through the beaded curtain and let the end of it travel up and over his shoulders.

"Nobody you know is in here, bub." He took Edward by the elbow. "Now, if you ain't going to spend any money, I think we just better call it a night. What do you think?"

"I have her things," Cakes said.

"Great. You send us a long letter about it." The man was moving him out the door, to the landing, the top of the stairwell. "Good night, bub."

Edward Cakes went down into the street and stood searching through his own pockets; he had one twenty-dollar bill, folded and crumpled, and a few pennies. He turned and looked at the building, then at the man in the long overcoat, who still tried to interest people in the photograph, the carnal secrets of the building. It was growing very cold, the wind biting down from the cold stars, and Cakes walked over to the train station, where it was warm. He got change for his twenty at the ticket counter and bought a ham sandwich from one of the machines. The ham was full of gristle, and, anyway, he had no appetite. He sat on a bench and watched the crowd empty out of an early morning train.

30

▲

It was full light before he got back to the house. The sky was clear and cold behind the trees of the park. In the grass there, dew had frozen and looked like a thin coating of snow. He had walked all the way, watching the sky soften to light, feeling the chill, coughing and wheezing, his feet tingling with the lack of circulation and warmth. He climbed the stairs, entered, and looked at the empty foyer. Somehow he had expected to find Ida Warren there. The fact that he found no one made him feel as though he might begin

weeping again, and he hurried up to his room, anxious not to be
seen this way. He had always been able to pull his dignity around
him like a coat, and now he felt exposed, stripped bare, with only
the small scrap of pride that made him hurry. He got to the room,
was inside, in the chilly safety and quiet. He leaned against the
door for a few moments, then gathered himself, moved to the bed,
took off his coat, let it drop. He sat down, breathed deeply once
and wiped his forehead with a folded handkerchief from the bedstand. It was very early. The house was asleep. There was no
sound from upstairs. He got up at last, and shuffled across to the
window and looked out. The street was empty, painted with
shade. Nothing moved. There wasn't a trace of a cloud in the
high, limitless blue. He sat in his chair, lay his head back and
remembered that Arthur was gone.

A moment later he leaned forward, turned the television on
and moved it on its stand so that it was directly in front of him. It
was news; someone standing in front of a weather map, and how
many people had passed on into the dark before this dawning
day? What a beautiful fall day it would be, the weatherman said,
smiling. The sun smiled on the whole country.

Edward closed his eyes, perhaps slept, and was awakened
abruptly by the sound of someone moving around behind him in
the room. He came fully to, sat up, gasping, turning. He thought
it was Ida Warren.

But it was the girl.

She was bent over into the closet, and now she straightened,
with the canvas bag in one hand. When she saw that he was
awake, she said, "You didn't lock your door. I didn't want to
wake you."

He didn't move. She carried the bag to the table and set it
down, then went back to the closet.

"Been meaning to get these things," she said. "I'm going to
be living with Terry you know—we got back together. I'm going
to start college and all. Go to school with him."

"It's all there," Cakes said.

"Pardon?"

"There's nothing else there."

She had begun to root around in the closet. Now she came back to the table and began to open the bag.

"It's all there," he said.

"I know," she said, "just want to get it tied tight."

"Why did you bother coming back?" he asked.

She paused. "What do you mean. I left my things here—just got sidetracked is all."

He shook his head.

"Look, you were nice to me," she said. "But that doesn't give you the right to—" She pulled the cord on the bag tight. "You just don't have the right to criticize me."

"You don't have to worry about that," he said.

"I'm not going to worry about it."

"Well," he said, "that's fine."

"You bet it is."

There was a moment, then, when he thought she might whirl and leave him there. But she didn't; she put one hand up to her eye, gingerly rubbed the discolored skin just beneath it, and looked at the tips of the fingers of that hand.

"You're not pregnant anymore," he said.

"I am. But not for long."

As he got to his feet, he wondered if there were not some terrific significance to the fact that he had found her in that accidental way; he sought for words to tell her about it: he was absolutely certain that she would never have come back again if he hadn't seen her. "Listen," he said, "you can stay here. I don't care about anything else, I'm too old to care about it. But I found you there, and you came back."

"I just came to get my things."

"My friend Arthur," he said, not looking at her. "My best friend—I lost him yesterday."

"I'm sorry," she said.

"I was just wandering around. Arthur said something about riding in a cab again, taking a train. I went to the train station, and—I found you."

"Yes."

"Don't you see?"

She shook her head.

"What were you doing in that place?"

"I don't know what you're talking about."

"You just said—you said yes. When I said I found you, you said yes."

She was silent, watching her hands fumble with the cord at the top of the bag. "I told you I had friends near the train station."

They were quiet a moment.

"Why, Mary?"

She spoke through her teeth. "Maybe I want it—okay?"

"What about the baby?"

"That's my business."

"What about me," he said.

She looked at him. "You don't even know me."

"I know you," he said.

"No."

"Well, I want to know you."

"When I was a little girl," she said, "I used to think grown-ups were people that had the secret, you know. Somebody told them the secret and that made them grown-ups—they had got the secret. And—and the secret was something that made you not afraid, and when you forgot it, you became a child again. Like my mother. I didn't know what the secret was going to be, but I had my mind made up that once I found it out I wasn't ever going to let go of it, not ever. And I did find it out, too. The secret is not to care. That's what being real grown-up is—you don't care anymore so much, and everything's the same, smooth, like a napkin in your lap maybe or like a table. Everything's—level, like. I mean, my mother—my mother got so absolutely everything mattered to her, everything was life and death, and she'd lay in bed for days, all curled up like a baby. I couldn't even stand to look at her. I couldn't even stand to come home every day from school. And— and then one day I figured it all out. I just stopped myself—I said, 'Mary Virginia, here's where we get off.' And you know, it was easy."

He was quiet. They were facing each other, on either side of the table.

"Look," she said, "I promise there's nothing horrible or secret or terrible or anything like that. I'm not doing anything against my will, and if you don't believe me, that's your problem. Besides, I was just visiting that place. I—I have a friend there. I told you, Terry and me are getting back together."

"I'm happy for you," he said.

"Right. Send us a bag of rice."

"Where should I send it?"

She was tying the cord on the bag now. "It's just an expression, okay?"

He said, "Mary—I found you there."

"You were looking for me?"

"No. Something—something led me there, though. Something must have."

"Why?" she said.

"Well, think about it. Out of all the people in this city—all the places to go, I wound up there."

"Okay," she said. "And—?"

"And—you came here. You came back."

"I came back to get these things." Her face was blank. "Look, what's the point?"

"But—" he said. "You—you didn't come back to get these things. You came back because I saw you go into that place. And you came here and—and lied to me about this—getting back with Terry. Why did you feel you should lie?"

"Maybe I didn't want to hurt your feelings."

"But you're here," he said. "It's not just to pick these things up."

"All right," she said, "it's not."

They looked at each other.

"Well?" she said.

He sighed. "Then—why? Why did you come?"

"I don't know why."

"Don't you see," he said, "I went all that way, I took a cab, I wound up on a street corner and there you were. It has to mean something."

"What do you think it means?" she said.

"I don't know."

"Well, then I don't know, either."

"Maybe it means we should stick together."

This seemed to amuse her. "Really?"

"Well," he said, and though he was embarrassed, he kept his eyes on hers.

She looked down. "You sweet old man."

"Well?"

"That's what you want it to mean."

Now he looked down.

"Isn't it?"

"Maybe it is," he muttered.

"You sweet old man." She shouldered the bag.

"Wait," he said.

She stopped, looking at him as one might look at a child.

"Maybe—maybe we need each other."

"You know what?" she said. "I don't want to hurt your feelings—really I don't. But I've got to go now, okay? You were nice. I'm grateful—all right? You don't really know me, any more than those—any more than anyone else—let's just leave it at that."

"But—you came back," he said.

"I'm clearing things. That's all. Look—you know how when you read in the newspapers somebody killed somebody or took a shot at somebody, and right away they start looking for the reasons? Some guy takes a shot at the President and they start trying to figure where it all started, like back with his parents or something. Like maybe his mother never gave him a Twinkie with his lunch and he got humiliated at school, and that adds up to shooting at the President. You know what I mean, Cakes?"

He said nothing.

"You know what I mean. Well, it's not like that at all, is it. I mean there's people out there getting beat up every day, you know, and terrible things happening to them, and they're not going to go shooting anyone. Do you understand me, Cakes? My mother was nervous. It doesn't add up to me. I'm not somebody's creation. There's nobody to blame but me."

"But if you know this—" he began.

She came back toward him a little, letting the bag drop down to her lower arm. "Listen, working hours are over, you know, but I could make an exception this morning if it'll—if you want."

"I—" He couldn't look at her.

"Oh hell, Cakes. I'm nothing. I'm not that—that girl in your picture there, you know? I thought I could make it work with Terry—I'm not what you think. I've been with a lot of guys, Cakes. An awful lot of them before Terry. It's not always for desperate reasons people do these things."

"But why," he said.

"Maybe because I know what I'm doing and because I'm going to make a lot of money at it and because I like it. Maybe that, too. Look—you got what you wanted out of this."

"Don't—don't say anymore," he said.

"Well?" She took another step toward him. "That's the way things are."

He sat down on the bed.

"You never really saw *me*, Cakes."

"No."

"I was just—somebody young."

"No," he said. "You're wrong."

"I don't think there's anything bad about that."

"It's not so," he said.

"You loved me, right?"

He was shaking his head.

"You know," she said, touching his shoulder, "you did make me feel good, sort of. You were so courtly, and scared of yourself and worried about me."

"Please," he said, "please go."

She let her hand drop. "Yeah."

"Please," he said.

"You're humiliated."

"For the love of God," he said.

"You don't have to be, you know. We can be friends, still. I know where you live, after all."

He was silent.

When she had hefted the bag again, she said, "Poor Cakes. Maybe I do wish you'd come along a lot sooner."

"Goodbye," he said.

At the door she turned. "Listen, if—that stuff about my father. It's—it's not true. If he comes here—or anyone comes here looking for me, you never saw me."

"No," he said. "Right—I never saw you."

"Thanks."

He did not speak.

"You saved my life, Cakes."

He couldn't look at her.

"They don't like it when somebody just—you know, freelances. I got my black eye just for asking around."

"I'm afraid I don't know quite what you're talking about," he said.

"Can't even look at me now, can you."

He did so.

"Friends?" she said.

He nodded.

"Kind sir."

And she was gone. He watched from the window as she went on up the block, past the square and beyond. The sun poured down like summer, though there was still the snowy look to the grass in all the cold patches of shade. It dawned on him that the television was still on, and he switched it off, and then he lay down on the bed, on his side, facing away from the window. Max was dead, the family would have its own service and Cakes would not attend, even if the family thought to invite him. Now he must find something to do with his days. He turned in the bed, sobbed, once, and put his hands behind his head. From the room above came the strains of old jazz, and in a little while he would get up. Ida Warren was dancing again. He listened to the soft scuffle, the scratchy notes, and then he sat up and put his feet down on the floor. He had to tell Ida about it all. He went into the bathroom, cleaned his teeth, ran cold water over his red, tired eyes, shaved and combed his hair. He put on a clean shirt, and his good wing-tip shoes. Then he went to his door, hearing the commotion of arrival in the hall, on the stairs—Paula and Denise coming home from the night shift. He met them on the landing; they were flushed and excited and young and full of plans, the cold air in their clothes and coloring their cheeks.

"Good morning, Baby Cakes," Paula said.

Edward said, "Hello."

They stared at him. "Are you okay?"

"He's got a nice crisp clean white shirt on," Denise said.

"Yeah, but look at his face. Cakes, you look like a pall-bearer." And now Paula took him gently by the arm. "Are you all right?"

"Fine," he mumbled. "Fine."

"Come on, Paula, let him alone. We got four days off. Let's live it up. Cakes, you're invited to our party tonight. You and anybody else you want to bring."

Paula squeezed his elbow. "You come tonight, you hear?"

"Fine," he said.

He watched them go into their apartment, dropping scarves and packages and whirling in the enthusiasm of the beginning of a good time, and when they had closed the door it was a moment before he realized that he was standing alone there in the hall. He took a deep breath and climbed the stairs. The music was slow now, someone singing in a tinny voice about a satin doll. Edward Cakes knocked on the door, waited, breathless and quite still, beginning to think what he would say when the door opened, as it presently opened, and Ida Warren smiled at him, delighted, in the center of music, dancing there in the doorway, wearing, as he'd hoped she would be, the dress he had recognized as the one.

Fairfax, Virginia
April–August 1983